AN UNEXPECTED MOMENT

Lucian caught Catherine's wrist, nipping it around behind her back before she knew what was up. He pulled her to him in a kiss that drove all the breath from her body.

For a moment, the world spun so madly about her that Catherine thought she would faint, but his arms held her captive, steadying her as his lips, softer now, explored hers, begging her, willing her to respond to them.

She was powerless to resist. After the stresses and strains, the emotional ups and downs of the past few days, after having her carefully arranged world thrown into disorder by his sudden appearance, all she could do was cling to him and marvel at how wonderful it felt to be held in someone's arms again. But she was not just being held in the solid reassuring way that Granville had held her from time to time. She was being enfolded, caressed, treasured, held close as though she had always belonged there, as though she were part of him. . . .

continued . . .

The Scandalous Widow

Evelyn Richardson

A SIGNET BOOK

SIGNET
Published by New American Library, a division of
Penguin Group (USA) Inc., 375 Hudson Street,
New York, New York 10014, U.S.A.
Penguin Books Ltd, 80 Strand,
London WC2R 0RL, England
Penguin Books Australia Ltd, 250 Camberwell Road,
Camberwell, Victoria 3124, Australia
Penguin Books Canada Ltd, 10 Alcorn Avenue,
Toronto, Ontario, Canada M4V 3B2
Penguin Books (N.Z.) Ltd, Cnr Rosedale and Airborne Roads,
Albany, Auckland 1310, New Zealand

Penguin Books Ltd, Registered Offices:
80 Strand, London WC2R 0RL, England

First published by Signet, an imprint of New American Library,
a division of Penguin Group (USA) Inc.

First Printing, April 2004
10 9 8 7 6 5 4 3 2 1

 REGISTERED TRADEMARK—MARCA REGISTRADA

Printed in the United States of America

PUBLISHER'S NOTE
This is a work of fiction. Names, characters, places, and incidents either are the product of the author's imagination or are used fictitiously, and any resemblance to actual
persons, living or dead, business establishments, events, or locales is entirely coinci-
dental.

To Carol, who has struggled for the past eight years to put a roof over our heads at Cary Library

And to Carolyn, who has been holding us all together for as long as we can remember

Chapter One

*N*aturally, I cannot help but find it mortifying in the extreme. Surely there is something that can be done to stop it. Do you not agree, Charlmont . . . ? Charlmont . . . ? Lucian!"

The sound of his own name jerked Lucian rudely back to the present in a way that could not be ignored. He had, for the moment, been so wrapped up in calculating his horse's chances of winning at Newmarket that he had completely succeeded in wiping all consciousness of his present situation from his mind. What madness had possessed him to make him agree to appear at Almack's this evening?

He loathed the place, and the company—dull, predictable, and smug. And he had assiduously avoided it since his salad days, when he could have been forgiven for not knowing any better. He glanced hopefully around the room, but the dowagers putting their turbaned heads together sharing scandal broth and the half-eager, half-shy glances of young misses in their first Season only served to confirm his worst fears. This was not a dream. He truly was at Almack's. It had not changed the slightest bit. And he was waltzing. His eyes focused at last on the full red lips and delectable bosom of his partner, also his latest mistress, the thoroughly delicious and very lovely Lady Granville.

"I beg your pardon. I was not attending."

"I am well aware of that, you dreadful man." His partner's lips pursed in an enticing moue of frustration.

He was tempted to kiss those lips at that very moment. They were certainly far better suited to kissing than to conversation; besides which, he was beginning to have the very distinct and thoroughly unpleasant sensation that those lips were about to ask him to do something that he did not wish to do.

"And what, pray tell, was preoccupying you to such a degree?" The playful note in his partner's voice was sharpened by just a hint of irritation.

"I was wondering what in God's name I was doing here and thinking that nothing but the presence of the most beautiful, the most enchanting woman in all of London could have drawn me here, as it has." He grinned as he watched the spark of annoyance in her blue eyes melt into gratified amusement.

"It was you who suggested we meet at Almack's."

"Did I? I must have been crazed ... or thoroughly foxed."

"Well, certainly the latter. But you had such excellent reasons for doing so that I was convinced you knew what you were about. You assured me that it was bound to insure the success of my reputation in the *ton* if I were to appear here, especially in your company."

Lucian glanced quickly around. "The last is debatable. Certainly my company has got you noticed, for it is a well-known fact that nothing—well, almost nothing, would induce me to visit an establishment where the entertainment is so utterly tame. On the other hand, it is precisely because I seek out other, er, *less* tame amusements that makes the success of this foray somewhat dubious. When people see you here with me they will wonder what sort of woman you are, aside from one who is extremely beautiful and turned out in the highest kick of fashion. Why, at this very moment I see Mrs. Drummond Burrell glowering at us. Come, my dear, let us beard the dragon in its lair."

And taking his partner's arm in his, Lucian led her through the crowd with the confidence of a man who truly did not give a damn what was going on behind the vacant stares of the people who parted to make way for them. "But, forgive me, I quite forgot. Something was troubling you. What was it you wished to ask me?"

However, there was such a crush of people at Almack's that evening it was impossible to converse as they made their way across the room, and by the time they had reached Mrs. Drummond Burrell, Lucian's partner was too bemused by it all to realize how effectively he had forestalled any possibility of her reopening the discussion.

"Well, Charlmont, to what do we owe this dubious pleasure? I had thought you considered us far too respectable to appeal to your rackety taste." The stately patroness fixed him with a glare that would have reduced lesser men to stammering incoherence.

Lucian smiled sweetly. "I admit that I have been remiss in my attentions, but that should make you all the more delighted to welcome me back to the Marriage Mart—prodigal son sort of thing, you know. In truth, my presence at Almack's is solely attributable to the fact that I knew Lady Granville would be here and I knew that as someone new to London who has just received a voucher, and someone far too modest to put herself forward, she was in need of encouragement. So here I am."

"Maria!" Mrs. Drummond Burrell snorted. "She is softhearted to a fault."

"Lady Sefton may have been responsible for procuring Lady Granville her voucher, but everyone knows that only you can convey the true seal of approval. Surely the wife of Lord Granville, a man so respectable that he chooses the careful administration of his estates over pursuit of a frivolous existence, is worthy of your notice. Until now, Lady Granville has led such a sheltered existence and knows so few people in London that she is in need of a powerful sponsor such as you to offer her guidance in a milieu that can be truly terrifying to the uninitiated."

"Ah." Almack's most cantankerous patroness surveyed the lady in question thoroughly. Truly she made an exquisite picture in her simple yet fashionable frock of British net draped over a blue satin slip. Elegant yet unpretentious and clearly in the best of taste, it was a gown designed to appeal to Mrs. Drummond Burrell's critical eye. In fact, the patroness became so absorbed in gauging every detail of the supplicant's appearance that she quite forgot to wonder how it was that the Marquess of Charlmont, who had only recently succeeded to his brother's title, and had previously shown very little inclination for any of the haunts of good society, was the one responsible for bringing Lady Granville to her attention.

Lucian could not help admiring Lady Granville's calm endurance of the patroness's scrutiny, a scrutiny that was thorough to the point of rudeness. In fact in anybody else it *would* have been condemned as rudeness. This show of courage in the face of such outright callousness proved beyond a doubt the level of Lady Granville's determination to win a place for herself among the very highest ranks of the *ton,* no matter what it cost her.

It was this determination, coupled with the lady's undeniable beauty, that had caught Lucian's attention and piqued his interest in the first place. Her appearance on the scene had also coincided somewhat fortuitously with developments in his own life.

Lucian had become rather bored with his previous mistress, an opera dancer whose tastes had begun to run to the expensive, bordering on rapacious, and whose demands had crossed the boundary from flattering to incessant. Therefore, he had been casting around rather aimlessly for a replacement when Lavinia, Lady Granville, had suddenly appeared on the scene.

Lucian had first caught sight of her at the opera, where her pale blonde hair and fragile beauty had instantly captured most of the masculine attention, while her magnificent pearls and a gown whose style and décolletage appeared to have come directly from Paris excited the envy of the female contingent. But it was her half-flirtatious, half-defiant air that had intrigued Lucian and made him wish to know more about this latest arrival to the metropolis.

The more he inquired, the more he discovered that very little was known about Lady Granville except that her husband, an obscure gentleman from some northern county, had recently succeeded to his uncle's estate near Bath, as well as an estate in Somerset and sizable interests in mines and canals.

Those who had met the lady in question had pronounced her charming enough in her own way but had withheld their final approval until more could be discovered about her antecedents. And it was these antecedents, as Lucian soon found out, after he had managed an introduction, that were responsible for the defiant lift of the chin and the determined set of her ladyship's delicately rounded jaw. Quite simply, there were none. Or, to be more exact, there were none who lent any cachet or credibility to someone who had set her sights on becoming a glittering ornament in the very highest circles of the *ton*.

For the beautiful and elegant Lady Granville was nothing more than a provincial banker's daughter, an enormously wealthy and powerful banker's daughter, but a provincial banker's daughter nevertheless. And though she had certainly captured the attention and admiration of one and all at every local assembly when she had first made her come out, there had been no one there whose interest was worth attracting. None of the neighboring landowners had titles or estates worthy of a woman who was determined to become a diamond of the first water.

Desperate for a wider audience, Lavinia had begged her papa for a Season in London, but Mr. Matthews, banker that he was, could not foresee a large enough return on an investment that would require a considerable outlay of capital. It was only after the forcible representations on the part of Mrs. Matthews that her husband finally agreed that Bath offered a far better ratio of exposure to eligible society in relation to expense than did London or the provinces.

It was in Bath that Lavinia had managed to snare the

marginally eligible Hugo Granville, who, if he had neither
title nor vast estates, was at least first in line to inherit a
considerable amount of both. And with that Lavinia was
forced to content herself, for she had discovered that no
matter how much eligible gentlemen might admire a beautiful face or indulge in flirtation with a charming young
lady, they never could be persuaded to commit themselves
to anything more binding than the reservation of a dance at
the public balls on Tuesdays and Fridays. Gentlemen were
more than happy to feast their eyes on a provincial nobody,
but they were not about to ally their families or their futures
with one.

While it was true that Hugo Granville's wife was now
welcomed in far more select company than Miss Matthews
ever had been, it still did not begin to resemble the future
that Lavinia had envisioned for herself. But fate had been
kind; not a year after the marriage, Lord Granville had died,
struck down in his prime by a putrid fever contracted while
riding home in the rain. The donning of mourning clothes,
purchased from the most fashionable establishments,
seemed a small price to pay for having gained a title and an
estate to call her own at last.

But for Lavinia, the estate and the title were only the
means to an end. And that end was to take what she considered to be her rightful place in the most select gatherings
of the *ton,* a place where her beauty, her taste, and the exquisite manners she had cultivated her entire life would
have their proper setting.

However, much to her dismay, she soon found that estates and title were not sufficient to get her what she
wanted. She had her box at the opera and invitations to the
larger balls, routs, and masquerades, but the rest continued
to elude her until Lucian, Marquess of Charlmont, appeared
in her box at the opera one evening in the company of one
of the *ton's* most lively young matrons.

Lady Robert Thornhill's manners might hover on the
edge of scandalous, but her birth was impeccable and her
position as daughter of Lady Widmore, one of the arbiters

of Bath society, and Lord Widmore, owner of most of the land near Bath that did not belong to the Granvilles, assured her of the sort of position in the *ton* that Lavinia so desperately craved.

"My dear Lady Granville, I was not aware that you had arrived in town or I certainly would have called on one of Mama and Papa's nearest neighbors."

It was the merest fabrication of course. Lady Robert Thornhill had endured only the briefest of introductions to Lavinia when a visit to her parents had happened to coincide with the new Lord and Lady Granville's ceremonial calls on the local gentry in the vicinity, and she had never done anything subsequently to acknowledge the acquaintance. But fabrication or not, it was a miracle, and Lavinia knew instantly that the source of this miracle was the tall dark-haired gentleman standing at Lady Robert's side. There was something about him—Lavinia could not decide whether it was the knowing glint in the deep set gray eyes or the ironic twist of his lips—but something about the man told her that he had observed and understood her predicament completely.

Ever since that moment, doors had begun to open, slowly at first, but steadily enough to reassure Lavinia that she was well and truly on her way to taking her place in the *ton*. She had never asked Lucian why it had amused him to pave her way but had simply taken it as her due, the natural result of being born a beautiful woman, a beautiful woman who knew just what to do to capture and hold a man's attention.

Pleasing men had never been Lavinia's problem; bringing them up to scratch had. Men were always eager to pay homage to her lovely face and exquisite figure; however, they were far less eager to ally themselves permanently with someone whose background smacked of trade.

Naturally a woman who possessed as strong a sense of self-preservation as Lavinia Granville did kept the liaison between herself and the Marquess of Charlmont discreet, but the fact that she had managed to capture and hold the attention of a man whose fickleness was legendary only served to add to the growing acknowledgment that Lady Granville was "something of a beauty," though of course her lack of truly ancient and respectable blood kept her from being declared a diamond of the first water.

The beauty was now doing her best to appear both charming and respectful under the unflinchingly critical stare of Mrs. Drummond Burrell, but it was heavy going in the face of the patroness's notoriously unbending attitude toward anyone ill-bred enough not to have been born into the Upper Ten Thousand.

Fortunately, the Marquess of Charlmont had been born to that select group, his birth and breeding being superior even to Mrs. Drummond Burrell's. In addition to that, he possessed charm in abundance, which, whenever he chose to use it, could be extremely effective, as it was at this particular moment.

Lucian favored the patroness with a smile that caused the rigidly disapproving line of her lips to curve ever so slightly into something approaching an answering smile. "But now, if you will excuse us, we must not be selfish and take all your attention when it is plain to see there are others clamoring for it." He turned to his lovely partner. "Come, Lady Granville, I see Lady Robert Thornhill looking in our direction and it would never do to ignore one of your Somerset neighbors."

Sketching a casually elegant bow to Mrs. Drummond Burrell, he held out his arm to Lavinia, steering her deftly toward the opposite corner of the room. "There, now, you may consider yourself to be thoroughly launched. And if you do not find yourself the toast of the town within this Season or the next, I shall be very much surprised."

Lady Granville sighed gently. "It is very kind of you Charlmont, to do this, but . . ." The beauty paused to look up at him in a way that had never failed to melt even the most unsusceptible of masculine hearts.

"But what?" Too late, Lucian realized that he had fallen into the trap that he had been so carefully avoiding since their arrival at Almack's, the request that had been hovering on Lady Granville's lips all during their waltz. He had managed to distract her with the promised introduction to Mrs. Drummond Burrell, but even a diversion of that magnitude was futile in the face of Lavinia Granville's resolve.

Sighing, he gave in to the inevitable. "Very well. You had better tell me what is troubling you now so that I have the rest of the evening to ponder it."

He was instantly rewarded by a brilliant smile and a grateful squeeze of his hand. "Oh Charlmont, I *knew* I could depend on you. You are always so generous, so . . ."

"Cut line, my dear. I am nothing of the sort. Now, what is it?"

"It is Lady Catherine."

He looked blank.

"Granville's widow."

This enlightening explanation did not appear to elucidate the situation. The marquess continued to stare at her blankly.

"She has begun a school."

"Surely that is an admirable and proper thing for a widow to do."

"This is not a charity school for children of the local village. It is an academy where young ladies *pay* to be educated, an academy that she styles Lady Catherine Granville's Select Academy for Genteel Young Ladies. It is utterly mortifying to have one's name connected with trade. Granville, of course, is furious. Now that he is head of the family, the responsibility for maintaining the reputation of the Granville name falls entirely upon his shoulders. Naturally, he made the most forcible representations to her about the scandalously inappropriate nature of this enterprise in the first place, and then when he discovered how she had chosen to style her establishment, why . . . Well, not to put too fine a point on it, he was horrified."

"And the widow?"

"Paid not the slightest attention. She is excessively strong-minded."

"Something of a dragon, is she?"

"Worse." Lady Granville shuddered delicately. "She is a veritable bluestocking."

"An intellectual woman? How dreadful for you."

The ironic gleam in the marquess's eye was lost on his companion. Wringing her hands she cast a pleading glance at him. "Now you see why I am desperate for your help. If she will not listen to reason from the head of her own husband's family, she . . . ."

"Is not likely to listen to it from a complete stranger."

"But Charlmont, *everyone* listens to you." Lady Granville's eyelashes fluttered charmingly and she shook a playful finger at him. "And you know very well, my lord, that there is not a woman alive who can resist you. Why even Mrs. Drummond Burrell . . ."

He saw that it was hopeless. "Very well, Lavinia, what is it that you are hoping I will be able to do?"

"Go to her. Speak to her. Make her see that she cannot do this. It will ruin everything for me to be known as the relation of a woman who runs a boarding establishment in Bath."

"If Granville's argument was not sufficiently compelling to make her change her mind, I fail to see what reasoning *I* can lay before her that will make her do so."

"I know you will think of something. Everyone says that you are excessively clever."

The marquess was silent for a moment, thinking. "It *is* true that my niece, who has been allowed to run wild since her father died, is in desperate need of an education and that her mother is most concerned about the hopelessly inappropriate friendship she seems to have formed with the squire's son. Perhaps I should pay a visit to this academy for genteel young ladies on her behalf."

Lucian was rewarded by a brilliant smile. "The very thing! I knew you would save me. Believe me, I am grateful indeed for this and all that you have done. You know that if you were to call on me, say, ah . . . later this evening . . . I could prove to you just how grateful I am."

"I have not solved your problem yet. I have still to meet the dragon, you know."

"I have every confidence that you will bring her around. You know that no woman is proof against your charm, even a dragon."

Chapter Two

*T*he dragon, however, was far from charmed when a week later a letter arrived from the Marquess of Charlmont informing her of his impending visit.

"Oh dear," she gasped faintly as her eyes fell on the crest adorning the heavy cream paper and the boldly scrawled "Charlmont" at the bottom.

"What is it, Catherine? It is not Granville causing more trouble again, I trust?" Her companion looked up from the stack of bills she had been organizing.

"No, worse. The Marquess of Charlmont is considering sending his niece to the academy and is coming to inspect it." Lady Catherine Granville glanced hurriedly through the letter. "Tomorrow!"

"But surely that is excellent news. Not only is the marquess the biggest landowner in two counties, but the family has been one of the leading families since they came over with the Conqueror. To have Charlmont's niece as a pupil would be a feather in your cap indeed!" Margaret Denholme, the local vicar's daughter, mathematics instructress at Lady Catherine Granville's Select Academy for Genteel Young Ladies, and Lady Catherine Granville's closest companion, looked up from the bills she had been sorting.

"If it were the marquess's daughter, perhaps, it would be." Frowning thoughtfully, Catherine gazed out the window. It was clear from the faraway expression in her eyes, however, that she was not looking at the rose bushes in the garden behind her office but at something a good deal further away in space and time. "But his niece?" She shook her head. "I . . . er . . . was *introduced* to Charlmont's brother Lucian Verney during my Season in London and at that time, he had a reputation that did not bear looking into."

"Ah." Margaret watched with great interest as the faintest tinge of color crept into her friend's cheeks. Lady Catherine Granville, mistress of a vast estate for eight years, widowed for two, and founder of a steadily growing academy for young ladies was not the sort of person whose sensibilities caused her to blush at the mere hint of scandal. Though still young, she had always been an independent thinking, practical, and competent woman who welcomed and even sought out the challenges that life brought her way. It was unlike her to cavil at a man's reputation, even if it were out of concern for the reputation and good name of her fledgling establishment.

"But it is quite possible that, now, as the father to a school-age daughter, the Marquess of Charlmont's brother has mended his ways. Perhaps he is now a pattern card of respectability."

"Perhaps." Lady Catherine sounded doubtful, and the blush, instead of fading, grew deeper. She continued to focus her gaze on the scene outside the window with an intensity that told Margaret she was deliberately avoiding meeting her friend's eyes.

Silence reigned once again in the library that now functioned as the office of Lady Catherine Granville's Select Academy in Bath's elegant Royal Crescent. Margaret again bent her head over her accounts while Catherine perused the other letters the post had brought. But there was something in the way Catherine kept looking up from her correspondence and staring off into space from time to time that told Margaret her mind was not on the rest of the letters in front of her. Surely there was more to this than met the eye?

From the moment Catherine's husband had died so unexpectedly and she had been hustled off by his heir to the dower house without so much as a by-your-leave, Catherine had fought to remain involved in the world in which she had played such a vital part as Lord Granville's wife, a world that the new heir was equally determined to divest of her. She was no longer welcomed at Granville Park where the staff's clear preference for its former mistress made it difficult, if not impossible, for the new Lord Granville to establish any authority over them. And in the surrounding countryside where Lady Catherine's popularity was constantly being thrown in his face, the heir had made it abundantly clear that he considered it the height of impropriety and a blot on the family name to have a recently widowed woman so constantly in the public eye. All Catherine's protests that it was charitable work and not social interaction that took her out among her neighbors had fallen on deaf ears, and in the end, she had been forced to curtail even those minimal activities.

For the past two years Margaret had watched her friend simmer with frustration as she sought other avenues in which to invest her abundant energies. When at last the mourning period was over, she had thrown herself into new projects with the force of a whirlwind, hardly pausing to rest. All this—the seething discontent and the ensuing activity—now made this sudden fit of abstraction seem all the more remarkable and out of character for a woman whose every waking moment proved her to be a creature of enormous vitality and a possessor of a restless, inquiring mind.

Margaret did not for a moment believe that it was the prospect of a student whose parent's name was associated with long-ago scandal that was causing this unusual reflectiveness. No, it was much more than that. After all, if Lord Granville's accusations were to be believed, the very existence of Lady Catherine Granville's Select Academy for Genteel Young Ladies was a scandal in and of itself and a blot on a noble name that had existed unsullied for over five hundred years without any member being remotely connected with "trade," as Lord Granville termed it. It almost seemed to Margaret, nibbling thoughtfully on the end of her pencil as she observed the faraway look in her friend's eyes, that there was some sort of connection between the widow and this man of unsavory reputation, something beyond the mere *introduction* that had been alluded to.

Margaret forced herself to continue sorting the bills in front of her, but her mind was seething with questions. What possible connection could a woman like Lady Catherine— sober, respectable, and intelligent, widow of an equally sober, respectable, intelligent, and responsible landowner— have with a man of the *ton* whose "reputation did not bear looking into"? It was an intriguing question, and Margaret, who had spent her entire life in a quiet country vicarage looking after a widowed father of reclusive, studious habits, adored intriguing questions.

In fact, it was this fondness for intriguing questions that had drawn her to Lady Catherine Granville in the first place. The minute she had encountered Lord Granville's young wife the morning Lady Catherine had come to call on the parish's spiritual advisor, Margaret had recognized a mind and a spirit as restless as her own, another person burning to make a difference, no matter how small, in the world. She was another woman who disliked sitting idly by while there were poor cottagers to feed, village children to educate, the sick and infirm to visit, and a whiff of political reform in the air.

None of the women with whom Margaret was acquainted read anything more daring than *Ackermann's Repository,* if they read at all, much less a newspaper, but she soon discovered that Lady Catherine Granville not only absorbed every scrap of news to be gleaned from the *Times* each day, she also devoted herself to *Blackstone's* and the *Edinburgh Review.* In addition, she thoroughly enjoyed a spirited discussion of topics as wide ranging as the poor laws, parliamentary reform, the slave trade, or the beneficial effects of crop rotation.

From that moment on, the two women had become close companions, sharing their hopes and their dreams as well as the minutiae of village life while they ministered to the poor and afflicted and expanded the efforts of the local school so that the older children were able to further their education in the evenings.

Margaret and her father had long applauded Lord Granville's responsible administration of his estates and constantly reminded the parishioners how fortunate they were in having a landlord who was not only a fair and honorable gentleman but someone whose passion was the improvement of his estate and the implementation of modern agricultural practices. In fact, the only criticism anyone could voice concerning Granville Park or its owner was that it lacked a feminine touch. There had been great rejoicing when it was announced that on a trip to Yorkshire to look after his interests in a joint venture in a canal Lord Granville had met a young lady and decided to make her his wife.

The prospective bride was the only daughter of the Earl of Hunsford, a personage of enough importance to be known even in rural Somerset, and it was generally accepted that in marrying the only daughter of such an ancient and respected family, Lord Granville was making a most advantageous match. It only remained to see the lady in person to make this marriage the finishing touch to a man already loved and honored by his tenants and his neighbors.

Lady Catherine had not disappointed expectations. A decade younger than her husband, she was all that was charming, equally friendly and easy with the cottagers and the gentry, but retaining a touch of reserve that gave dignity to her youth and her position.

And if she was not so fashionable nor so much of an Incomparable as some of the more romantically inclined members of the female population had hoped, she was decidedly pretty, with large, sparkling, hazel eyes, a fresh complexion, and a lively expression that drew everyone to her. Her clothes were like her person, in quiet good taste, becoming rather than à la mode, but obviously of the very best quality.

In short, the countryside had almost instantly approved, and Lady Catherine Granville had soon become a much beloved fixture in the community, so beloved that when Lord Granville died and a new Lady Granville appeared on the scene, she was not welcomed with any evidence of enthusiasm, despite her outstanding beauty and the decided air of fashion so lacking in Lady Catherine.

It was this lack of enthusiasm which had prompted the new Lord Granville to move his uncle's relict to the dower house as quickly as possible, isolating her as best he could from the devoted servants and adoring tenants of Granville Park.

However, removing a beloved mistress from the immediate vicinity had done nothing to improve the popularity of the new Lady Granville, who with her London airs and graces had soon alienated even those initially attracted by her fashionable appearance. And the new Lady Granville had only made matters worse by declaring herself utterly bored with the country. She had soon returned to London, leaving her husband to deal with the rustics of Granville Park as best he could.

"But you would still welcome the marquess's niece as a pupil at the academy in spite of her father's reputation, would you not?" Margaret broke into her friend's reverie.

Catherine did not answer. Staring blindly off over the gardens of the houses around them she saw neither the graceful Lombardy poplars in the garden next door, nor the elaborate espalier on the garden wall of the house on the other side; instead she pictured an angular aristocratic face whose gray eyes glinted with ironic amusement and whose lips curled in a mocking smile except when they had smiled at her. Then the eyes had been warmed with the gleam of shared humor and the smile had been a private acknowledgment of the ridiculousness of it all.

Lucian's daughter. It was not the reputation of the father that gave her pause. Oh no, it was something far more unnerving than that. It was the thought of his flesh and blood there in her world, the calm, quiet, orderly world she had worked so hard to create for herself after he had disappeared from it. What would happen to that world of hers if she had to see his eyes looking at her every day or watch his smile transforming the face of one of her pupils? What would become of that calm, orderly world then?

Chapter Three

*C*atherine dressed with greater care than usual the next morning, which is to say that she spent time selecting her gown. It was a plain round dress of black bombazine trimmed in black crape whose sole ornamentation, a white crape frill that stood up around her throat, only emphasized the sober respectability of her attire. She pulled her hair into a braid and coiled it on top of her head, but no matter how ruthlessly she pulled it back, she could do nothing to keep a few dark curls from escaping.

She frowned at her reflection in the looking glass—too youthful by half. If only she had a pair of spectacles to counteract the softening effect of the curls clustering at her temples. There was simply no help for it; she would just have to adopt a suitably severe expression and hope for the best. Primming her lips she tried to school her features into a look more appropriate to a headmistress but succeeded only in appearing what she was, a lively young woman trying to look older and more serious than her years.

Shaking her head at her reflection, she gathered up her bonnet and gloves and taking a last sip of chocolate from the cup her maid had brought her, headed down to the waiting carriage. However little else had been stipulated in her husband's will, it had been left so abundantly clear that the dower house included a carriage and pair that even the effrontery of the new Lord Granville did not extend to denying her that luxury. She had taken full advantage of that provision to order the most beautifully sprung, well-appointed carriage she could from Bath's finest coachmaker and had provided it with a team that was the envy of every whip in the surrounding countryside.

Surveying the magnificent equipage now she permitted herself just the tiniest smirk of satisfaction as she allowed John Coachman to help her into the carriage.

In the days following her husband's death, Lady Catherine had felt so utterly powerless in the face of Lord Granville's ambitions that she had savored every little victory she had been able to achieve, every scrap of freedom and independence that she had been able to hang onto in the face of his determination to cow her into subservient insignificance and respectability.

"The academy, my lady?" John helped her up the step and closed the door behind her.

"Yes, John, but first I should like to stop at the home farm."

"Very good, my lady." The coachman grinned as he climbed onto the box. His mistress could no more pass the home farm without stopping to see the baby than she could spend a day without taking a vigorous walk in the countryside, whatever the weather. And why shouldn't she take pleasure where she could in spite of his lordship's determination that her life should be as dull and confined as he could possibly make it?

A few minutes later the carriage pulled into the neat-looking farmyard and a liver-colored hound ran out to greet them, barking energetically. John had not even reined in the horses before the mistress of the establishment came bustling out of the kitchen. "Good morning, my lady. Come to see the baby, have you? Betty is just finishing up with the milking, but our Tom is feeling fine as fivepence this morning, cooing and smiling with all his wee might. I never did see such a contented baby as our lad here." She led Catherine into a kitchen filled with the enticing smells of baking bread and bramble preserves and stooped over the cradle near the fire from which came happy gurgling sounds, inter-rupted now and again with an occasional chirp.

"My, we are looking chipper today, are we not?" Cather-ine stroked the soft cheek and held out a finger to be clutched by one of the chubby waving hands. "I do believe he has grown since I saw him last."

Mrs. Griggs smiled fondly at the cradle's occupant. "That he has, my lady. It's a right good appetite our boy has."

"And Betty?"

"Merry as a grig and that grateful to you for taking her in when her time came. That family of hers . . . Farmer Griggs's wife shook her head resignedly. "To think that they would deny a child of theirs in trouble. You know me, my lady, I am as respectable as the next person, but when being respectable comes down to turning away your own flesh and blood, well, I am against it. But then the Wantages always did hold a very high opinion of themselves, and what with Mrs. Wantage giving herself airs because her daughter had become maid to a great lady of fashion, well, I say that such pride was well served when her daughter returned home car-rying the great lord's baby. But to turn her out in disgrace, a girl six months gone without a penny to her name, why, it is downright cruel, not to mention unchristian. I am surprised they can hold up their heads in church. And I shudder to think what would have become of Betty and the baby if you had not taken her in."

Mrs. Griggs also leaned over to stroke a downy cheek. "And to think they would deprive themselves of this little laddie here, all for the sake of their precious respectability. I ask you, is there any one among us who has not made a mis-take in their lives that we can be so hard on those who have?"

Catherine's gaze traveled from the baby's big dark blue eyes to his button nose and rose bud lips and, smiling, she shook her head slowly. "No, Mrs. Griggs, there is not."

Even though this was the answer her rhetorical question had anticipated, the farmer's wife was somewhat surprised at her visitor's tone of regret. That, and the hint of sadness in her eyes, almost made it appear as though the young widow herself were thinking of some past indiscretion of her own. But it was impossible to imagine someone as levelheaded and sensible as Lady Catherine Granville ever giving in to youthful folly, or folly of any kind for that matter. In fact, it was difficult to picture Lady Catherine as anything but the perfect image of well–brought up gentility whose unshakable decorum could be counted on to carry her through even the most unnerving and distressing of situations with coolness and aplomb.

In fact, Catherine felt all her coolness and aplomb evaporating as she bestowed a last kiss on the baby's cheek. Casting a reluctant glance around the cheery kitchen, she sighed gently. "Well, I must be off. I shall just stop by the pasture on my way out."

Betty was just filling the last of the milk pails when she caught sight of her benefactress. "Good morning, my lady," she called, her fresh, open face lighting up at the sight of Catherine standing in the gate between the farmyard and the pasture. "Have you been visiting our Tom? Is he not a dear wee thing? Such a delight as he is to his mama's heart and so good. If you had told me six months ago what a comfort to us all that lad would be I would have thought you fit for Bedlam, but there, life is funny, is it not?"

Betty gave a final pat to the cow's sleek rump, rose, and wiping her hands on her apron picked up her stool and her pail. "Nor would I have believed you if two years ago you had told me that I would be able to say that I prefer a simple existence in Somerset to all the excitement of London." Her blue eyes shone suspiciously and she blinked rapidly. "And it is all owing to you, my lady. If you had not taken me in in my hour of need and let me help out at the dower house until the baby came, I do not know what would have become of me. Young Tom and I owe you a debt as we can never repay, and we shall never forget it."

"Think nothing of it, Betty. I am only sorry that my household is too small to need another maid on a permanent basis."

"Oh no, my lady. Farm work is what I truly love. There is something honest and true about it, hard as it is, that makes it more satisfying than waiting on the finest lady in the land, your ladyship excepted, of course. And the Griggses are that kind. I could not be happier where I am, nor more grateful. But now, if you will excuse me, our Tom will be wanting his breakfast."

Catherine bade the young mother goodbye and climbed back into the carriage well satisfied that both mother and baby were flourishing. Indeed, as she recalled Betty's proud smile when she spoke of the baby and the air of contentment she radiated, Catherine could not help feeling the tiniest bit envious. If she had been fortunate enough to have a child, her days would have been a good deal less lonely and a good deal more busy than they were now. Of course she had the academy to keep her occupied and the welfare of her students that required her attention, but it was not the same as having a family of one's own to belong to.

And, an ignoble little voice in her head reminded her, if the child had been a son, she herself would still be at Granville Park and Hugo Granville nothing more than a harmless country gentleman living out his insignificant existence in a small manor house in an obscure corner of Gloucestershire. Ruthlessly Catherine stifled this unworthy thought, forcing herself instead to concentrate on the impending visit of the Marquess of Charlmont.

This man would expect an air of capability in the headmistress of the establishment to which he was willing to entrust the education of his niece. She must not betray any feminine weakness, no matter how much he reminded her of—no, she would not think about it, any of it, not her Season in London, not her husband, not the quiet years of married life. It was gone, all of it, buried in the past. There was nothing left but the present to attend to.

The carriage pulled up in front of the graceful classical facade of the Royal Crescent and halted at the door of Lady Catherine Granville's Select Academy for Genteel Young Ladies. The academy's footman, her one concession to ostentation, hurried out to help her alight, and head held high, chin up, back straight, Lady Catherine marched in, prepared for any and all of the challenges the day might bring her.

Entering her office she pulled off her bonnet, removed her pelisse, stripped off her gloves, seated herself at her husband's impressive mahogany desk that had been dismissed by the current Lady Granville as being too heavy and old-fashioned, and opened her account books. There was nothing like adding up columns of numbers to steady a person and take her mind off whatever worries might plague it. It also would not be a bad thing for the Marquess of Charlmont to see that the head of Lady Catherine's Academy was a businesslike woman with a practical turn of mind.

There was a slight sound in the doorway and Catherine looked up as the tall, lean figure entered the room. The blood drained from her face. Her heart seemed to drop to her feet, and the pen slipped from her fingers, spilling ink on the neat columns of figures on the ledger before her. "Lord Charlmont!"

Chapter Four

*S*ummoning every ounce of strength she had, Catherine
rose to face him. The planes of the angular face were
sharper, the lines of dissipation were deeper, and there was
a touch of gray in the jet-black hair, but the gray eyes still
held their ironic gleam. Yes, it was indeed Lucian Verney, an
older Lucian than the one who occasionally haunted her
dreams, but the same Lucian Verney, nevertheless.

"But you are not the Marquess of Charlmont!"

The twinkle in his eyes deepened. "And I might say the
same thing of you, Catherine. You are apparently no longer
Lady Catherine Montague, but times change. Unfortunately,
I am now indeed the Marquess of Charlmont, my brother
having been so uncooperative as to suffer an untimely and
fatal attack of apoplexy last year."

The voice, deep with a hint of laughter, was having the
same effect on her that it always had. Her knees, already
weak at the sight of him after all these years, buckled under
her and she sank back into her chair with what little grace
she could muster. Drawing a deep, shaky breath, she ges-
tured to the chair opposite. "Your letter said that you wanted
to look at the academy for your niece."

She was unprepared for the wave of relief that washed
over her as she realized the full implication of her words. It
was the Marquess of Charlmont's niece, not Lucian's daughter after all.

He watched as the color rose in her cheeks. So the real

Catherine was there after all, hiding somewhere within this sober stranger. Yes, there were still traces of Lady Catherine Montague to be found if one looked carefully enough. The large hazel eyes, though shadowed, were as knowing and intelligent as ever. The determined chin was a shade more determined now, and the slender nose and delicately arched brows lent it the character that had once distinguished her from all the other young misses in their first Season. Only the mouth was different. The lips that had once seemed always on the verge of curling into a smile were straight and serious, as though they had been compressed in silent protest too many times, and the liveliness about her had vanished. To be sure, the air of vitality remained. Lady Catherine, whether she was Lady Catherine Montague or Lady Catherine Granville, would never lose that vitality, but now her energy seemed to come from determination rather than a zest for living. What had become of the Catherine he once knew?

The slender dark brows rose questioningly and it was his turn to look discomfited. She was still waiting for an answer. "Oh, er, yes, my niece. Well, she is sadly in need of an education. Her mother, an amiable woman who is no match for her daughter, has let her run roughshod over a series of governesses, drawing masters, music masters, and tutors, with the end result that she has, at best, acquired only a smattering of the knowledge she should have. You, no doubt, would consider her a perfect little heathen."

Ignoring the glancing reference to a past acquaintance that she was desperately trying to forget, Catherine clasped her hands in front of her and assumed what she hoped was a suitably impressive expression. "Here at the academy we are dedicated to providing a full range of instruction that will equip young women to fulfill their roles as mistresses of their estates, wives, and mothers in the most responsible fashion. We are not a finishing school that puts a few artistic touches on a decorative object in order to raise its value on the Marriage Mart."

His lips twitched. "I did not for a moment think you were.

My niece is decorative enough already. She needs the solid foundation of a more classical education. In short, she needs to be taught to think."

"I would not have thought that *you* would want a woman . . ."—Catherine bit her lip—"Er, I mean, that is a most laudable goal, my lord. I trust that it will be realized."

"However, considering the ramshackle character of her uncle, you have your doubts."

"I did not say that."

"You did not need to. Your face was always most expressive and you were never good at dissembling. I always found that transparency to be one of your most charming traits." He watched with a good deal of satisfaction as her cheeks grew pink once again and she struggled to keep her countenance. There, he had almost made her smile.

In spite of the years that had passed, she looked absurdly youthful in her widow's garb and definitely out of place. She should be indulging in all the country pursuits she had so missed when she was in London—galloping rides across the fields, long walks in the country, working in the garden—not sitting behind a desk on such a glorious day, faced with the cares and responsibilities of running an educational institution.

"Confess it, you were thinking it impossible that someone like me should be head of a family now."

This time she did smile in spite of herself. "And brutal frankness was always one of *your* traits, my lord. Yes, it is rather difficult to picture you in that role."

"Well, it was not by choice, I'll admit, but when a role is thrust upon one, there is no alternative but to do one's best."

The hint of a smile tugging at Catherine's lips broadened into a real one. Lucian, no matter what else he might be, had always been a realist, and it was this willingness to look life in the face instead of consulting the fashion of the moment or prevailing opinion that had originally drawn her to him and made him such an easy person to talk to and to share things with. No, Catherine admonished herself, she would *not* think those things this time. She had done that once before and had nearly broken her heart in the process.

Drawing a deep breath, she squared her shoulders resolutely. "Then you will forgive me for sounding boastful, but I will say that in selecting this academy for your niece you are doing the very best for her. I have gathered some of the most accomplished teachers it has ever been my pleasure to encounter, and we give our students a very thorough preparation in history, rhetoric, geography, French, and mathematics, as well as music, painting, and drawing. And for those who are so inclined, we also offer Latin."

"A most impressive program indeed. A young lady who has paid even the slightest attention during her stay here ought to emerge from your establishment a very thoughtful young lady indeed. And since it was you who taught me that there is nothing so enchanting or, unfortunately, so rare as a woman who can think and speak for herself, I am sure you do an excellent job of it."

Again, he was pleased to see the tinge of pink creep along her cheekbones. Good. It meant that in spite of the responsible position she had chosen for herself and the severely businesslike exterior she tried to maintain, the vital, passionate girl he had once known had not entirely vanished or been replaced by this somber stranger.

"What? Er, yes, if I dare say so myself, we do strive to accomplish all that here. But you must see for yourself." In her haste to rescue the conversation from straying into the dangerous channels where it seemed to be heading, Catherine rose too quickly, nearly upsetting the inkwell in the process. Biting her lip, she caught it just in time, restored it to its proper place, and struggling to cover her confusion, tidied the papers on her desk. Then drawing herself up as straight and tall as she could and adopting her most gracious lady-of-the-manor air, she sailed to the door. "If you will but follow me, my lord."

She led him into the hall past marble statues from Greek and Roman mythology and etchings of classical Roman antiquities to the drawing room at the front of the house. The light pouring in through the numerous large windows made the spacious, airy room seem large despite the row of tables lined in the center and the harp and pianoforte that dominated the wall opposite the door.

Every available space along the walls was covered with either maps or book shelves, and several globes stood ready to reveal their geographical complexities to eager young minds.

At the moment, there were four eager young minds all focused on a large map of ancient Greece at the right hand of an impressive looking woman of indeterminate age who seemed to hold the undivided attention of her well-groomed pupils. "So you see, girls, what an extremely perilous voyage Odysseus was forced to undertake. One can only imagine the adventures that could befall one on such a journey. Now, as we read together, I want you to ask yourselves what you would have done in similar situations. Would you have been as clever as the wily Odysseus should you have been faced with the trials that he was?"

Lucian ruthlessly stifled the grin that threatened to rise to his lips. It seemed that Catherine was not the only redoubtable female in the establishment.

From the drawing room they proceeded down the staircase to the dining room, now doing duty as another classroom. Here another group of slightly older girls was listening to one of their members reciting verses in Latin with a fervor that Lucian could not ever recall having felt during his own Latin lessons.

He listened intently for a moment. "Horace?" Then he turned to Catherine, one quizzical dark brow raised in mock dismay. "Love poetry? You are using love poetry to teach them their Latin?"

She chuckled. "What better way? Every young girl has romantic notions of some sort or another. Better to admit that fact and try to use such notions to teach something instead of having them spend their time haunting the circulating libraries."

"I always said you were the cleverest person I knew. I can see that at least *that* has not changed."

For her part, Catherine could not decide whether she was gratified to be remembered as clever or dismayed to think he found her changed and, from the tone of his voice, apparently not for the better. But what he had thought of her then or what he thought of her now was utterly immaterial, just so long as he approved of her establishment.

Nodding blindly at Miss Compton, who was conducting the class, she led him quickly from the room.

Across the hall in a smaller study room, the oldest girls were clustered around a large table busily working at what appeared to be a mathematical problem.

As Lucian and Catherine entered the room, the instructress was admonishing the youngest girl in the group. "No, no, Lucinda, you must stop and consider the problem carefully. Here, perhaps if I were to put it to you in a more practical way you will find it easier to figure out. Suppose you were placing a bench on the lawn near a copse of trees. Naturally, you would wish it always to be in the sun. Now, if you have the height of the tallest tree in that copse, then you can calculate the farthest distance it could possibly cast a shadow and you could then place the bench beyond that point. So you see, the study of mathematics can be extremely useful to anyone."

Hearing their footsteps, the woman straightened and glanced around in their direction.

"Do not let us interrupt you, Miss Denholme; I am just showing the Marquess of Charlmont around our establishment."

The instructress quickly returned her attention to her student, but not before directing a glance in Lucian's direction, a glance that made him feel as though she harbored something more than a normal curiosity about him. It was as though she saw him as something more than a possible patron of the establishment. Had Catherine mentioned to her that she had once been acquainted with the Marquess of Charlmont's brother—well acquainted, in fact? Lucian was surprised to discover how much he hoped that this was the case.

Continuing the tour, Catherine led him to two more rooms, in one of which the girls were poring silently and intently over books in front of them and in another where they listened spellbound as a rather frail older woman, clad in the fashion of some twenty years ago, declaimed the immortal lines of Corneille's *Phèdre*.

Everywhere he looked, from the simple but elegant furnishings to the well-stocked school rooms, revealed the careful thought and attention that had been lavished on the establishment. Though he would have expected no less from Catherine Montague—no, he corrected himself hastily, Catherine Granville—he was impressed in spite of himself. There was, however, one detail that was notably lacking in Lady Catherine Granville's Select Academy. "Do you employ no male preceptors in your academy, then?" Lucian wondered.

She turned and looked him full in the face, a hint of a smile hovering at the corners of her mouth. "Now, how can a young woman be expected to think for herself or rely on her own intelligence if everything she learns is taught to her by a man? No, my lord, the young ladies of this establishment are not just learning their sums or their geography, they are learning that females can excel at things to the same degree that males can, and that is no small lesson."

"If your fiercely competent mathematics instructress is any sort of an indication to go by, I would say that your pupils will not only learn to rely on their own intelligence, they will dispense with the need for masculine companionship altogether."

The hint of the smile broadened into a full-fledged grin and the hazel eyes began to twinkle. "Oh no, we are not such Amazons as all that. I would never go so far as to encourage my girls to eschew male company completely. We do have a Monsieur D'Antoine as our dancing master, a most accomplished one too, I might add."

"So we men do have our uses after all, I see. Not many,

but enough to justify our continued existence, for the time being, at least."

She chuckled at that. "*For the time being,* most assuredly."

Chapter Five

*T*he Marquess of Charlmont left the establishment at the Royal Crescent well satisfied with both the quality of the instruction and the accommodations to be had at Lady Catherine Granville's Select Academy for Genteel Young Ladies. He was not, however, satisfied with the state of its proprietress.

Lucian had always possessed a sixth sense where women were concerned. It was what made him so hugely popular, not to mention devastatingly effective, with the female sex. And this sixth sense was telling him that despite her air of cool authority, all was not well with Lady Catherine Granville.

It was not simply that the spirited and independent Lady Catherine Montague had grown into the calmly competent Lady Catherine Granville, for that sort of thing was to be expected after ten years. But this was not a question of inexperienced youth ripening into sedate maturity. It was more fundamental than that. Something vital had been lost along the way, and Lucian, in spite of all the warning bells going off in his head, in spite of the promptings of his own good sense—a good sense gained at considerable cost during the turbulent years of a somewhat checkered career—was determined to find out what it was that had been lost and why.

In a thoughtful frame of mind he returned to his lodgings at the White Hart to lay plans for the next day, plans that included inquiries, not so much into the academy itself, as into the sort of person the late Lord Granville had been, and, if possible, the sort of relationship he had had with his wife.

As to the academy, Lucian had few doubts that it would do his headstrong niece a world of good to be placed in the care of the strong-minded ladies he had seen there. Not only was Arabella bound to learn more than the desultory interest in water colors and smattering of Italian songs that were all her current governess, the ineffectual Miss Mitton, seemed to have instilled in her charge, but Lucian was reasonably certain that the good ladies at Lady Catherine Granville's Select Academy would exercise a beneficial effect on a romantical young woman who was, according to her mother, determined to ruin herself with the squire's son.

When he had first been told of the Marchioness of Charlmont's fears concerning her daughter's attachment to young Foxworthy, Lucian, already a most reluctant head of the family, had dismissed them as the nervous imaginings of a weak woman who was still overwhelmed by the untimely loss of her lord and master. But her constant fretting had finally worn on his own nerves to the point that he had engineered a casual encounter with young Foxworthy at the taproom of the local hostelry. He had not the least interest in confronting the young man about his intentions toward Arabella. He merely wished to discover what sort of person the lad was and to learn if he truly had designs on Lucian's niece or if it was nothing more than anxious delusions on the part of a mother who was anticipating a brilliant match for a girl who was as pretty as she was well born and as wealthy as she was pretty.

What Lucian had discovered had not reassured him. The young man was handsome enough to appeal to any young woman, and being possessed of a somewhat exalted sense of his own worth was bound to appear masterful and bold to an inexperienced young girl like Arabella. However, in the more worldly eyes of her uncle, Tom Foxworthy seemed selfish rather than masterful and a braggart rather than bold. In fact, Foxworthy reminded Lucian of no one so much as the brutal self-styled "husband" of his first mis-

tress, the talented and much sought after actress Miranda
Delahunt. And despite the number of years that had passed
since Lucian's involvement with the lady, he had not lost
one whit of his anger at the mistreatment she had suffered
at the hands of that man. It was an anger so deep that it had
ultimately spurred Lucian to devote his energies in ways he
had never thought possible to insuring that such men were
deprived of the power they so unfairly possessed over
women like Miranda.

One glance into the emptiness of young Foxworthy's
eyes, one look at the stubborn set of his jaw, had convinced
Lucian that this callous and selfish young man was fully capable of making Arabella as miserable as William Delahunt
had made Miranda.

However, Lucian also knew that sharing these misgivings
with his niece was more likely to make her fly to the defense
of her beloved than to give him up, hence his plans for her
immediate removal from the vicinity and admission into the
care of a strictly supervised educational establishment. The
fact that this plan had coincided so nicely with Lady
Granville's demand that he pay a visit to Lady Catherine's
Academy had been so fortuitous as to make him accede to
Lady Granville's wishes more promptly than he ordinarily
would have considered wise.

Having jotted down notes as to all the inquiries he still
wished to make, Lucian strolled down to the taproom in
search of refreshment.

He had barely crossed the threshold when the innkeeper's
wife, catching sight of a guest whose presence was bound to
bring further business to her establishment, hurried forward
to see to his comfort, even going so far as to fetch the forti-
fying glass of ale he ordered herself instead of leaving it to
the barmaid.

"It is an honor to have you as our guest, my lord. You
must let me know if there is anything we can do to make
your stay here more comfortable. Of course, the White Hart
enjoys an excellent reputation, but it has been some time
since we have been honored by a guest of your lordship's

distinction. I do hope you will think of the White Hart again should you happen to be in Bath in the future. But perhaps you are considering setting up an establishment of your own in town? There are many who consider Bath to be quite eclipsed by Brighton, now that the Prince Regent has made it so fashionable, but there are still a number of notable families who prefer to come here to refresh their health. Why, I could tell you the names of any number of families who patronize our fair city."

Clearly the woman considered herself an authority on the comings and goings of Bath's more illustrious visitors. Perhaps she was an equally authoritative source of information on some of its inhabitants as well. Favoring her with the smile that had never failed to put women at ease, whether they were scullery maids or duchesses, Lucian decided to put her knowledge to the test. "I do, in fact, expect to be an occasional visitor to the city as my niece is to become a pupil at Lady Catherine Granville's Academy."

He was instantly rewarded for his trouble. The innkeeper's wife nodded her head sagaciously. "An excellent choice, my lord. Even though it was but recently begun, the establishment already enjoys the highest of reputations among the best families in these parts. There is no one more loved or respected in the surrounding countryside than Lady Catherine, though you would not think it after the shabby treatment she has received at *his* hands."

"His?"

"The new Lord Granville, and as clutch-fisted as they come, he is, at least where everyone else is concerned. For himself and to further his own ambitions, he spares no expense. It was a sad day for us all when the old lord died, not that he was so old, for a finer gentleman and more generous landlord you never did see. And it was an even sadder day for her, poor thing, packed off to the dower house and forced to take on pupils to earn her keep. I tell you, it does not bear thinking of." The innkeeper's wife sighed gustily and shook her head. "And she who was so kind and good to everyone, hurried out of the Park where she had been mistress for all those years before the master was even cold in his grave."

"She seems to have succeeded in providing for herself, however. The academy certainly looks as though it is doing well." But while he was speaking of the present, Lucian was busy thinking over the past, Catherine's past. The innkeeper's wife had referred to her husband as "the old lord." Surely she would not have done so if Lord Granville had not been considerably more advanced in years than his wife. Then it must have been a marriage of convenience rather than a love match.

Lucian did not want to admit to himself how relieved he felt. Encountering Catherine so unexpectedly after all these years had been unsettling enough already. He did not need to be further unsettled by examining his own reactions more closely than he already had. As it was, he found himself looking forward far too much to seeing her again tomorrow when he would stop at the academy to make final arrangements for enrolling Arabella.

"She has done an excellent job of running the place. Many of her pupils are from the best families in the county. But it is still a crying shame to see a fine lady like that being forced to work for a living, especially when there is no need for it, if certain folks were not so greedy, that is."

Lucian suppressed a start of surprise. He had completely forgotten the existence of the innkeeper's wife, so absorbed had he been in his own thoughts. "Does she have no other relatives with whom she could live or who could offer her support?" Dredging back into his past, Lucian thought he remembered an elder brother being mentioned, but he could not be sure. He did remember reading in the *Times* that the Earl of Hunsford had died a matter of months after his wife had.

"I never heard of any, but even if there were, what woman who has been mistress of an estate like Granville Park wants to become the poor relation in someone else's establishment?"

What woman indeed? Certainly not the fiercely independent Catherine who had chafed against the confining expectations of proper behavior for a young miss in her first Season. How much more she would resent living by the rules of someone else's household, no matter how closely related she was to that person. Far better for someone as energetic as Lady Catherine to be in charge of her own academy, no matter how hard she had to work or how much risk it entailed. At least she was in control of her own destiny as the proprietress of Lady Catherine Granville's Select Academy.

Or was she? Even as he was arriving at this conclusion, Lucian remembered his original purpose in coming to Bath, not for the sake of Arabella's education but because the new Lady Granville wished him to persuade Lady Catherine Granville to give up her establishment and behave with the decorum and propriety expected not only of Lord Granville's relict but of anyone connected with one of the most respected names in the county.

Anyone faced by the determination of the socially ambitious Lady Granville as well as the reputed greed of her husband was bound to feel uncertain as to the degree of control she actually did exert over her own life. As someone who had spent much of his own existence rebelling against the expectations of his family in particular and the dictates of society in general, Lucian could sympathize heartily with the frustration Catherine undoubtedly felt. She and he had always been independent thinkers. In fact, it had been their recognition of this independence in one another, coupled with their fervent desire to create lives of their own, that had initially drawn Lord Lucian Verney and Lady Catherine Montague together a decade ago, establishing a friendship that had made the rigors of the Season not only bearable but almost enjoyable for both of them.

But later that day as Lucian once again sat in the headmistress's office overlooking the gardens lying behind the majestic curve of the Royal Crescent's severely classical facade, he could not detect even the slightest indication that Lady Catherine Granville was not supremely in command of her establishment and her life. She answered every one of his questions with an assurance and an authority that would have been impressive in a sixty-year-old man, much less a woman who was less than half that age.

In fact, it was Catherine and not Lucian who posed the truly uncomfortable question in the interview. "And what other establishments are you considering for your niece's education, my lord?"

He hoped his face did not betray the sheepishness he felt as he relied. "None."

"What, not even one? I would be remiss in my duties as an educator if I did not urge you to examine at least one other alternative. If you are truly concerned about your niece's future, it is imperative that you select an establishment that will suit her."

"Believe me, there is no need. The moment I entered your office, er, I mean the minute I entered this clearly excellently managed academy I knew it would suit her and I feel no particular need to look elsewhere, for it would be the merest waste of my time."

"Believe me, I appreciate your flattering assessment of our institution, my lord, but I must reiterate my concern over a decision so hastily made."

"Your concern is indeed commendable, but I am more than satisfied with my choice."

"Then I thank you for your confidence in the academy."

There was no mistaking the ironic note in her voice. Clearly she recognized the firmness of his resolve and gave in to it. Just as clearly she recognized that he had selected her establishment for reasons that had nothing to do with his niece, reasons that he was not about to divulge or even examine himself. Lucian felt an uncomfortable flush rising to his cheeks.

Unable to think of a suitable rejoinder Lucian executed an impressively formal bow and strode from the room, leaving her to stare thoughtfully after him.

Chapter Six

*I*t would have done Catherine a considerable amount of good to know that his thoughts were in as much turmoil as hers, that his air of cool detachment was no more real than hers.

She had hoped that after recovering from the initial shock of seeing Lucian again she would adjust to the idea of his being the Marquess of Charlmont, the uncle of a prospective student, and that she would be able to relegate him to the ranks of the rest of her patrons who possessed the good sense and discriminating taste to entrust their female relatives to her care. In other words, he would represent nothing more or less to her than a business proposition.

Unfortunately, or fortunately, as the case might be, business propositions did not make her heart pound and her knees go weak. The Marquess of Charlmont, however, did, even after eight years of marriage and two years of widowhood.

It was not a weakness Catherine liked to admit, but admit it she did. She had always done her utmost to be brutally honest with herself, struggling on a regular basis to face issues squarely and deal with them accordingly. This had been easily enough accomplished when, admitting to herself that she was not what the world would call a beauty and recognizing that she was far too independent to inspire masculine protectiveness or devotion, she had settled for a marriage of convenience to Lord Granville. Fully aware of what she was doing, she had accepted respect instead of love, shared interests instead of mutual passion. It was a great deal more difficult, however, to admit now that someone who never should have played a significant role in her life and in her consciousness had, in fact, never left them.

Shaking her head vigorously, Catherine looked back down at the account book in front of her. She had been young and inexperienced, just a girl, when Lord Lucian Verney had first upset her peace of mind. Then, she had been powerless to combat the deep impression he had made on her. Now she was no longer young and impressionable. She could choose to ignore the way he made her feel. She would focus on her own life, her own goals of turning her academy into a place that shaped women's lives into something of value and satisfaction instead of a frenetic search for fashion and social status.

But at the moment, Catherine needed more distraction than the account books in front of her could offer. She needed other people, other conversations. Closing the book in front of her with a decisive snap, she went in search of Margaret Denholme, who shared the carriage ride home with her as far as the vicarage every afternoon after school when Catherine returned to the dower house.

The instructress was gathering up her students' papers and several obscure-looking mathematical treatises as Catherine entered the room. Making rather more work than was necessary out of stuffing it all into a serviceable-looking satchel, Margaret tried unobtrusively to read the expression on her friend's face with little success.

It was not until they were both finally in the carriage and rolling off down the Royal Crescent toward home that Margaret, unable to contain her curiosity any longer, spoke up. "From the little I saw, the Marquess of Charlmont appeared to be favorably enough impressed with us yesterday, but what person of taste and refinement would not be? And he definitely seemed to be a person of taste and refinement. I trust that upon his return today he was decided upon the academy for his niece?"

Catherine was silent for some time, and Margaret, her gaze still focused on her friend's face, thought she detected just the hint of a blush spreading over the delicate aristocratic features, but perhaps it was just the warm hues of the late afternoon sunlight pouring through the carriage window.

"Ah, er, yes he did." Catherine blushed even more deeply as she looked up to discover Margaret surveying her closely.

It was a most unsatisfactory answer, especially for a young woman born with an intellectually curious nature. "Odd that he has the care of the young lady. I suppose that he mentioned why it is he who is looking after his niece instead of her mother or father?"

"The father is dead."

"How sad. An accident, I collect? However, you did say that he was a man of dubious reputation. People of dubious reputations are more prone to such things than the rest of the population."

"That is undoubtedly true, but such is not the case where the Marquess of Charlmont is concerned. That is, I mean he *is* the Marquess of Charlmont, but not *the* Marquess of Charlmont, if you know what I mean."

Margaret's blank expression was irrefutable proof that she did *not* know what her friend meant.

"What I *mean* to say is that the man you saw today is the man you presumed to be dead. He is the man I formerly knew as Lord Lucian Verney, brother to the Marquess of Charlmont."

"The rake?"

Catherine nodded slowly, and this time Margaret was certain that the rosiness suffusing her companion's cheeks had nothing to do with the sun and everything to do with Lord Lucian Verney, who was apparently now the Marquess of Charlmont.

"Perhaps he is not so rakish as he once was. After all, he must have mended his ways to some degree if he is now concerning himself with his niece's education."

"On the contrary, he is as irresponsible as ever. Do you

know he even admitted to me that he is not looking at any other establishments beyond ours? It is *that* sort of heedless behavior that once made me . . . We—er—never mind. After all, what business is it of mine if he does not exert the proper attention in the selection of an educational establishment for his niece as long as it is to our benefit?"

"So he in fact *was* an acquaintance of yours at one time." Margaret could not hide the satisfaction in her voice. From the moment Catherine had mentioned the rakish younger brother of the Marquess of Charlmont, Margaret had suspected that it was more than a casual introduction that was responsible for the self-conscious expression that crept into her friend's eyes every time the subject came up in conversation.

That self-conscious expression was most definitely present now. "Well, we did become acquainted during my one and only Season, but it was only the most casual, the briefest of friendships, thank heavens, for in the very middle of it . . . the Season, I mean . . . he utterly disgraced himself by running off with an actress. So you see why I was not necessarily ecstatic at the thought of his daughter entering . . . Well, never mind. Undoubtedly I refine upon it too much, but where a fledgling enterprise such as ours is concerned, one can never be too careful of one's reputation."

They were silent during the rest of the journey, Margaret entertaining a variety of wild speculations concerning the history of the relationship between Lady Catherine Granville and the Marquess of Charlmont, formerly Lord Lucian Verney, and Catherine trying desperately to fix her mind on anything but that relationship.

Such concerns were immediately wiped from both their minds, however, as they pulled up in front of the vicarage to discover another carriage in the drive.

"Granville? Here? He is up to some sort of mischief if he has managed to overcome his distaste for your father's 'liberal principles' enough to call on him," Catherine commented grimly.

Margaret was equally uneasy. "Certainly he is up to no good, but then, he never is. You had best come in with me and find out what it is."

Margaret's father was looking decidedly uncomfortable as they entered the vicarage's cozy sitting room, and he welcomed his daughter and her companion with obvious relief. "There, you see, my lord, here are my daughter and Lady Catherine now to answer your question."

"Question? There is no *question* about it! The woman is a disgrace, and her presence is an affront to every decent citizen in the community." The already florid face of the vicar's visitor took on an even more alarming hue as he pointed a stubby finger at the community's moral preceptor. "And I would expect a vicar worthy of his living to do something to rectify the situation immediately."

He glanced triumphantly at the two young women after this pronouncement, but the gasp of dismay he was so clearly hoping for did not come.

"How odd. I would think that the first concern of any spiritual advisor would be Christian charity." Catherine refused to pretend ignorance of the topic of discussion, which was clearly the presence of Betty and her baby, and she refused even more adamantly to betray even the slightest sign of weakness.

Looking Lord Granville straight in the eye, she continued. "Surely a vicar can find no better way to save the souls of his parishioners than by encouraging them to follow our Lord's own precept, 'He that is without sin among you, let him cast the first stone.' And surely Betty, who is now living as sober and industrious a life as any of us, repents of the indiscretion that cost her her dream of becoming a fashionable lady's maid."

Ignoring her completely, Lord Granville continued to focus his attention on the vicar. "As you see, sirrah, the situation is dire indeed when gently born ladies are so far gone that they forget what they owe to their name and countenance this sort of loose behavior. Such an attitude is nothing short of scandalous. Not only do they not shun this fallen woman with the proper horror of respectable women, they offer her aid and sustenance. Furthermore," he added, warming to his theme, "failing to establish the proper moral tone in their own lives, they now have the audacity to set themselves up as preceptresses to other young woman. All of which, sirrah, can lead me to only one conclusion, and that is that we are sadly in need of a new spiritual leader in our little corner of the world."

This time a moment of shocked silence did follow his outburst. Then Catherine, struggling to contain her rage, finally found her voice. "How dare you, sir, speak to a gentleman in this way, a gentleman who has cared for the sick and the poor, consoled the suffering, and done more for his parish in a day than you have done in your lifetime! And as to my audacity in educating young women, I can only say that *I*, at least, am doing something useful with the inheritance left me by my Great-aunt Belinda, which is more than I can say for the inheritance that was entrusted to *you!* Now, if you have done insulting the vicar in his own home, I suggest you leave."

Lord Granville was no match for her righteous indignation. Standing erect, shoulders back, chin up, her eyes blazing with the intensity of her purpose, Lady Catherine looked like an avenging angel. If the truth were told, Lord Granville had always been a little in awe of her absolute confidence, a confidence born out of her own personal convictions, rather than arising, as he attributed it, from being born the daughter of an earl, a fact that his own nagging sense of inferiority would not let him forget.

"I shall be happy to quit the company of those whose utter lack of moral responsibility fills me with disgust." Lord Granville had intended to match Catherine's high moral tone, but he failed entirely and once again, in spite of his efforts, he found himself on the defensive, a position that made him feel distinctly uneasy and robbed him completely of what little dignity he did have. Sweat beaded his brow, and his voice, which was petulant at best, had risen to a high pitch more characteristic of a fishwife than the lord of a vast estate. There was nothing left to do but retire before what little superiority he possessed disappeared entirely.

Turning on his heel, he stomped out of the room, slamming the door behind him.

"Oh, dear." Margaret put a hand to her lips. "I do believe that we have gone too far this time. He truly could choose to bestow Papa's living on someone else."

"Nonsense. If he is foolish enough to do that—which he is not, for the entire countryside would be up in arms and he has too strong a sense of self-preservation to risk that—we shall just hire your papa to teach Greek and religion at the academy. In fact, it might be a very good idea to have him do so anyway."

But for all her bold words and defiant looks, Catherine was nearly as shaken as the vicar and his daughter. "That man may turn me out of my home, may even enrich himself on the shares from the canals that came as part of my dowry, but I will *not* let him bring harm to my friends or to the community that welcomed me here as a bride. He is forever throwing my 'lack of respectability' in my face, but I have too much respect for myself and for all that Granville and I tried to accomplish over the years to let that grasping, pompous, fool . . . Well, never mind."

She smiled reassuringly at the worried pair in front of her. "Forget about him. Concentrate instead on preparing your lessons for tomorrow, Margaret, and I shall call for you in the morning at the usual time."

Chapter Seven

*B*ut in spite of her brave words, Catherine was worried. The new Lord Granville was a bully and a fool, but he had already managed to make her life difficult. And though most people treated her with the same love and respect they had always accorded her when she was the mistress of Granville Park, there were some who were willing to espouse whatever opinions her husband's heir happened to voice simply because he was Lord Granville and he was a man.

Catherine sighed wearily as she surrendered her bonnet and gloves to her waiting maid. She wished desperately that she had someone to talk to.

The maid hung the bonnet on a peg, laid the gloves on a side table, and returned to light the fire in the library. "You just take a seat before the fire, my lady, and I shall bring you some tea."

"Thank you, Lucy. It has been a long day."

The maid shook her head. "You work too hard, my lady. It is that school of yours. It will make you old before your time. Far better to have taken your great-aunt's inheritance and gone to London to find yourself another husband."

"Lucy!"

"I know, I know. You do not want another husband. But you are too young and too pretty to hide yourself in the countryside and waste your youth on good works. Time enough for that when you are old and ugly. Besides, you need a man to take . . ."

"Take over my affairs? Thank you, no. What I *need* is to be left alone to manage them by myself. I have men enough as it is interfering in my affairs."

"It is not Lord Granville again?" Lucy had been one of the servants lucky enough to have an excuse to leave Granville Park when the heir took over, but she had heard tales enough from those left behind to thank her lucky stars that she had been one of the few servants for whom the mistress had had a place in the dower house. And from that privileged position she had been witness to her mistress's many battles with the new Lord Granville. If she had not been an active witness to the encounters, certainly she had been a witness to their effects. Lady Catherine's compressed lips and angry frown were just the sort of effects that proved, as she had seen time and time again, that such a battle had taken place.

"Yes, it is Lord Granville again." Catherine had always accorded what the new Lord Granville called 'a dangerous familiarity' to her personal servants. In those first lonely days at the dower house, that familiarity had saved her from the crushing sense of loss and purposelessness that had threatened to overwhelm her. It was the ready sympathy and understanding of people like Lucy that had carried her through that dark time. People of her own social standing, her peers, had viewed the move to the dower house, the ceding of responsibility for Granville Park to its new master, as the natural course of affairs. To them, it made perfect sense for her to lose so many important aspects of her life and they had congratulated her on shedding the various tasks and responsibilities of the mistress of a vast estate. To them, it signified freedom. To her, it meant emptiness.

Only those accustomed to making their own way in the world—people like Lucy and Margaret—understood what it had been like to lose the very purpose of her existence. But even Lucy had thought she was crazed to go so far as to take on the responsibility of Lady Catherine Granville's Academy.

"If only Madam's brother lived closer, he would put his lordship to the rightabout. Perhaps if you were to write to him . . ."

"Robert? What could Robert do? Robert is a good man, but he is no match for Hugo, er, I mean Lord Granville, and he utterly lacks the imagination to appreciate the situation. He simply would not see any harm in consigning a widow to a hopelessly boring existence. Nor would he understand in the slightest. I do not want any man telling me what to do or offering his advice on this question. *Or on my life,* Catherine added silently, as the vision of a tall dark-haired man with penetrating gray eyes rose before her. Now, here was a man she truly did not want in her life. Lord Lucian Verney had caused problems enough when he had appeared in it for the first time. True, she was no longer the impressionable young girl she had been then. She had outgrown her naiveté, but she had not outgrown the way he affected her. His smile still made her feel just as breathless now as it had ten years ago, and that sense of the special understanding between them remained as strong now as it ever had been ten years ago, in spite of his betrayal.

Blast! Catherine set down the cup of tea that Lucy had brought her and picked up the latest edition of the *Edinburgh Review.* She refused to let the past overwhelm her. What was done was done, and if Lord Lucian Verney had chosen to run off with an actress rather than pay court to Lady Catherine Montague, well, that was his affair, and she was not going to waste one more moment's thought on it or on the question of who, if anyone, had become the new Marchioness of Charlmont. All she needed to know at present was that the marquess's niece was soon to become a pupil at Lady Catherine Granville's Academy and if she were happy there, everyone in the Upper Ten Thousand would be clamoring to send their daughters, nieces, sisters, and granddaughters to that select educational establishment.

As for the Marquess of Charlmont, he was gone, back to Charlmont or wherever he had come from. And with any luck, she would never see him again. The niece would arrive

in the family carriage with her maid and possibly her mother
as a companion. The bills and correspondence would all be
handled by the new marquess's man of business and Catherine would very likely not have any further contact with him.
So why did she not feel relief at this prospect? She should
be happy and proud that she had faced a ghost from her past
and had survived with dignity intact. Instead she merely felt
dull and dispirited.

"Will Madam be requiring anything else?"

"What? Oh, no, thank you." Catherine shook her head
groggily. She had been so lost in her own thoughts that she
had completely forgotten Lucy hovering at her elbow.

"Very good, Madam." Lucy gave a final poke to the fire
and then, closing the door silently behind her, left her mistress alone with her thoughts.

And those thoughts appeared to be more upsetting than
usual. Lucy had watched sympathetically as one by one her
mistress's responsibilities had been stripped away and the
small indignities had piled up.

First, the servants had been ordered to refer any command, even the simplest of requests for the stoking of a fire
or the saddling of a horse to his lordship. Then had followed
the abrupt dismissal of anyone, from the butler to the lowest
scullery maid, who had been inclined to look favorably on
their former mistress or refer to the way things had been
done under her tenure. Finally, there had been her removal
to the dower house, with every stick of furniture begrudg-
ingly bestowed. And through it all Lady Catherine had
maintained an air of aloof dignity that only those who knew
her best could penetrate enough to see the hurt and outrage
seething just below the calm, collected surface.

But this evening Lucy sensed that there was more to her
mistress's mood than yet another outrage perpetrated by the
grasping 'Ugolino' as Lady Catherine had dubbed him in a
moment of particular frustration with the man who, bit by
bit, was destroying all the trust, all the respect, and all the
good that she and her husband had carefully built up over
the years.

No, there had been a wistful note in her ladyship's voice as she had dismissed her maid, a hint of regret, almost sadness, in her eyes as she had gazed into the fire. While it was true that Lord Granville made Lady Catherine angry on a continual basis, he had never made her sad. He was far too despicable a creature to affect her that way. So if it was not Lord Granville who was upsetting Lucy's mistress, then who or what was it?

Eschewing the warmth and companionship of the kitchen where Cook was busy preparing her ladyship's supper, Lucy climbed the stairs to her own room under the eaves and picked up her basket of mending. It was chillier here than in the kitchen, but it was quiet, and Lucy wanted to be alone to sort out her thoughts.

During the entire time following the shock of Lord Granville's sudden death, the precipitous descent of the new heir and his wife into their lives, the unexpected inheritance of her great-aunt's fortune, and the subsequent establishment of Lady Catherine Granville's Select Academy for Genteel Young Ladies, Lady Catherine had moved toward her goals with an energy and a purposefulness that, even for someone as vital and dynamic as she, had been remarkable. Why now should she suddenly look so weary and disoriented? Why now, when she had withstood so much, should she appear more worn out, more grave and thoughtful than ever?

Lucy was almost as determined a young woman as her mistress, and at the moment, she was determined to find out what was bothering Lady Catherine. Born into a large family of ne'er-do-wells, Lucy had always had her mind set on bettering herself, and at a tender age had, with great audacity, convinced the cook at Granville Park to take her on as a scullery maid. Lucy's willingness to do any task asked of her and her quiet, cheerful efficiency had quickly endeared her to everyone in the kitchen and she had soon been promoted to kitchenmaid. She had even impressed the housekeeper to such a degree that when one of the chambermaids left to marry a farmer, Lucy had been asked to take the girl's place.

Again, her diligence and her willingness to take on any task paid off and she became the chief downstairs maid, where she caught the eye of Granville Park's young mistress, who had taken a serious interest in the young woman's ambitions.

And when the time had come for Lady Catherine to move to her new home in the dower house, she had asked Lucy to come with her as a replacement for her own maid, Rose, who was longing to return to her family in Yorkshire. Rose had returned home with sufficient wages to last her a year and recommendations glowing enough to earn her a place in any household, while Lucy, who could not believe that she had reached a status so exalted that it exceeded her wildest dreams, had taken up the duties of maid to her ladyship, vowing to repay Lady Catherine's kindness with undying gratitude for as long as she drew breath.

It seemed to Lucy as though now might be the moment she had been waiting for to demonstrate this gratitude. Clearly something was upsetting her mistress, something more than a problem at the academy or even Lord Granville's perfidy; she would have elaborated on any of these, but instead she had been quiet, quieter than usual. There was nothing to do but watch and wait for some clue as to what was troubling Lady Catherine. In the meantime, though, she could at least brighten her mistress's day with the news that yet another servant had left Lord Granville's employ and come to beg her former mistress for a job.

Lucy had warned Mary as kindly as she could that the dower house was too small an establishment to need another servant, but the girl had been so distraught that she had promised to let her speak with Lady Catherine herself, knowing full well that her kindhearted mistress would think of some excuse to keep the girl on for a little while at least, until she had managed to find her a position elsewhere.

Neatly snipping a thread, Lucy smiled grimly as she re-called her conversation with Mary. It would be small consolation after being dumped so unceremoniously at the dower house, but Lady Catherine was sure to take comfort from the fact that she was so sorely missed at Granville Park that servants still begged her to find them a position in her household.

But now was not the moment to inform her mistress of the new arrival. Better to let her sort out what was troubling her and then tell her about Mary in the morning. For no matter how tired or dispirited Lady Catherine was, she always seemed to be able to put her troubles behind her and rise the next day filled with renewed energy and purpose.

For Catherine, however, staring unseeing into the fire, energy and purpose and the future were a long way off. At the moment all she could see before her was Lady Almeria Northcote's victorious smirk one evening ten years ago as she announced the latest scandalous *on dit.* "It is said that Lord Lucian Verney has run off with an actress. Have you ever heard anything so outrageous?"

"Not if she were very pretty." Catherine had replied calmly enough, but it had taken every ounce of her strength to ignore the dreadful sinking feeling in her stomach and the chill that crept over her as she looked into Almeria's pale, humorless eyes. Fortunately, her loathing for the prudish, sanctimonious gossip was strong enough to make her forget everything for the moment except her desire to retain her dignity at any cost in front of a young woman who had never lost an opportunity to demonstrate her superior knowledge of the *ton* from the moment Catherine had arrived in London.

Lady Almeria's pale eyelashes blinked rapidly. "Have care, Lady Catherine. You know very well you have made a fool of yourself in setting your cap at that man, and all your pert responses will only make it look the worse for you. One must be infinitely careful in one's first Season, for a reputation is a fragile thing. Once shattered, it can never be repaired. You would do well to listen to the wisdom of those of us who have been on the town for more than one Season and know the ways of the fashionable world."

Catherine gritted her teeth. "But why would I listen to the advice of one who has had several Seasons? Surely, anyone who was truly knowledgeable would be so successful as not to need more than one Season to make a brilliant match."

"Why you—you brazen little. . . ." Lady Almeria managed to gasp at last. "How *dare* you speak that way to me when you have only managed to attract the notice of a man who is so dead to propriety that he runs off with an actress and is such a fool that he will probably marry her."

And to Catherine's infinite relief, Lady Almeria had turned on her heel and stalked away, leaving her to survive as best she could the anguish that seemed to be squeezing all the blood from her heart.

But she had survived in spite of her absolute conviction that she could not live through the loss of her closest friend and his total betrayal of her trust.

Catherine's eyes focused at last on the flickering flames in front of her. The searing visions of that awful night receded into that part of her soul that she had thought she had locked away forever. Now she knew she could take those corrosive memories out again, reexamine them in all their pathetic detail, lock them back away, and still survive. Surely this was the last time she would have to do it, for no matter how intriguing and clever Lord Lucian Verney had once thought her, he now found her sadly changed. Had he not hinted as much?

Having selected a fitting educational establishment for his niece, he had no reason to reappear in her life. Undoubtedly he would be glad to shed that particular responsibility so that he could return to his many others, which, if they happened to include a wife and a family of his own, were no concern of Catherine's.

Chapter Eight

*I*n fact, Catherine's speculations were entirely incorrect. Far from being eager to shed his responsibilities, Lucian was at that moment increasing them as he informed the Marchioness of Charlmont that he had not only found a suitable place for her daughter, but he also intended to escort her there.

"That is very good of you, Lucian. You have been all that is kind in finding a place for Arabella, but there is no need for further effort on your part. Surely at such a time, a young girl is in need of her mother's support." The marchioness, clutching her ever-present handkerchief, dabbed gently at the corner of each eye. "Though I still see no reason for her to go so far away. Surely, if Miss Mitton is as ineffective as you say she is, it is merely a matter of finding another governess, and . . ." Her voice trailed off helplessly.

"I thought you were concerned about Arabella's growing friendship with Foxworthy's son?"

"I am, but Arabella is a good girl and most biddable. It is enough that I point out to her how unsuitable it is for her to encourage him. Do you not think so?"

Lucian, who knew his lively and determined niece far better than her mother did, did *not* think so, but it was useless to remonstrate. The marchioness was a woman of limited intelligence and even less resolve who saw only what she wished to see.

"Believe me, Arabella is not likely to forget about

young Foxworthy when he is intent on capturing a wealthy bride. He is well aware of his good fortune. Such a prize, so close and so ripe for the picking, is not to be sneezed at, and I assure you he is determined to take advantage of his situation."

"Oh, surely not. Surely he is aware that their difference in station makes such a thing impossible?"

"I am convinced that he thinks nothing of the sort."

"Oh, dear. Whatever shall we do? Arabella will be most distressed, I am sure."

"Trust me, Louisa, removing her from his influence is the only answer. Do not worry about it. I assure you that once Arabella has been introduced into the companionship of other girls and the delights of shopping in Bath, she will forget all about young Foxworthy. And the quicker she is introduced to them, the better. I shall be happy to escort her there on Saturday."

"Saturday! But that is only three days' time! We can never be ready in three days' time."

"*You* have no need to be ready, as I intend to accompany her."

"But she must have her mother with her for support."

Privately, Lucian was certain that Arabella was far more likely to consider her mother a burden than a support, but he smiled reassuringly at the marchioness as he patted her shoulder. "Your concern is only natural, but think of the fatigue of the journey. I shall be returning to London soon at any rate, and Bath is but a stop along the way for me. For you, it would mean not only the journey there, but a night at an inn and the return trip alone without the company of your daughter."

The marchioness shuddered.

"So you see, your offer, though all that is admirable, is entirely unnecessary, and I promise I shall not have leave Bath until I have seen to it that Arabella is safely ensconced at Lady Catherine Granville's Select Academy for Genteel Young Ladies."

The marchioness raised swimming eyes and smiled

tremulously at her brother-in-law. "Thank you, Lucian. You have been so good. Ever since Herbert left us, I have not known how to go on. I hate to ask yet another favor from one who has already done so much, but I think it would be a great deal better coming from you—*the news,* I mean."

"I shall be happy to inform Arabella of *our* decision."

"Oh, would you? You are too generous." The marchioness reached for her vinaigrette and lay back on the sofa where she had been reclining with a book of sermons when Lucian sought her out.

It was nothing even remotely like generosity that compelled Lucian to return to Bath, but there was no point in disabusing the marchioness of that notion. The more she believed him to be acting in their best interests, and the more she relied on him for guidance and support, the better off they would all be. Her impulses were always the best; however, the marchioness was a kind but weak mistress whose indecisiveness had nearly reduced the household to utter confusion before Lucian had been able to get there and set things back to rights again after receiving the news of his elder brother's death.

No, it was not generosity, or even concern for the welfare of his niece, who would be perfectly well protected on her journey with the coachman, her maid, and several burly outriders, but an intense desire to see Catherine again that made him volunteer to accompany Arabella to Bath.

Lucian had forgotten what a potent effect Catherine had always had on him, but it had all come rushing back to him in a moment as he had stood staring at her across her desk that first day at the academy. There was a vitality about her, an intensity, and a sense of purpose that had always intrigued and challenged him. It was her eyes that had first attracted him. Filled with a lively intelligence and lit with a sparkle of humor, they told him that their owner was a person worth knowing.

He smiled as he remembered their first waltz together. They had immediately become involved in such a heated discussion of the importance of common lands and the economic effects of the Speenhamland System that at one point they had stopped dead on the floor while the other couples swirled around them like so many butterflies, as Catherine argued that supplementing wages with parish poor rates would bring disaster.

Lucian had never known any other woman, or man, for that matter, who was so interested in so many things, and he had sorely missed their conversations after he had left London, but other events and other concerns had soon overtaken him, and over time he had forgotten how much he missed those conversations until he saw her again.

He admitted to himself that after ten years there was still no other woman who could stand up to him as she did, and certainly no one clever enough or strong-minded enough to make him feel foolish. He could not help chuckling as he recalled her shocked disapproval as she questioned him about his selection process of schools for his niece. 'What? Not even one?' Even though his own lack of thoroughness in reviewing other possible choices for Arabella's schooling was all to her advantage, Catherine could not stifle her innate integrity. And who else among his acquaintances would have dared to call him to task for his intellectual laziness or would have cared that he find the best possible place for his niece, regardless of personal interest?

Rejecting the offer of a servant to fetch his niece, Lucian himself went in search of Arabella, whom he eventually located in the rose garden, though he suspected from the lopsided angle of the bonnet, its carelessly tied ribbons and the muddle of scissors and gloves in her otherwise empty basket that she had arrived there only moments before.

Clearly she had wished him to find her there. And just as clearly she had chosen to pose in the role of country gentlewoman for some particular purpose. The last time he had seen his niece, she had been equally determined to prove to him that she was an avid equestrienne. Unlike her weak and vacillating mother, Arabella never did anything by half measures, and never without a reason, obscure though that reason might be to the rest of the world.

"Uncle Lucian! How delightful to see you. I vow it has been an age since you were at Charlmont."

Lucian ignored the gracefully extended hand. "Cut line, Arabella. It has been less than a month; furthermore, you are quite aware of how long it has been and all the reasons for it."

"Ah yes, the enchanting Lady Granville, I believe. Undoubtedly she grew bored without the flattering attentions of her latest flirt."

"You know full well that my presence in London was required for other reasons, business reasons. But that is quite beside the point. What sort of company are you keeping that amuses itself by wasting its time spreading idle gossip? You sound like the worst of the town tabbies."

Arabella glanced at her uncle nervously. His tone was light enough, but there was a hint of steel underneath. "I was merely repeating what is common knowledge. Lady Partington and her daughters were speaking of it not long ago, and naturally I informed them that it was business and not pleasure that had recalled you to town."

Lucian hastily stifled a grin. She might widen her eyes, the picture of artlessness, but despite her innocent tone the defiant tilt of the chin betrayed her; there was no doubt that Arabella was a minx or that her weak-willed mother was simply no match for her lively daughter. It was high time that his niece was sent someplace where she would not be able to ride roughshod over everyone.

"Then it is Lady Partington and her daughters who sound like the worst sort of town tabbies, and it is time you were introduced to more fitting company. Fortunately, I have come to speak to you about that very thing."

"You have?" Arabella eyed him suspiciously.

"Yes. A young lady of your expectations should be expanding her horizons, growing beyond the provincial sort of thinking that inevitably pervades country society."

"But I like the country. It is peaceful here, and I am happy with simple country pursuits." She waved a dramatic arm to include the vista of green fields dotted with sheep as well as the basket that she had laid at her feet.

So that was it, the reason behind the carefully staged scene in the garden! She knew he had come to take her to school and this was her way of convincing him that it was a waste of time. "I am more than seven, you know, Arabella. You would insist on being a nun if it suited your purpose. And I do recall that not long ago you were equally insistent that life at Charlmont was intolerably boring."

"That was ages ago. I have grown up a great deal since then."

"Yes, all of six months ago, I believe. And I know you have grown up since then," he responded grimly, thinking of young Foxworthy. "However, it is high time you acquired knowledge commensurate with your age. I have found a place that will give you all that, believe me. It will also prepare you for a future that encompasses a world far beyond Charlmont."

"But I have no wish to leave Charlmont. I do not want to become some lady of fashion who spends her entire day at her toilette in the hopes of being more à la mode than her rivals. There is no need for me to have a Season in London, for I plan to spend the rest of my life in the country. And surely if you are concerned about my wasting my time 'spreading gossip like the worst sort of town tabby,' it would be more sensible to keep me here in the country away from the influence of town tabbies," Arabella concluded triumphantly.

Lucian was silent for a moment, picturing another strong-minded young lady many years ago who insisted she had no use for the *ton*, who had resisted her parents' efforts to give her a Season. But surely, Lady Catherine had enjoyed that Season just a little bit? Certainly it had been the most memorable Season in Lucian's experience. Every Season after that had been a stale repetition of the one immediately before it. "No," he responded slowly, "I do not wish you to waste your time in trading gossip and the latest *on-dits*, which is precisely why I am escorting you to Bath, where you will learn to think for yourself, to develop a mind that can appreciate many things beyond mere *on-dits* and the latest whims of fashion."

"Bath? You are taking me to Bath?" Arabella looked thoughtful.

"Yes, that is where the academy is."

"Oh." It was almost a sigh of relief.

Lucian could almost see his niece's mind working feverishly. She knew him to be a man of his word, a man who was immune, or nearly immune, to the machinations of females far more sophisticated than she, and she knew there was no resisting him. She also knew that Bath was a good deal closer to Charlmont than other places he could have selected. Further resistance would arouse his suspicions and perhaps make him think seriously about sending her some place farther away.

"Very well, but I must be able to come home to visit Mama. She has been suffering a great deal from her nerves since Papa's death."

"I will make sure that whenever I come to Charlmont I shall stop along the way to pick you up and bring you with me." Lucian did not think for a moment that the Marchioness of Charlmont's nerves, her chief claim to anyone's attention, were any more present after her husband's death than they had been before, but regular visits to Bath would give him the opportunity to pursue interests of his own, and that was reason enough for him.

Chapter Nine

*O*nce Arabella had submitted to her uncle's plans for her future, she appeared biddable enough, and if she remained closeted in her chamber for long periods with her maid, it was presumed that she was supervising the packing for the trip.

On Saturday she bade her mother and the assembled servants at Charlmont a fond but cheerful farewell and composed herself for the journey with such equanimity that Lucian's suspicions were immediately aroused.

He kept a weather eye out for lone riders along their route, but none appeared, and he was forced to conclude that either her relationship with young Foxworthy had cooled considerably or she was far more skilled at clandestine relationships than he had given her credit for.

They pulled up in front of number 16, the Royal Crescent, late that evening just as the sky was deepening from pink to azure and the stars were beginning to come out. The academy was ablaze with light and the butler opening the door smiled benevolently at them. As he ushered them upstairs to Lady Catherine's office, the sounds of laughter drifted enticingly down the stairs.

Closely observing his niece, Lucian was pleased to see the carefully bored expression Arabella had maintained throughout the trip brighten into one of curiosity and interest until she felt her uncle's eyes upon her and the mask of boredom came down again.

Lucian was not the only one to see beneath this carefully assumed appearance. As Catherine greeted her prospective student she studied her carefully. It was a merry face with a generous mouth, a hint of dimple at one corner of it, and large brown eyes that were clearly more accustomed to examining the world with frank curiosity than remaining fixed demurely on the carpet as they were now. Obviously this was a young woman of spirit who was doing her utmost to hide that fact under the best imitation of a meek exterior she could manufacture.

"I am delighted that you could join us here at the academy, Lady Arabella." Catherine rose and extended her hand. "I do hope you will enjoy the girls as much as I do. They are a lively bunch so I am sure you will soon feel quite at home." She smiled at the sparkle of interest that flashed in her prospective pupil's eyes despite her best efforts to remain expressionless.

"In particular, I expect you will enjoy Olivia, the Countess of Morehampton's daughter. She was one of our first pupils and is about your age. As she lives very near here, I count on her to be your guide to the shops in Milsom Street and the many delightful walks in the area. She is also an excellent student, though I imagine that is of less interest to you. Shall I ask for her to show you around? You are far more likely to learn what you wish to know about us from someone your own age than from one of the teachers or the headmistress of this establishment."

"Oh, yes, please. I would like that." Arabella smiled shyly. There was no resisting Lady Catherine's frank, easy manner and her genuine concern for her new pupil's future happiness. In fact, Arabella quite forgot her resolve to maintain her air of meek indifference and was soon responding readily to Lady Catherine's questions about her journey, the number of trunks she had brought with her, and her concern for her horse whom she had been forced to leave behind.

"At the moment we have no accommodations for horses as we are but a small establishment. As we grow, however, I fully intend to offer stabling for our students, as I know I could not do without my regular exercise, and walking is just not the same thing as riding. Ah, here is Olivia. Olivia, may I introduce you to Lady Arabella, who has just arrived. I hope you can show her around, introduce her to the others, and make her feel welcome. I have already assured her that you are our authority on the best shops to be found in Bath." Catherine turned to welcome a tall young woman with masses of golden hair and a decided air of fashion which clearly made an impression on the newcomer. There was no mistaking the envious admiration in Arabella's eyes as she took in the higher waist, tighter shape, and long sleeves that proclaimed the gown Olivia was wearing to have been very recently created by an extremely skilled modiste.

"I shall be happy to show her around." Olivia smiled in the friendliest of fashions as she led Arabella towards the door. "It will be delightful to have another member of the academy who is the age of the older girls. Is this your first time in Bath, Arabella?"

As Catherine turned back again to Arabella's uncle, the sounds of girlish laughter wafted up the stairs. "I think I can safely say that at the very least your niece will enjoy the companionship here. In addition to Olivia, we have two other students who are very close to her age as well as a few who are only slightly younger, and they all appear to be on the best of terms."

"Credit for which I am sure is due to you and your instructresses. Nevertheless, I intend to remain in town several days to ensure that Arabella is feeling quite at home before I return to London."

Catherine's eyebrows rose in faint surprise. There was no need for his concern. Though Arabella's attitude had at first been rather unforthcoming, it had been quickly discarded in favor of one that was far more animated the minute she had become involved in conversation. Catherine did not have the slightest worry about the new pupil's fitting right in with the rest of the girls. In fact, she was willing to wager a good deal that the girl would prove to be the most redoubtable of a group that had already been characterized by any number of people as "extremely lively."

"It is just that she has never been away from home and it has not been a year since she lost her father." Even to Lucian's ears this sounded like the merest excuse.

"I see. Well, we shall do our very best to make her feel at home, then—not that we do not try to do so for everyone." Catherine remained unconvinced of the need for this extra solicitude on the marquess's part. There had been something—undue emphasis in his voice, just the hint of self-consciousness in his expression, a certain look in his eye—that led her to believe that Lucian had reasons of his own, entirely unconnected to Arabella, for remaining in Bath. Did he not trust her to care for his niece? If he did not, then why had he chosen Lady Catherine Granville's Select Academy for Genteel Young Ladies as the place to educate Lady Arabella out of the hundreds of others, some of which claimed to offer all the advantages and more than her establishment did?

"Ah, then perhaps I had better tell you the time that is best to visit us is after morning lessons. We encourage exercise and fresh air after a morning spent in the schoolroom, so at noon you can expect your niece to be free to see you. And now if you will excuse me, I have some things I must attend to."

In the face of such a clear dismissal, there was nothing he could do but bow and leave. However, he paused when he reached the doorway. "I trust that if the academy encourages fresh air and exercise for its students after a busy morning, then the same goes for its headmistress, who must be even more in need of such diversion. And if she instructs by example, then surely she can be enticed into a short drive in the country with me."

"What? I mean, there is certainly no need . . . That is to say, it is most gracious of you to offer, but I am sure that your niece would prefer to be alone with you since she is so recently arrived at the academy."

"Oh, I was not intending for her to accompany us. It is

you I wish to induce to join me. It strikes me that a head-mistress who takes her duty as seriously as you obviously do, and far more seriously than my niece will ever take her lessons—or anything else in her life, for that matter—is in much greater need of a break from her tasks than any of her pupils."

And without giving Catherine a moment to recover from her confusion, much less frame a reply, Lucian flashed her an impish grin and closed the door behind him, leaving her, he hoped, prey to a whirlwind of conflicting emotions, the same sort of conflicting emotions that were playing havoc with his own well-ordered existence.

Not since he had met Catherine the first time had he been so unsure of a woman, so uncertain as to what was going on under that coolly professional exterior of hers. And not since he had met her the first time had he been so determined to find out. Surely there was more there than the rigorously re-sponsible headmistress? Surely that passion, that quick ap-preciation for the ridiculous in all things, that lively curiosity, that urge to learn everything, had not vanished en-tirely in the sober owner of Lady Catherine Granville's Se-lect Academy? And surely if such a vital creature still existed under that somber exterior, the Marquess of Charl-mont was just the man to discover it. He would start that dis-covery tomorrow.

In the meantime, it had been a long day spent in the com-pany of a determined young lady who had done her best to adopt a suspiciously false demureness, so suspicious that her uncle had found himself constantly on the alert for the ap-pearance of a young gentleman at every crossroad and every hostelry they passed. After hours of such enforced watchful-ness, Lucian was most definitely in need of the excellent re-freshment and all the comforts to be found at the White Hart.

Chapter Ten

*U*nfortunately for Catherine, she did not have the distraction of the taproom of the White Hart. After tidying up her desk for the evening, she checked with the footman to see that Arabella's things had been delivered to the chamber she was to share with Olivia. Then, having assured herself that the two girls were engaged in a lively discussion of where the very best gloves, bonnets, ribbons, and all the other necessities of life were to be found, as well as the competing merits of Bath's numerous circulating libraries, she went in search of Margaret Denholme in the hope that her conversation during the journey home could be counted on to obliterate all thoughts of the Marquess of Charlmont from her mind.

When Catherine had said goodbye to Lucian after his first visit to the academy, she had chided herself for allowing her relief at his return to his own life to be tempered by just a hint of regret that he would have no reason to return to Bath once he had selected a school for his niece. Now that he had, she was equally as disturbed by his presence as she once had been by the prospect of his absence. What was wrong with her? And why did the thought of riding alone with him in a carriage the next day plunge her into such a state of agitation?

Margaret's presence in the carriage on the way home did offer diversion of a kind, for she was still fretting over Lord Granville's veiled threats to her father's living. "You know

Papa as well as I do; he would never consent to being bullied, even if his principles were not being challenged, but they are. And he is too proud to ask any of his more powerful and influential friends and acquaintances for assistance."

"Have no fear," Catherine reassured her. "We are fortunate in one thing, and that is that Ugolino is an even greater coward than he is a bully. And the two things he fears most are his wife and the loss of his reputation. After our little, er, *discussion* with him at the vicarage, I wrote a note to the Countess of Morehampton, who immediately assured me that she will sing your father's praises so loudly everywhere that Granville will not *dare* say a word against him and will very likely begin complimenting himself on being the benefactor of a man who is held in the highest regard by all the best families in the county. The countess assures me that he acts the veriest toady in her presence so I feel certain that she will succeed in cowing him into submission."

Margaret shook her head in admiration at this strategy. "I must say, you can be very clever when you wish to. One might even go so far as to call you devious."

"I have had to be. That *man* has done his best to destroy all the good that Granville and I worked so hard to accomplish, whether it was fencing in the common land that we had given over for the villagers' use or letting loyal servants go after years of faithful service to the family. Why, just this morning, Lucy begged me to take on another poor unfortunate who was summarily dismissed. I have told Mary that she can stay at the dower house for a while until I can find something for her, but I have no place for her in my household. The poor girl was so desperate at being let go without the least warning and so grateful to me for helping her that she promised to put her hand to anything."

Catherine was thus distracted until they reached the vicarage, and for the rest of the evening she managed to occupy herself with domestic issues great and small, but the next morning she could not prevent herself from waking to the thought that this was the day for her drive with Lucian.

Once again, in an effort to remind herself that she was no

longer an impressionable girl but a grown woman with responsibilities, she donned a carriage dress of impressive respectability and selected a modest crape-trimmed bonnet.
She even went so far as to hide her hair under a lawn cor-
nette edged in black.

As she took a final glance in the looking glass before
heading down to the carriage, she told herself she was
pleased that her somewhat restless night had left her paler
than usual with faint smudges of fatigue under her eyes. It
only made her look that much older and more responsible,
to look in fact what she was—a woman whose life was dedicated to serious pursuits, a woman who was far too busy to
indulge in something as frivolous as a drive simply for the
pleasure of it.

But all morning long she could not help glancing at the
clock on the mantel and watching the hands creep inex-
orably toward noon. It was an exceedingly fine spring day,
and it had been an age since she had enjoyed a leisurely
drive in an open carriage. Even the garden below her window looked inviting as a gentle breeze stirred the leaves on
the trees and the occasional butterfly flitted by.

She was still gazing out the window when the butler announced, "The Marquess of Charlmont to see you, my lady."

Catherine jumped guiltily as she turned to see Lucian in
the doorway. She was lost now. There was no way she
would be able to convince him that she was far too busy to
join him in a drive, not when he had caught her staring wist-
fully out the window.

"I am delighted to see that you are longing to be out of
doors on such a beautiful day." Frowning slightly he strode
over to the desk and looked searchingly at her. "And I would
venture to say, judging by your looks, that you spend far too
much time in your office and far too little indulging in your
own fresh air and exercise, however much you may advo-
cate it for your pupils." He took her arm, raised her to her
feet, and propelled her gently toward the door.

"What makes you . . ." Catherine just managed to snatch

up her bonnet from the peg as she passed through the door. "I mean, why do you say that?"

"Because, Madam Headmistress, you look sadly pulled. Now,"—he paused for a moment, took the bonnet from her hands, set it carefully on her head, and tied the bow with an expertise that betrayed years of practice in such things— "you are to forget about everything—the accounts that need balancing, bills crying out to be paid, provisions to be stocked, letters to be written—and let someone else see to the disposal of your life for the moment. In an hour or so you may reassert that commendable organization and control that distinguishes whatever you do, but for the time being, you are in my care, and"—he held up an admonitory hand before she could open her mouth to protest—"not another word until we are in the carriage."

He smiled down at her reassuringly as he led her downstairs and out the door, handed her into the curricle, and took the reins. But instead of heading through town toward Sydney Gardens, he turned the horses away from the city to the hills that encircled it. "Unless you have changed a great deal in the past few years, I thought you would prefer the more natural vistas of the country and a chance to spring the horses to a tame roll through the crowded and cultivated paths of the public gardens."

How well he understood her, even after all this time. "Oh, infinitely, though there would be far more talk if I were to be seen driving with you in Sydney Gardens."

"Talk?" He looked at her curiously. There had been no mistaking the bitterness in her voice. "Talk? About the headmistress of a genteel educational establishment?"

"According to Ugolino, I am constantly courting ruinous gossip with my scandalous behavior."

"Ugolino?"

"My husband's heir, the new Lord Granville, though I never call him that if I can help it. He does not deserve the title of Lord Granville. His real name is Hugo, but I call him "Ugolino," after the villain in Dante's *Inferno* and a far more fitting appellation in my opinion. It is *he,* not I, who is the blot on the family escutcheon."

"Scandalous behavior? You? What have you done, revealed your ankles to all and sundry in Milsom Street?"

Catherine sighed. "No, nothing like that. I simply exist and that is apparently insult enough to the family name, though until Ugolino appeared, I had thought I was upholding the honorable traditions that Granville worked so hard to establish over the years, traditions like charity, responsibility to the tenants, stewardship of the land, and . . ."

She stopped so abruptly that Lucian turned to look at her as she fixed her eyes fiercely on the scene unfolding before her, but her rapid breathing and determined blinking betrayed her.

He slowed his team to a walk and laid one hand over hers. "My poor girl. You seem to have had rather a bad time of it."

She was totally unprepared for his ready sympathy, but then, that had always been the most disarming thing about him. He had always possessed a singular appreciation for whatever was bothering her.

"Well, to be fair to him, it is as much Ugolino's wife as it is he. She is a frivolous creature totally devoted to carrying on her own fashionable existence and he is so grateful to be married to such an exquisite beauty that he will do anything to see that she gets what she wants. It is quite clear to me that Ugolino lives under that cat's paw."

"He does, does he?"

"Yes, he does. Lady Granville, like so many beauties, is clearly accustomed to having her way where men are concerned."

"She is, is she?"

"*I* think so. Undoubtedly, she is constantly surrounded by countless men in London who are all pathetically eager to do her bidding."

"Now, how would you arrive at a conclusion like that? Surely *you* do not listen to idle gossip."

"Certainly not." Catherine sniffed haughtily.

"I am glad to hear it." Lucian heaved a tiny sigh of relief.

"But I know the type. She is used to getting what she wants. And what she wants is to become one of the leading lights of the *ton,* which encompasses the stifling of what she considers to be disreputable behavior in her husband's relatives, such as educating young women, for example. For Ugolino's part, he is mostly excessively greedy and he has made sure that he has secured for himself not only the entire profit from the estate, but all my canal shares. My father naively gave them as part of my marriage settlement without setting them up in trust for me, since he knew my husband was a gentleman who could be counted upon to see to it that I benefited from them. It was only the death of Great-aunt Belinda, who unexpectedly left me her entire estate, that allowed me to establish the academy. But we have talked enough of me. Tell me more about Arabella . . . and her family."

There was silence for some minutes as Lucian appeared to be lost in thought. "Oh, ah, Arabella. Yes. She is an only child whose liveliness has been allowed to go unchecked by a rather weak-willed mother. Her father's death has left her without any restraining influence in her life."

"Except for her uncle."

"Except for her uncle, whose affairs keep him in London a good deal of the time."

"And are there no other uncles, cousins, or . . . ah . . . aunts to provide a stabilizing influence?"

"No. William, my younger brother, was killed at Water-loo. He was not married."

"Ah. I *am* sorry." The carefully neutral tone of his voice told her how deeply this loss was felt. Struggling to remember, Catherine recalled a vague image of a handsome, laughing young man in regimentals who stood in considerable awe of his older brother's reputation as a noted whip and Corinthian. So apparently there had been no Lady Lucian Verney who had suddenly become the Marchioness of Charlmont? Catherine chided herself for suddenly feeling so lighthearted when the faraway look in Lucian's eyes told her

that the loss of his younger brother continued to be a freshly
felt pain.

"I know he was very dear to you." It was her turn to lay a
sympathetic hand on his arm.

"Very dear, but"—his smile twisted—"he would be the
first to scold me for mourning him. To him it was all a glorious adventure, and Waterloo, undoubtedly, the most glorious of all. He always told me he wanted nothing more than
to be a hero . . . and that is what he was."

They were both quiet for some time, alone with their
thoughts, yet sensible of the sympathetic presence of the
other. It had always been this way between them. They had
always managed to share their thoughts without the least
self-consciousness, each secure in the confidence of being
accepted and appreciated by the other.

It was Lucian who broke the silence at last. "But I am
here to see that you enjoy yourself. I am also here to prove
to you that I am a serious fellow who is entirely capable of
acting as responsibly toward his niece as any guardian in the
land. Now, tell me more about your academy. How did you
begin and where did you find what appear to be your dedicated and excellent instructresses?"

"What? Did you make *no* inquiries at all as to the history
and reputation of my academy before you decided upon it
for your niece?" She shot him a teasing glance that for a moment transformed her into the Catherine he remembered—
spirited, lively, confident of her own cleverness and
resourcefulness.

"It was, er, a rather sudden decision," He admitted. "I had
been absent from Charlmont for some time, and when I finally paid a visit, I could see that the situation was rapidly
getting out of hand. Your academy is close enough to Arabella's home that her family can visit should she fall into a
decline, and Bath itself has enough distractions to amuse
her, should your instructresses fail to engage her attention."

"They will not fail."

"You seem remarkably confident of their ability."

"I am. The woman you saw teaching *Phédre* was my own

dear governess, Madame de St. Alembert. She and her husband barely escaped from France with their lives, and when her husband died soon after their arrival in England, she came to us in order to earn her living. She was a remarkable teacher, and when I went to London for my Season, she became an instructress at an academy in Harrogate. Naturally, I sought her out immediately when I began my academy here. I count myself very fortunate to have lured her here, along with some of her fellow instructresses."

"I imagine that Bath does have a good deal more to offer than Harrogate."

"Perhaps, but I also pay a wage commensurate with their talents—something that is all too rare even in male educational establishments, much less female ones."

He smiled at the fierceness of her tone. "Forever the reformer. No wonder Ugolino is afraid of you. You will turn his precious little world of wealth and privilege upside down before you're through."

"I certainly hope so."

"You always were a fire-eater. I am glad you have not changed. I knew it the first time I saw you at Almack's. While all the other young ladies were pinning bright welcoming smiles on their faces, you were scowling like a thundercloud, and I knew you were the one for . . . ah, I knew we were all in the basket. You seemed to see right though all the fashionable pretenses and it was painfully obvious that you had no use for the company in general or the Marriage Mart in particular, as indeed you did not. Clearly Lord Granville made your acquaintance elsewhere." It was a pitifully obvious ploy to discover more about her husband and her marriage. He knew it, but at the moment it was all he could come up with.

"Granville was a friend of Papa's. Like Papa, he was convinced that canals were the key to many things—industry, commerce, travel, even agriculture. He agreed with Papa that investing in them was investing in the future of England. He came to Yorkshire to inspect some of Papa's canals and that is how we met."

"And having met you, he was immediately taken with your wit and beauty and determined at once to make you his wife."

She cast him a pitying look. "You make me sound like some helpless creature from a novel. Granville and I discovered that we shared many of the same interests. I could see he was a man who took his responsibilities seriously. He worked hard to make his estates and his investments prosperous, which in turn made his tenants and his laborers prosperous as well. And he could see that I was equally serious about such things."

"Ah. I see, a truly madcap affair, then."

There was something in his look, Catherine could not quite say what it was, that put her on the defensive. "You may sneer if you like, but Granville needed a wife who could help him fulfill his dreams for his estate. He appreciated what I could do for him, the schools I wished to establish, the charitable plans I . . . In short, I would venture to say that there are very few husbands and wives who trusted and respected one another as we did."

"There is no need to fly into the boughs. Believe me, I meant no disrespect." Lucian himself could not say what had prompted him to make such an ironic comment in the first place. "Relationships of mutual trust and respect are far less common between men and women than madcap affairs. You are fortunate indeed to have found such a helpmeet. But tell me more about how Lady Catherine Granville's Select Academy for Genteel Young Ladies came into being."

And deftly steering the conversation toward less dangerous territory, Lucian was soon able to reestablish the tone of easy openness that had always distinguished their discussions.

However, after he had returned Catherine to the academy and had had time to reflect on their entire conversation, he found he was able to take a certain amount of satisfaction from her bloodless description of her marriage. Respect and trust were all very well, but they were not everything. The Lord knew, he had enjoyed precious few relationships, if any, that had been characterized by either respect or trust, much less both—except for the one he had enjoyed with her so long ago, until he had destroyed it. But had he ruined it entirely, or was there still something left after all those years? It was far too early to say, but he knew that he hoped so.

She still had the power to affect him strongly, but did he affect her in the same way? He was not sure. He pulled into the stable yard of the White Hart, a grimly ironic smile on his face. Who would ever have thought that the notorious Lucian Verney would ever be unsure of a female? Not since the age of twelve, when he had kissed his first chambermaid, had Lucian ever suffered a moment's doubt where woman were concerned. Young or old, rich or poor, peeress or peasant, they all were attracted by his frank appreciation, his dashing good looks, his ironic smile, and his genuine interest in them. With this woman, however, he had never been sure of himself. She was far too clever, too independent, and too dedicated to her own interests to make him feel even the least bit sure of himself with her.

There was nothing for it but to remain in Bath until he could find out for certain how she felt about him, for he was most uncomfortably aware of how he still felt about her. He might have been able to put her out of his mind for a time, but he had never forgotten how her quick wit, her ready smile, and her appreciation of whatever topic he happened to introduce made him feel as though he had at last met a soul mate in a world where everyone else was wasting time on the petty pursuit of wealth, or fame, or fashion.

Chapter Eleven

*L*ucian was not the only one to return from the drive in a reflective mood. Slowly stripping off her gloves, Catherine climbed the stairs to her office. After the bright sunshine and fresh air, the book-lined room seemed cramped and stuffy. For the past two years it had always been her place of refuge, the one place where she felt truly herself and not some powerless pawn to be shoved aside because she was inconvenient or in the way. Now, however, the cozy room seemed confining instead of protective, and she felt stifled instead of free from all outside pressures.

It had been glorious to be out of doors among the trees and flowers, with the blue sky and fluffy clouds overhead, glorious to be bowling along in a well-sprung vehicle driven by someone who could both drive to an inch and carry on an intelligent conversation at the same time. She had reveled in the luxury of being with a driver who made her feel as though she were a person of interest instead of a nuisance, a driver who made her feel full of life again, and, yes, a driver who made her feel attractive and special.

Pulling off her bonnet, Catherine ran her fingers through her hair. She had not felt so alive in a long time. A quick glance in the small looking glass on the wall next to a bookshelf confirmed this. Even to herself, she suddenly looked quite five years younger. She looked hopeful and excited, as though she had something to look forward to in life.

Surely a simple drive in the country could not be entirely

responsible for such a change? *Be careful,* a cynical little voice in her head warned her. *You know what he is, here one day and gone the next.* But she was older and wiser now, a widow, no longer vulnerable to the dangerous schoolgirl fancies that had once turned an attractive man into a knight in shining armor. Now she expected nothing from Lucian except friendship, friendship and nothing more. But surely friendship was not too much to ask?

A knock on the door saved Catherine from having to answer this particular question for herself.

It was Arabella. "Excuse me. I did not mean to disturb you, Lady Catherine." Arabella looked suddenly and uncharacteristically ill at ease. "But you *did* ask me to come see you at this hour."

"Did I . . . ? Oh, yes. Please sit down." Quickly smoothing the hair disordered by her bonnet, Catherine indicated a chair on one side of the fireplace while she settled in the one opposite. Indeed, she had completely forgotten that she had set this time for a talk with Lucian's niece to discover how she was getting on.

Sitting very straight, her hands demurely folded in her lap, Arabella examined her new headmistress anxiously.

"You need not look so apprehensive. I merely called you in to see how you are settling in. The first few days can be rather trying for anyone. I trust, however, that Olivia and the others have made you feel welcome."

Arabella relaxed visibly. "Oh yes, indeed. They have been most kind, Olivia especially."

"And your lessons? Not too overwhelming, I trust. All our instructresses are highly proficient in their fields and I can see how they might appear somewhat intimidating, but I assure you that their first concern is always for the well-being of their pupils."

"Ye-es." Arabella sounded less certain on this point. "Miss Denholme is very clever, is she not?"

"Exceedingly. But do not be put off by her formidable intellect. Underneath she has a heart of gold and is fiercely devoted to all her students, whether or not they share her enthusiasm for mathematical formulae."

Clearly this was a relief to the academy's newest arrival. She remained quiet for a moment as she regarded Catherine with a half-curious, half-appraising look.

Catherine looked back. She had seen this expression on several of her pupils' faces, and generally these girls were the ones most inclined to think for themselves. They were young women who, if given the proper instruction and encouragement, would grow into woman to be reckoned with some day. "And now you are wondering about me."

There was no need for an answer. Arabella's expression of blank amazement was all the response necessary.

"It is plain to see that you are not accustomed to being around people, or at least females, who are in the least curious or observant."

Arabella nodded slowly.

"And what are you wondering?"

"I do not know. I mean, that is . . ."

"Lady Arabella, one of the things I hope to teach every girl here, no matter how clever or how dull she may be, is to organize her thoughts quickly and express them clearly. In your case, I would say that you are a young woman who is already well accustomed to speaking her mind. Now is not the time to be missish."

"Very well." Arabella drew a deep breath, her full dark brows wrinkling in concentration. "I do not understand why you do it. It cannot be because you have to. I mean, the establishment is most comfortable and well appointed. And the girls say—that is to say, it is well known that you are already mistress of your own establishment so you do not need to work." She paused as her eyes traveled to Catherine's gown which, though it might not be in the first stare of fashion, was clearly made of the very best materials.

Taking pity on her obvious confusion, Catherine chuckled. "Why, since I appear to be a woman in sufficiently comfortable circumstances, do I do something that most people would only do out of necessity? Because, quite simply, I wish to do something useful. If I did not have any purpose to my life I would be intolerably bored. And it has been my experience that women who are bored either become excessively silly or turn into perfect harridans. As I have no wish to become either, I decided to start this academy to stop other perfectly intelligent young women from falling into the same vicious pattern. The more we women learn to think and to do things for ourselves, the less likely we are to meddle in other people's lives or demand they look after us and take care of us."

"Now," Catherine rose, "I can see that I have given you quite enough to think about for one day at least. I suggest you ask Olivia to distract you with an introduction to some of the more enticing shops on Milsom Street."

She ushered a somewhat dazed Arabella to the door, nodded encouragingly, and then returned to her desk where she attacked the day's correspondence with a good deal more energy than she actually felt.

If she had given in to her own desires, Catherine would have put her bonnet back on her head and gone for a long leisurely ramble across the hills outside the city in order to clear her mind before tackling business, but she was nothing if not her own sternest taskmistress, and she concentrated on the task before her, forcibly emptying her mind of all thoughts of a beautifully sprung curricle pulled by an exquisitely matched team held in check by strong, skillful hands, not to mention the memories of an ironic smile and gray eyes that seemed to see everything and understand everything about her. Brutally she reminded herself that if Lady Catherine Granville's Select Academy for Genteel Young Ladies was going to be successful in teaching young women to lead purposeful lives, then its headmistress had better set an example worth following by taking hold of her own wayward thoughts.

And so, for the next several hours, she answered letters from anxious parents, assuring those who cared about such things that the instruction offered at the academy was equal to what they might hope for for their sons. Others she directed to Miss Chamberlayne's establishment in Queen's Square, where they could be confident that the very best dancing masters, singing teachers, and instructresses in needlework and watercolors would return to them a product as completely accomplished, aesthetically pleasing, and highly marriageable as any hopeful parent could possibly wish.

From the stack of correspondence, she proceeded to greengrocers' bills, butchers' bills, and accounts from stationers, linen drapers, and coal merchants, adding columns of figures, subtracting, projecting income and expenses until she thought her eyes would glaze over at the sight of another number. But at last she rose triumphant, the stack of bills recorded, letters answered, and accounts paid, all piled neatly before her on her desk and ready to be filed away the next morning.

And what did she have to show for it all? she asked herself wearily, as she surveyed the piles of paper in front of her. What indeed did she have except tired eyes, cramped fingers, aching shoulders, and an orderly heap of work waiting for her in the morning?

Catherine rubbed her forehead wearily. *It is what you wanted, after all,* she admonished herself sternly, *and there is no one to blame but yourself now that you have it.* With a tired sigh, she closed her office door behind her and went in search of Margaret.

The mathematics instructress was still in her schoolroom, bending over one of the younger girls who was struggling over her multiplication tables, her face the picture of misery. "I cannot, Miss Denholme," she moaned. "I simply do not understand figures."

"Very well then, Cordelia, let us look at it another way. Stop thinking of them as just numbers on a piece of paper. Think of them as . . . as . . . Well, what do you like?"

"Like?" Twisting one long chestnut curl unhappily the girl stared blankly at her teacher.

"Yes, like. Do you like flowers? Ponies?"

"Cats. I like cats."

"Cats it is, then. Now suppose you had five cats and every day you put out a saucer of milk for each cat. But then suppose you found out that all these cats were going to have kittens. You would want a saucer of milk for each kitten as well, wouldn't you?"

The girl nodded slowly.

"So, what would you do?"

"Find out how many kittens there were going to be?"

"Excellent! So you might ask someone very knowledgeable who might tell you that at most these cats would have five kittens each. How many saucers would you then have to have if each cat had five kittens?"

There was a long silence.

"Ummmm, twenty-five?"

Margaret patted her encouragingly on the shoulder. "Sometimes it helps if one stops thinking of them as figures and starts thinking of them as things. Then it does not matter if you are dreadful with figures or not.

The girl smiled shyly at Margaret. "Thank you, Miss Denholme. I shall try that."

"There's the spirit. Now, run along as it is time for tea."

As Cordelia scampered off, Margaret turned to Catherine with a rueful smile. "It is fortunate for me that she is far too young for zoology; undoubtedly Letitia would have my head for suggesting that litters of kittens are always so predictable."

"I shall make sure that she does not hear of it. However, scientist though she may be, I feel sure she would allow you some latitude when your cause is good."

Margaret looked doubtful. "Letitia Grayson is the soul of rigor. That is what makes her the accomplished scientist she is, in addition to being a superb zoology instructor."

"We are all of us here souls of rigor."

Margaret looked at her friend curiously. "You do not sound as though you consider that a good thing. Surely if it were not for rigor, or determination, none of us would be where we are today. And surely where we are and what we are doing today is a good thing?"

"I hope so."

"But you *know* it is! Why, even the Marquess of Charlmont's niece appears to be settling in and enjoying herself and she looked utterly bored and disenchanted when she arrived," Margaret protested. It was not like Catherine to sound bitter or despondent. What could possibly have occurred to make her sound that way now? Even Ugolino, pompous and bullying as he was, had never succeeded in making her sound this way. If anything, his criticisms only made her more determined to succeed.

Margaret grabbed her cloak and satchel and followed her friend down the gracious staircase to the waiting carriage. As they passed one room after another filled with girls chattering together or poring over books by themselves and in groups, she wondered at the somber expression on Catherine's face. Surely if she desired proof of the value of what she was doing she need only look around her, for there was proof in abundance everywhere.

But in spite of Margaret's best attempts to distract her during the carriage ride home, Catherine remained in a sober, reflective mood, and it wasn't until she was getting ready for bed that night that she realized that though she had teased Lucian for making no inquiries about educational establishments other than hers, it had never occurred to her to ask him how he had come to hear of Lady Catherine Granville's Select Academy in the first place.

Chapter Twelve

*C*atherine not only went to bed in a sober mood that night but she awoke to it again the next day. Somehow, her outing with the Marquess of Charlmont, brief though it had been, had put her in a questioning frame of mind. Something about the way he had made her feel, even for the briefest of moments, recalled the happiness of times past. It made her wonder if in spite of all that she and Granville had accomplished, and all that she had managed to accomplish on her own, she was missing something. Had she, in her desire to pursue a life of meaning and purpose, neglected to live?

And it did not help the next morning to have the footman deliver a note from the Marquess of Charlmont requesting the honor of her company on another drive into the country. The moment she recognized the bold writing on the envelope, Catherine became mired in an agony of self-doubt. What sort of person was she that a mere invitation to go driving could make her feel suddenly lighthearted and free, could make her look forward to the day in a way she had not for as long as she could remember? Was her own desire to live a useful life and to justify her own existence by the performance of good works no longer enough to satisfy her? What was wrong with her? Had she strived her entire life to develop into a person of values and ideals only to degenerate into a woman whose sum total of happiness was to be seen in the company of a highly attractive and eligible man?

No, she amended, she did not care a farthing for being

seen in his company. In fact, she preferred not to be. What she *did* look forward to, however, was his companionship. And by the time the appointed hour rolled around, she had made quick work of all the tasks with which she had planned to fill her entire day.

"Much better," Lucian remarked, as he strolled into her office a few minutes after she had signed her name to the last letter in her pile of correspondence.

"Better?" Catherine had mentally prepared herself for any of half a dozen things he might say. She had even thought up a number of impressively convincing excuses as to why she could not possibly find the time to go for a drive with him, but his obscure comment drove them all completely from her head.

"Your costume. It is far less sober and infinitely more in your style than the stiflingly respectable attire you selected yesterday when you *knew* you were going out for a drive with me. But surely you know that there is not the slightest need to convince *me* that you are a serious-minded woman who is highly qualified to run a superior educational establishment. I have always had the utmost respect for you capabilities."

"I had no need . . . Well, I mean, it *is* true that I was not expecting to see you today." Catherine could feel the blush rising in her cheeks as she glanced down at the double flounce of her high-necked muslin dress and then over at the blush-colored spencer hanging on the peg. There was no denying the truth of the statement. Lucian Verney had always been uncomfortably acute, and that acuteness had been one of the things she had found most attractive about him, until now.

"I, on the other hand, have come fully prepared to prove to you beyond a doubt that I am not the slipshod ramshackle fellow that you think me. While you have been poring over your accounts and your correspondence this morning, I have visited no fewer than four extremely respectable institutions for the education of females, including Miss Chamberlayne's in Queen's Square, which came highly recommended to me by no fewer than three terrifying-looking dowagers I encountered taking the waters in the Pump Room, but I assured them that it could in no way compare with Lady Catherine Granville's Select Academy for Genteel Young Ladies."

"You didn't!" Half scandalized, half amused, she raised a hand to her mouth to stifle the laugh that rose to her lips.

"I assure you, I did. No, do not look so horrified. I promise you I have done your academy's reputation no harm for I am extremely respectable now. I grant you that if Lord Lucian Verney had recommended your establishment, it would have been quite another matter altogether, but believe me, when the Marquess of Charlmont puts his seal of approval on a place, its success is assured."

"You are incorrigible!" She did laugh this time and he laughed with her.

"Good. I am glad that you have not completely lost your sense of the ridiculous. Now, come, before we waste any more of this beautiful day indoors."

He was right; it was a glorious day, and as they drove to the top of Kingsdown, Catherine felt all her self-doubts and her sober mood vanish with the soft breezes that wafted the faint sweet scent of dog roses from the hedgerows now bursting into bloom. She could not help drawing a deep, satisfying breath as she gazed at the broad panorama below them. It seemed ages since she had paused long enough to take pleasure in the beauty that was all around her.

Watching her closely, her companion seemed to sense this. "You should not wall yourself around with your duties, you know. An afternoon's escape now and then will not undo everything you have strived to create. All your tasks will still be waiting for you when you return, and you may just find yourself so revived and refreshed by your break that they will seem far less burdensome to you."

She turned to find the gray eyes fixed on her, no longer teasing, but filled with genuine concern. "Yes. I know, but . . ."

"But what?" He pulled his team off on a convenient cart

track that led off across a field, jumped down, tied the horses to a nearby tree, and then came to hand her out of the carriage.

"There is so much to be done." She allowed him to help her down and pull her hand through the crook of his arm as he led her to the brow of the hill.

"Catherine, in your life, there will always be much to be done. If you do not stop to enjoy yourself now and then, you will spend your time finding even more things for you to do, so that you never have time to take pleasure in anything and everything will become a duty."

How well he knew her. How well he understood the struggle that was always with her—the wish to accomplish more and more and the longing to pause and appreciate what already existed.

"But if I stop, who knows what will happen? What will become of the academy?"

"Nothing will happen." He covered her hand reassuringly with his. "Believe me, I am not advocating abandoning your responsibilities, or even ignoring them. All I am suggesting is that you give yourself a moment to escape from your duties long enough to reflect on the things you have accomplished and to give yourself credit for them. After all, what is the point of accomplishing them if you yourself can not appreciate it. I know, I know." He held up an admonitory hand as she opened her mouth to speak. "At the outset there was a great deal that needed to be done in order to establish the academy and see to it that it ran efficiently. But now it *is* running efficiently. I have seen a fair amount of the world, you know, and some will even tell you that I have seen too much of it, but I have seen enough to know when an establishment runs like clockwork. Lady Catherine Granville's Select Academy runs like clockwork, I assure you of that. And my explorations of this morning have only served to confirm that impression."

"I suppose you are right, but . . ."

"Of course I am right. Even Ugolino, as you call him,

could not possibly fault you on the reputation for excellence that the academy is beginning to acquire."

"He would if he could."

"But he cannot." Lucian turned her to face him. "Is it . . . ? " He hesitated for a moment as he looked deep into her eyes, frowning slightly as though he were about to ask a question he seemed to have answered already for himself.

"Is it what?"

"Nothing. Tell me, did your husband also find it difficult to tear you away from your responsibilities?" He drew her arm back through his and began walking back toward the curricle.

"No. Granville understood that I had my own obligations that were as important to me as his were to him. He respected them and encouraged me in all that I tried to do."

"A paragon of understanding in fact."

"Well, yes he was, and I . . . I was most fortunate. Few husbands take the time or effort to understand their wife's life or ambitions, or share in them."

"He does not sound like a very passionate man to me."

"Oh, but he was. He was a man of deep convictions who tried hard to live up to the position he was born to. He was highly sensitive to his duties as a landlord and a neighbor, and those who relied on him for their livelihood were fortunate indeed. But, then . . ." She faltered as some fleeting expression she read in his eyes gave her pause. "But then, I am not a passionate creature myself."

"Not a passionate creature? I am more than seven, you know. I have been acquainted with a number of passionate woman in my life, and—"

"I know." Her tone was frosty and she lifted her chin to stare defiantly at him.

"And you *are* a passionate woman, very passionate indeed."

"I am not!"

"Oh no?" He took a step toward her, but she, defensive, and oddly defiant, refused to move an inch. "How can you castigate Ugolino for being 'greedy' and a 'blot on the family escutcheon,' how can you be so quick to insist that your academy is not some place that merely puts 'a few artistic touches on a decorative object' if you are not passionately devoted to your ideals of good stewardship and the necessity for female education? Yes, you *are* a passionate woman, and I suspect that much of that passion was wasted on a husband who could not appreciate it."

"How dare you!" She raised her hand to slap him.

He caught her wrist, nipping it around behind her back before she knew what was up. "My point exactly. Slapping a man is not the way to demonstrate a lack of passion."

And with that he pulled her to him in a kiss that drove all the breath from her body.

For a moment, the world spun so madly about her that Catherine thought she would faint, but his arms held her captive, steadying her as his lips, softer now, explored hers, begging her, willing her to respond to them.

She was powerless to resist. After the stresses and strains, the emotional ups and downs of the past few days, after having her carefully arranged world thrown into disorder by his sudden appearance, all she could do was cling to him and marvel at how wonderful it felt to be held in someone's arms again. But she was not just being held in the solid reassuring way that Granville had held her from time to time. She was being enfolded, caressed, treasured, held close as though she had always belonged there, as though she were part of him.

For a moment Catherine gave herself up to the wave of longing that washed over her, a longing that had invaded her heart the first time Lucian Verney had smiled at her, that crooked, half-ironic, half-humorous smile that told her he saw the world exactly the way she did, a smile that told her he knew her and understood her as well as she knew and understood herself. It was a longing for him that she thought she had banished years ago, but now she knew she had not. It had simply been hidden all this time, buried under her chosen existence as the honored wife and helpmeet of a respectable country gentleman. But now it reasserted itself with a vengeance, the longing to be as close to him physically as she was mentally, to know his body as well as she knew his mind, to trace the square line of his jaw, to revel in the strength of his arms and the warmth of his hands, to have him want her as much as she wanted him.

For a moment she gave in to it, and then reason returned. "How dare you! I am not one of your countless flirts who considers a drive wasted if she has not indulged in some sort of dalliance." She wrenched herself away and stood there shaking, too overwhelmed by it all to do anything but gasp for air.

"Of course you aren't. You are an intelligent woman with strongly held opinions of her own, opinions so strong that I was forced to try to change them by way of example, for no amount of discussion would."

When she was at last able to catch her breath, she drew herself up as proudly as she could manage with her entire body trembling and, willing herself to speak calmly, coldly, and dispassionately, she addressed him as if she were addressing a student accused of some minor infraction. "That is ludicrous. I know that you will go to any lengths to prove a point, my lord, but this is absurd. The example of my distaste for Ugolino and my views on education were sufficiently compelling to convince me of your assertion. Now, if you excuse me, it is high time I returned to my work."

And praying that her knees would continue to support her, Catherine turned, stalked back to the curricle, and climbed in with as much dignity as she could muster.

Stifling a grin, Lucian untied the horses and climbed in beside her. For a few minutes he was too occupied with handling his team as he turned the carriage and made the way back along the cart track to spare a thought for his companion, and by the time they had gained the road, she appeared to have recovered her equanimity. In fact there was nothing but two small spots of color on her cheeks to betray the fact that anything out of the ordinary had occurred.

But Catherine's mind was racing as she struggled to come up with some topic of conversation that would bring everything back to normal. "I am indeed impressed that a team as high-spirited as yours would consent to stand idly by while their owner secured them with nothing more than reins loosely tied to a tree."

"Ah, but then my cattle are quite accustomed to drives in which I, er, indulge in 'some sort of dalliance.'"

"Oh, you are in . . ." Catherine closed her mouth with a furious snap.

"Insufferable? Impossible?" He slanted a teasing smile in her direction. "I know." The smile disappeared and his tone grew serious once more. "But I had to do something to shake you."

"Shake me? But why?" She stared at him incredulously.

"To see if the lively, passionate woman I once knew still existed under the serious and sober exterior of the head-mistress of Lady Catherine Granville's Select Academy."

"I fail to see what possible concern it is of yours what exists there. Furthermore, I should think that a responsible guardian would be delighted that the headmistress into whose care he was entrusting the welfare of his niece was serious and sober."

"It is my concern because I care about your happiness as well as my niece's. And while I am reasonably assured that Arabella's mother, in her own desultory way, is also concerned about her daughter's happiness, I do *not* see that anyone is concerned about yours."

"Oh." His concern for her was totally disarming, especially now when she felt so utterly alone, but she had been disarmed before and had suffered for it. "That is indeed kind of you, but I prefer to rely on myself for my own happiness since *I* am not likely to disappear from my own life for years on end without so much as a by-your-leave, or even a friendly note."

Blast! Catherine bit her lip in vexation. She sounded like the veriest shrew, one of those helpless, clinging women whose entire world depended on masculine attention and direction.

"I know. I should have written. And I am sorry. I behaved abominably toward you."

"You did nothing of the sort!" She furiously untied and retied the bow of her bonnet. "There was no need for you to write to me. There was nothing between us. I had no claim on your attention."

"No claim except the friendship I had grown to treasure and to rely on." Lucian slowed the horses to a walk. "Catherine, I doubt that you will believe me when I say I felt the loss of that friendship a great deal over the years, but I did. And I have no reason to expect that you will forgive me and say that we can be friends again except that it would make me very happy indeed if you would."

She tried her best not to look at him, to keep her gaze riveted on the road in front of them, on the meadowlark just taking flight, on the hills in the distance, anything but the gray eyes fixed so intently on her. But it was no use. She did look up, and she was surprised by what she saw, the questioning look, the loneliness, the emptiness that told her he too knew what it was to lose a friend, to miss that friend.

"Friends, then." She held out her hand.

"Friends." He raised it gently to his lips and then placed it carefully back in her lap and they finished the ride in companionable silence.

Chapter Thirteen

*H*e was gone the next day but not before stopping to say goodbye. Catherine and his niece were both waiting in Catherine's office to bid him farewell.

"I expect regular reports from you as to your progress, and I expect each report to be more erudite than the last." Lucian frowned ferociously at Arabella.

She laughed and smiled saucily at him. "Only if you answer those reports with letters of your own."

"You see?" He turned to Catherine. "I warned you that she is a handful. But she is your handful now, Lady Catherine." And he sketched a mocking bow in her direction. "However, I promise to stop by now and again to make sure that she has not driven you to total distraction."

Another bow, this time to both of them, and he was gone.

"He likes you, I think." Arabella smiled at her new headmistress in the friendliest of fashions.

"Since he will be only an infrequent visitor at this establishment, it really is of no importance if he likes me or not." Catherine sat back down at her desk and reached for her account books. "It would be far more useful if he respected me."

"But that is what I mean. Uncle Lucian would never like someone he could not respect. I can tell he likes you because he jokes with you. He only jokes with people he likes. He and Uncle William were always joking with one another, but he never joked with Papa, for which I certainly do not blame

. him. Papa was a prosy old bore and he did not like the fact that Uncle Lucian was far cleverer than he. He is clever, is he not, Uncle Lucian?"

"Very." Catherine responded dryly.

"I think that is why he has never married. He never found anyone as clever as he was. I am fortunate to have him as my guardian. Of course there are scores of women who are after him because he is so dashing and of course now he is a Marquess, but Charlotte Partington, who has had her first Season already and thinks she now knows everything there is to know about the *ton,* says he never pays the least heed to any women except his mistresses. And of course, with mistresses it is different for they are only supposed to be beautiful, not clever. And Charlotte says his mistresses are always exceptionally beautiful, but then one does not necessarily want cleverness in a mistress, does one?"

"I, er, expect not. But I do not think your uncle would appreciate your telling me all of this. I also know that Madame de St. Alembert will be wondering what has become of you, since I promised her you would return to your lesson immediately after you had finished saying goodbye to your uncle."

Catherine accompanied her admonitory tone with a quelling look, but it appeared to have no effect on the irrepressible Arabella, who rose cheerfully enough and headed off to her interrupted French lesson.

Arabella might claim that her uncle Lucian had never married because he had never met a clever enough woman, but Catherine was not so naive. She knew how much he valued his freedom and his independence. After all, he had once been very close to a clever young woman, or at least it had seemed so at the time, and then he had vanished completely from her life.

And in spite of the regrets he now voiced, he had effectively avoided becoming further involved with that clever young woman by running off with an actress. Had it been the irresistible charms of the actress or fear of becoming fur-

ther involved with the young woman that had made him de-
camp so quickly? Catherine was not at all sure.

Lucian Verney might have grown more responsible over
the years, he might even regret that friendship he had lost
with the clever young woman, but Catherine very much
doubted that even now he would react so very differently
from the way he had years ago.

He had assured both Arabella and Catherine that he would
be calling in Bath on a regular basis, but Catherine sincerely
doubted it. Once he had returned to the myriad distractions
of the metropolis, he was hardly likely to waste a second's
thought on a widowed headmistress, even a widowed headmistress he had kissed on the top of Kingsdown. He also
knew that he could rely completely on that widowed headmistress to take excellent care of his niece, so there quite
simply was no reason for him to return to Bath.

But in spite of her constant determination to be realistic
and honest with herself, Catherine refused to admit that the
likelihood of his remaining in London was more distressing
than relieving. She was not fool enough to cherish hopes for
the possibility of reestablishing their friendship, but just
being with Lucian made her feel ten years younger, hopeful,
and ready to enjoy life in a way that she had thought was lost
to her forever.

Catherine threw down the account book she had picked
up. There was simply no point in looking at it. She knew she
would not be able to concentrate. The only thing that was
going to drive these distracting thoughts from her mind was
a vigorous walk.

She rose hastily, sending papers flying everywhere,
snatched up her bonnet, jammed it on her head, yanked on
her spencer, and marched down the stairs, out the door,
and off to the fields in front of the Royal Crescent. It was
not so distracting as driving a curricle along the Bath-
London road as some people were now doing, but it was
better than nothing.

In fact, Catherine was wrong in thinking that even driving
a high-spirited team along the Bath-London road was

enough diversion to keep reflections at bay. Lucian discovered that even before he was able to fight his way free of the press of town traffic, and even at the speed he was eventually able to attain once clear of town, he found his thoughts returning to Catherine—Catherine trying desperately to appear severe in a headmistress sort of way, Catherine luxuriating in the fresh air and the freedom of a drive in the open country, Catherine laughing up at him, her hazel eyes glinting with amusement, Catherine in his arms, warm and pliable, kissing him at last.

With a start so noticeable that it even caused his team to toss their heads, Lucian sat even more upright on the seat of his curricle. He had not ever allowed himself to acknowledge it until this very moment, but he had been longing to hold Catherine in his arms and kiss her breathless since that moment ten years ago when she had first looked up at him and laughed and he knew he had found a soul mate.

How could he have allowed himself to lose all that? Why had he not written to her? The answer, he knew, was that he had been too afraid, too afraid of what she would say to him, too afraid to learn what she thought of him. For the first time in his life, he, who ordinarily did not give a fig for anyone's opinion, had truly cared what someone else thought of him, had truly respected someone else's intelligence enough for that opinion to matter very much to him. And then he had been too cowardly to put that opinion to the test. Either way, the result had been the same. He had lost her. And only now was he realizing what that had meant.

With Bath and Catherine receding into the distance behind him, the prospect of London in front of him did not seem so attractive as it once had. Nor did his affairs seem as pressing as they usually did. Ordinarily during his visits to Charlmont, he was on the verge of desperation by the time he left, a desperation born of irritation at the banality of his sister-in-law or just plain boredom, but this time, the prospect ahead, rather than the one behind, was the one that seemed empty and boring.

"I must be entering my dotage," he muttered, as taking a

firmer grip on the reins, he tried to focus as he usually did
on the work that lay before him or on his latest mistress. But
the thought of Lady Granville only reminded him again of
Catherine and how galling it must be to her to be replaced as
mistress of Granville Park by a woman who had no thought
for anything beyond the latest fashions in *La Belle Assem-
blée* and whose only social concern was the improvement of
her position in the *haut ton*.

This whole unfortunate train of thought only served to
make him recall that it was this very social concern of Lady
Granville's that had been responsible for his visit to Lady
Catherine Granville's Select Academy in the first place. Enrolling Arabella there was not precisely the outcome that
Lady Granville had had in mind when she had sent him
there. She was not going to be best pleased with the results
of his visit.

Lucian grinned as he thought of how much Catherine
would enjoy the look of horror on Lady Granville's face
when he broke the news to her that not only had he done
nothing to disassociate the Granville name from the educational establishment but he was ready to recommend that establishment most highly to anyone who cared to listen.

Somewhat cheered by the irony of the whole situation, he
eventually arrived back at his lodgings in Mount Street the
next day in a slightly better frame of mind. But several days
later as he headed first towards Brooks's and then, after the
theaters had let out, to a snug little villa in Marylebone and
the welcoming arms of the newest member of the corps de
ballet at the Theatre Royal, he realized that he would far
rather have remained at home in front of his own fire dis-
cussing the recent article in the *The Edinburgh Review* on
the "Causes and Cures of Pauperism" with someone whose
conversation could be counted on to be as interesting as it
was enlivening.

Catherine, he felt sure, would have her own decided opinions on the subject. She had been a fierce critic of enclosures
when he had first met her and he was reasonably certain that
her experiences as the wife of a landholder responsible for

the welfare of the villages surrounding his estate would only
have expanded her opinions on the possible solutions to the
plight of the rural poor.

But as it was, the only intellectual challenge he had enjoyed that evening had been to raise the stakes at whist
with Tubby Whitcombe, Lord Southwold, and Colonel
Wrexham.

The next evening had little more to offer except the
choice between *The Double Gallant* at Drury Lane or *King
Richard the Third* at Covent Garden, either of which carried
the added risk of running into Lady Granville, something
which he had sedulously avoided since returning to London.

Or he could go again to Brooks's where the company was
not particularly enlivening, but at least he could be assured
of avoiding all contact with females of any sort. So to
Brooks's he went, and though his heart was not in it, it did
serve as a distraction from the questions that seemed to
hover constantly at the back of his mind, which were *How
was Catherine doing? Was she happy? Was Ugolino continuing to annoy her? Had she forgiven him for kissing her?*
And, more importantly, *Did she long,* as he did, *for it to happen again?*

His thoughts were running very much along these same
lines the next day as he sauntered down Bond Street. In fact
he was preoccupied with them to such a degree that it took
him a moment to realize that it was his name he heard being
called with an insistence that could not be ignored.

"Charlmont, are you quite well?" Lavinia Granville's delicately arched brows hovered somewhere between concern
and annoyance when he at last turned around to face her. "I
have been addressing you this age, since you were in front
of Madame Celeste's."

"I beg your pardon. I, er, was not attending. I did not expect to be so fortunate as to encounter you here." Executing
a truly elegant bow, he raised the offended beauty's hand to
his lips."

"I had no idea you were back in town."

"Only just. In fact, I was only now returning to my cham-

bers to write a note informing you of my return when I had
the great good fortune to . . ."

"You could have called on me." The beauty's eyes nar-
rowed ever so slightly and her voice lost some of its husky
sweetness.

"And I would have called on any ordinary woman,
Lavinia. But you are not an ordinary woman. Indeed your
company is so much sought after that I would never presume to call on you without first of all assuring myself that
you were at home and, secondly, being certain that you were
alone, a prospect so unlikely that I would have to be mad
even to think it possible."

Somewhat mollified, Lavinia favored him with a hint of a
smile. "For you, Lucian, I am always at home . . . alone,"
she whispered so that only he could hear.

He bowed again. "As always, I am in your debt, but . . ."

"Stay." She laid a gloved hand on his arm ever so lightly,
but there was no mistaking her message. "Do not rush away
just yet. You must tell me how you found that Granville
woman. Was she as brown and windblown as ever? I vow,
every time I see her she looks as though she has just come
in from the fields. So dreadfully unladylike."

"No. Actually, she looked rather paler than I remember
her."

"What? But I thought you were not acquainted with her."

"I thought so too. The Lady Catherine I knew was Lady
Catherine Montague, not Lady Catherine Granville."

"Not so well acquainted then if she made so little impression on you that you did not realize she had married." Lady
Granville's face relaxed again into a self-satisfied smile. "I
would be surprised if you did remember her for she is certainly not your type—something of a hoyden and definitely
a bluestocking."

Lavinia was right. It was not an *impression* Catherine had
made on him, it was an indelible imprint, but he had not realized until recently how indelible it had been. It was subtle,
so subtle that he had not been aware that every woman he
met he unconsciously measured against Catherine and, find-

ing them all lacking, soon moved on. Yes, it had been subtle, but indelible, nevertheless.

"I trust that you were able to make her see that her behavior, no matter how consistent it is with her customarily cavalier attitude toward the dictates of good society, is not at all the thing and brings nothing but distress to the family."

"If the truth be known, I did not even attempt such a useless exercise once I became aware of her identity. Lady Catherine is a woman of strong principles and even stronger convictions."

"But I asked you to. . . ."

For a moment, Lucian caught a brief glimpse of the spoilt little girl beneath the exquisite exterior, the spoilt little girl who had only to stomp her foot to get her way with indulgent parents. Then quite suddenly the angrily compressed lips drooped pathetically, and the flashing eyes swam with tears.

"But I was so counting on you," she whispered huskily as she laid a pleading hand on his arm in a manner that had never failed to win her her way with parents and anyone else rash enough to consider denying her something that she wanted.

The Marquess of Charlmont, however, was made of sterner stuff, and he had a vast experience with women who dissolved in tears the instant their wishes were not fulfilled. "Relax, Lavinia." He patted her hand indulgently. "I have done one better and enrolled my niece in Lady Catherine Granville's Select Academy."

"You have what?" It was a barely muffled shriek.

"I have enrolled Arabella. And if I do not miss my guess, she will be much improved by the experience. So much improved, that parents of young women throughout the *ton* will be falling all over one another in an effort to send their daughters there. You wait and see, you will have women of the highest fashion begging you to use your influence with Lady Catherine to accept their precious darlings into her exclusive establishment. Now, if you will excuse me, I have a most pressing engagement with Lord Sefton who will un-

doubtedly inquire as to the welfare of my brother's family
and will naturally inform his wife that my niece is most happily settled at Lady Catherine Granville's Select Academy
for Genteel Young Ladies."

The mere mention of one of Almack's patronesses was
enough to silence all possible objections, and Lady
Granville was forced to bid him good day with as much
grace as she could muster.

Catherine would have instantly detected the ironic gleam
in Lucian's eyes as he left Lavinia, and she would have appreciated his consummate skill in handling the spoilt beauty,
but unfortunately, Catherine was not there to share the moment with him. Worse yet, she was probably so immersed in
her own life that she did not have a thought to spare for the
Marquess of Charlmont or his affairs. Shaking his head ruefully at his own weakness for a particular headmistress, Lucian continued his progress along Bond Street.

Chapter Fourteen

*L*ucian was entirely correct; Catherine was extremely involved in her affairs, but in this case, her affairs were closely allied with the Marquess of Charlmont's or, to be more exact, a member of his family.

As she did with every new arrival at the academy, Catherine was keeping a close watch on Arabella, checking to see that she was happy, that she was making new friends, and that she was not plagued by the homesickness that inevitably struck after the excitement of the journey was over and the thrill of being on one's own for the first time wore off. But no matter how closely she observed, she could find no indication that her newest pupil was not adjusting beautifully to the change in her situation.

In fact, Arabella seemed to be flourishing in her new surroundings. Her eyes sparkled with mischief, her complexion glowed with good health, and she seemed to be the gayest of companions to anyone and everyone—almost too gay.

Catherine frowned thoughtfully as she watched the laughing crowd of young women chattering away in the garden below her office window. It was not natural for a new arrival not to suffer any ill effects from the transition, to appear so comfortable, even exuberant so quickly. Something else lay behind the unusually high spirits, and Catherine was determined to find out what it was.

From the little she had seen of Arabella, Catherine had quickly identified her as a most determined young woman, charming to be sure, but determined all the same to have her own way and bind everyone else to it. Even her uncle, inured as he was to manipulative females and their charms, did not appear to be entirely immune to his niece's wiles.

The more Catherine observed Arabella's behavior, the more she was certain that the redoubtable young woman had some sort of plan for which it suited her—for the moment—to be enrolled in Lady Catherine Granville's Academy, but clearly she had some other goal in mind. For one thing, she took far more care of her appearance than any of her companions, the fashionable Olivia included.

Several days later, as Catherine was again looking out of her office window, her eyes fell on Arabella, who every once in a while paused in her chattering and looked around as though expecting something. Her senses on the alert, Catherine stepped back from the window out of view and watched carefully as one by one the girls drifted back inside. Just as Arabella turned to leave, Catherine caught sight of a flicker of movement directly below, too quick for Catherine to make out who or what it was, and in an instant, Arabella had also run beneath the window, but not so far that Catherine could not see her extend her hand to receive what appeared to be a note which she slipped immediately into the pocket of her morning dress. Then, glancing hastily around the garden behind her, she too disappeared from view.

A horrible premonition seized Catherine. Somehow, somewhere, Arabella had acquired an admirer. But how? Where? While it was true that the older girls attending the academy were allowed a certain amount of freedom, they were always accompanied by one of the instructresses on their trips to the shops on Milsom Street or to one of the circulating libraries. Furthermore, Arabella had not been in Bath long enough to establish an acquaintance of any kind, let alone attract an admirer to the degree that he would be writing her letters, unless her admirer were a previous acquaintance, someone she had met before who happened to live in Bath. After all, Charlmont was not so far from Bath that the family could not have had acquaintances in the city who visited Charlmont on a regular enough basis for Arabella to have developed a relationship.

Sighing gently, Catherine let the curtain she was clutching fall back into place. At this point, her misgivings were too vague to enlist the aid of anyone else. She would just have to keep as close an eye as she could on Arabella without arousing the girl's suspicions.

If, in the ensuing days, the academy's headmistress seemed to spend less time in her office and more time visiting the classrooms or joining the girls as they strolled in the garden, no one seemed particularly aware of the change in routine except for Margaret Denholme, who simply ascribed it to Catherine's recent meetings with the Marquess of Charlmont and her desire to show the academy's most important patron that everyone at Lady Catherine Granville's Academy, from the headmistress on down, was concerned for the welfare of its pupils.

But despite her increased vigilance, Catherine was able to discover nothing further, nothing beyond a certain air of expectancy that Arabella was at pains to hide whenever she happened to catch the headmistress's eyes upon her.

Then one day Catherine, who in search of a slight diversion of her own was returning from an expedition to a nearby stationer's, happened to notice a rather sporting-looking young man sauntering slowly along the Royal Crescent in a studied casual sort of way. Catching sight of Catherine, he swiftly turned his attention to the exquisite ionic columns of the facade, assuming a look of intent interest in Mr. Wood's architectural masterpiece and one of Bath's crowning glories.

He was a rather handsome young man, in a florid, square-jawed sort of way, the kind of man who was generally more interested in fox hunting than aesthetics and whose attention was more likely to be caught by horses and hounds than architectural detail. Furthermore, he had been sauntering along in the same casual manner when Catherine had left to go on her errand.

All the vague suspicions that had been plaguing her for

the past week came crowding back into Catherine's mind. She nodded abstractedly as Biddle opened the door and marched upstairs to her office, where she proceeded to pace back and forth across the Axminster carpet.

Now, what was she to do? All her instincts told her that the young man in the street was the reason behind Arabella's exuberant behavior, but how was she to prove it without compromising the girl's trust? Was the young man simply seeking an assignation or was he planning an elopement?

For the rest of the day Catherine wrestled with this thorny issue. It intruded on her thoughts well into the evening as she sat before the fire in her own library trying to distract herself with he latest issue of the *The Edinburgh Review*. And it certainly kept her from drifting off into the dreamless sleep she longed for. At last she was forced to conclude that there was nothing to be done except to proceed in the manner that she had already adopted of keeping the girl under close observation while watching carefully for further developments.

None of the other girls appeared to be involved in Arabella's secret. There were no exchanges of knowing looks, no whispered conversations that Catherine could see. Therefore, Arabella must not be meeting him during any of the group excursions into town but must instead be biding her time until she could snatch a moment alone. One of the academy's cardinal rules was that no young lady could leave the premises unescorted, and there was simply no way for anyone to slip past the watchful Biddle at the front door, which left the small gate in the back wall of the garden as the only possible means of egress.

And the best way for Catherine to keep an eye on that gate was to remain in her office, which afforded an excellent view of the entire garden behind the academy. Accordingly, she let it be known that she was catching up on a mountain of work and spent the next day and a half closeted in her office, keeping a weather eye out the window overlooking the back.

At last her perseverance paid off as late one afternoon a

few days later she noticed Arabella lingering in the garden while the other girls returned to their studies. Catherine watched breathlessly as Arabella glanced carefully around the garden and then very casually strolled toward the gate at the back.

Laying down her pen, Catherine hurried down the stairs and out the French windows across a small terrace and down the path that led to the gate. By this time, the gate was deep in shadow and her view of it was obscured by the slanting rays of the afternoon sun, but she was soon close enough to hear the click of the latch and she quickly stepped off the gravel path onto the grass in order to muffle the sound of her footsteps. The gate squeaked on rusty hinges as it swung open and then came the sound of lowered voices speaking earnestly to one another.

When she drew close enough to make out the two figures framed in the arched gateway, Catherine stepped back onto the path, slowing her pace as though she were taking a leisurely turn around the garden. A few yards from the gate, she executed a well-feigned start of surprise. "Goodness! I did not see you there, Arabella. How you startled me."

Catherine's start of surprise was nothing compared to the look of dismay registering itself on Arabella's face, but the girl quickly regained control of herself. "Good afternoon, Lady Catherine. I was just speaking with, ah, an old family friend who happened by. Is it not delightful? Mr. Foxworthy was in Bath on business and, recalling that he had heard Mama mention that I was attending school here, he stopped to inquire after me and bring me news from home." Arabella spoke as glibly as though clandestine meetings in the garden with young men were a perfectly natural course of affairs, but the unusually high pitch of her voice and the defensively raised chin quickly gave her away.

Mr. Foxworthy, however, was not about to dissemble. Stepping forward, his blue eyes blazing defiantly, his lips set in an obstinate line, he thrust Arabella behind him. "What Lady Arabella means to say"——he shot a quelling look at his companion—"is that I am not only an old family friend, but also her affianced husband, and—"

"Then it is a pleasure to welcome you to the academy, Mr. Foxworthy," Catherine broke in smoothly, ignoring his pugnacious stance and belligerent expression. "We are all very fond of Arabella and are happy to make the acquaintance of someone who appreciates her as much as we do. Will you not step inside? I think you will find it far more comfortable in the drawing room as there is a decided chill in the air."

"I can not stay long as I am expected home today. Arabella and I are to be married soon, and I merely stopped by to discuss some final arrangements." Foxworthy remained rooted to the spot, staring defiantly at the headmistress.

But Arabella, who had recovered from her initial surprise, smiled gratefully at Catherine and directed a pleading look at her fiancé. "Yes, do let us go inside. I think you will find it quite charming, Foxworthy."

"Oh, very well, but only for a moment, mind you. I must be getting back to my affairs," he muttered ungraciously, but he followed the women back inside docilely enough.

Seating herself in a chair by the drawing room fire, Catherine directed the pair to the sofa opposite her. "I am sorry that I did not know about your engagement. If I had known, I would have made the drawing room available to you. It is one of those longstanding family arrangements, I assume."

"Well, we have not—"

"Yes." Foxworthy cut Arabella off with another quelling look. "It is only natural, after all, for the two most ancient families in the county to ally themselves with one another."

"It is a pity the Marquess of Charlmont did not think to mention it. We could have spared you the discomfort of — ah—meeting in the garden."

Arabella looked distinctly ill at ease, but Foxworthy, no longer feeling at a disadvantage now that he saw that the headmistress was only a few years older than he, if that, cleared his throat importantly. "Naturally the Marquess, who has only recently come into the title, has far more important things than a wedding to occupy his time," he responded pompously, conveniently forgetting that one of the first things the new marquess had done was to engineer an encounter that even someone as unimaginative as Foxworthy had recognized as being more than pure happenstance, an encounter in which the marquess had made it uncomfortably clear that he was not impressed with the squire's son. "Therefore I have not seen fit to discuss the details with him, but he will soon be hearing from me."

"Of course, that would explain it."

Catherine's heavily ironic tone was entirely lost on Foxworthy, but not on his fiancée. Arabella flushed uncomfortably and looked somewhat abashed by his air of self-importance.

"But now we have detained you from your affairs too long, Mr. Foxworthy." Catherine rose majestically. "Do let us know when you will be in town again."

In the face of such obvious dismissal, there was nothing for him to do but obey her. However, he was clearly not happy. Rising with a little less confidence than when he had sat down, Foxworthy nodded curtly to them both and strode from the room with as masterly an air as he could muster.

Chapter Fifteen

$\mathcal{A}$rabella remained gazing at her headmistress with a mixed expression of awe and trepidation.

"A most forceful young man," Catherine remarked, taking her seat again. "Having grown up in such close proximity, you know one another quite well, I gather."

"Not all—er—yes, naturally we have known one another since childhood, and, well . . ." Caught off guard by the unexpected calmness of Catherine's reaction to the entire encounter, Arabella found herself totally at sea.

"Then I expect that you know what you are about. You seem to be a young woman who knows her own mind. Still . . ." Catherine shrugged expressively and made as if to rise again.

"What . . . what do you mean?"

"I mean that a young man who is so confident of a woman even before they are married, a woman whose wealth and station are so clearly superior to his, will only become more so once her entire fortune and person are his to dispose of."

"I do not understand you."

"What I mean is that, from the little I have seen of you, I would say that you are a spirited young woman, spirited enough to be saucy with your uncle. Yet now you are acting as meek as a lamb, obeying every look, every gesture of a young man who possesses none of your uncle's stature or intelligence. Nor does he have a natural right to your respect. Furthermore, you, who never appear to be at a loss for words in any other situation allow this young man to speak entirely for you, a young man who is far less articulate and, from what I can tell, far less clever than you are." Catherine paused to judge the effect of her words, but somewhat to her surprise, Arabella did not look mulish or defensive, as was naturally to be expected, but appeared instead to be thinking it over.

"It seems to me," Catherine continued, "as though one ought to begin as one intends to continue. And if you are the sort of person who wishes to defer to her husband on every issue, who wants a husband who clearly expects you to look to him as your lord and master, then it is all very well. But if not . . ." Catherine allowed her words to hang in the air. From her conversations with Lucian she had gained the impression that Arabella tended to ride roughshod over the easily influenced Marchioness of Charlmont. From observing her in conversations with the other girls she had also arrived at the conclusion that Arabella was a strong-minded young woman who would definitely not picture herself as a dutiful wife meekly adjusting her wishes to suit her husband's.

Arabella's eyes widened in surprise. Clearly the possibility of such an absurd state of affairs had never crossed her mind.

"Marriage is a good deal different from courtship, you know. And a man who has control over both your fortune and your person is far less likely to accede to your whims and desires than one who is still hoping to win you. In general, men who are married are far less biddable than men who arc courting. Then they are on their very best behavior since they have everything to lose if they are not. But naturally your uncle will see to it that when the marriage settlements are drawn up you are left with something to call your own. My own dear father, I fear, was far less worldly than you uncle and allowed everything to go to my husband. He trusted, rightfully enough, in my husband's gentlemanly nature to see that I was provided for in the manner in which I had been brought up. Unfortunately, what my father did not foresee was Granville's untimely death. Honorable though my husband was in the disposition of my fortune, his heir was far less so. All that I brought with me to our marriage is now in the hands of someone who is not at all as concerned with my welfare and happiness as my husband was. But I suppose that since yours is a longstanding arrangement, a good deal of thought has already been given to that sort of thing. No doubt your father and your fiancé's father had many conversations on the subject."

If Arabella had appeared uneasy before, she now looked distinctly uncomfortable. "I do not know. I mean I was not privy . . ." She faltered, thought deeply for a few moments, and then in a rush of confidence admitted, "He never spoke—I mean, we were not friends in *that* sort of way until after father died."

It was clear from the strain that could be heard in Arabella's voice and the unhappy expression in her eyes that she had arrived at the same distressing conclusion Catherine had, that it was Lady Arabella's fortune and connections rather than her charming person that were the motivating factors in young Foxworthy's courtship of her, and that worldly considerations rather than more tender emotions had driven him to seek her out—and to seek her out when he thought there was only the spineless Marchioness of Charlmont to object to his obviously unsuitable proposal.

"Then you think," Arabella's big brown eyes were suddenly awash with tears, "you think he only wants me for my fortune?"

Clearly this was a sadly lowering reflection for one who had been picturing herself as a heroine in a highly romantic escapade. "I do not know," Catherine responded gently. "Only you can know that for sure. But marriage is a rather big step, and a risky step for a woman, especially if she is not sure. Now, you have had a rather wearing day, and it is time for supper. I suggest that you think no more about it until you have had something to eat and some time to rest. Things are always much clearer in the morning when one has had the chance to sleep on them."

Silently Arabella rose and walked slowly toward the door.

As she was about to close it behind her, she turned to smile half-shyly, half-apologetically. "I will think about it in the morning as you suggest . . . and, thank you."

The door closed gently behind her and Catherine was left to gaze thoughtfully into the fire. She had done all that she could think of to avert what was clearly a disastrous relationship. Was it enough? Would Arabella see that the graceless young man would make a selfish, brutish sort of husband whose lack of consideration for his wife would make her life miserable? Or was that only a conclusion that could be reached by an objective observer whose judgment was unclouded by the rosy glow of youth and love? Was it enough simply to voice her concerns to Arabella to keep her from taking any rash steps, or should she inform Arabella's uncle of her suspicions?

The idea of writing to the Marquess of Charlmont was distasteful to Catherine for a number of reasons. First and foremost, a letter informing him of his niece's clandestine affair was tantamount to admitting failure on the part of Catherine and her establishment. Any academy that could not protect its students from the enticements of importunate young men was not fulfilling its goals in a number of ways, from instilling the proper values in its pupils, to occupying their time so effectively that there was no room for thoughts of importunate young men, to protecting their persons from the advances, welcome or unwelcome, of these importunate young men.

Second, it would be a betrayal of Arabella's confidence if Catherine wrote to her uncle. Even though the young woman had not asked Catherine to keep the incident a secret from either her uncle or her mother, the understanding had been implicit in their discussion, and Catherine knew that Arabella would have been far less forthcoming if she had not somehow felt that Catherine would keep their discussion a private matter between the two of them. Catherine knew very well that any influence that she might be able to exert over Arabella, any credibility that she had managed to establish with that lively young woman, would be instantly destroyed if Catherine were to divulge it all to the girl's mother or her uncle.

Catherine did, however, keep a very close watch on all her charges for the next several days, but not one exhibited the least sign of any untoward excitement or the slightest indication that she was privy to any romantic secret. There were no unexpected trips to Milsom Street or walks in Sydney Gardens. No notes were suddenly thrust into pockets or passed from hand to hand, and no one lingered in the garden after everyone else had gone inside.

Arabella herself seemed rather subdued and thoughtful. The intense gaiety, the air of suppressed excitement that had previously clung to her had vanished entirely, and Catherine did not think she was dissembling. Whenever she encountered Arabella, the girl exhibited none of the awkwardness of someone conspiring to run away or carry on a secret correspondence. Her gaze was direct, her manner friendly, and though Catherine was willing to give her credit for a great deal of resourcefulness, she did not believe that someone as young and unsophisticated as Arabella could be so skilled at deception as to fool Catherine completely.

It was too soon to congratulate herself on having successfully thwarted a disastrous misalliance, but Catherine did allow herself to hope that the most dangerous moment had passed and that further reflection on Arabella's part would only serve to convince the girl that Tom Foxworthy was a most unsuitable and unworthy object of her affections.

Chapter Sixteen

*I*f relative calm appeared to have descended in the Royal Crescent, it had utterly vanished from Charlmont. The day before Tom Foxworthy had appeared at the garden gate of Lady Catherine Granville's Select Academy the peace that hung over Charlmont had been shattered by the clatter of horse's hooves as Squire Foxworthy, riding at breakneck speed, tore up the drive, flung himself off his horse, tossed his reins to the boy who came hurrying from the stables, and strode up the marble staircase two steps at a time.

"The marchioness," he barked at the goggling footman who opened the door.

Arabella's mother, who was unused to interruptions of any kind, particularly from men who were clearly in a rage, regarded the squire with misgiving as she laid down her book and pulled her cashmere shawl more closely around her. "Is something amiss, Squire Foxworthy?"

"Amiss? Amiss? Your daughter runs off with my son and you ask me if something is amiss?" He roared.

The marchioness shuddered. "Do sit down and let me send for some refreshment." She nodded significantly at the hovering footman. "I am sure this misunderstanding will soon be sorted out. Arabella can not have run off with your son, sir. She is away at school in Bath."

The squire snorted derisively at this obvious piece of stupidity. "And where do you think it is that my son has gone, Madam?"

"Oh, no!" The marchioness turned pale and clutched her shawl even closer.

He nodded grimly. "Had it from one of the lads at the stable, I did. The designing minx has been after my son this past six months or more and I won't have it, I tell you. I won't have it! The Foxworthys are honest folk, good squires as far back as anyone can remember, and I won't have my son throwing himself away on some young woman who does not know her proper station."

"Oh, no," the marchioness reiterated faintly. "Arabella is a most biddable girl. She would never. . . ."

"Would she not?" The squire interrupted fiercely. "Aye, I thought as much. She *has* been setting her cap at my son. Well, I won't have it. I am going after them."

"No! Wait." The marchioness finally roused herself. "I shall send for her uncle. He will have far more success with both Arabella and your son than either you or I. Think of it," she pleaded. "You and I are both too old to go chasing around the countryside after them. Lucian is accustomed to traveling fast, and he is far more familiar with the roads and the inns than most people."

"Think, Madam. By the time you have sent to London for the marquess, and he has journeyed to Charlmont, three days will have been lost at the very least, three days that I can put to good use searching for the wretched pair."

"My dear sir, if you would just be reasonable for a moment. Luc—er, the Marquess of Charlmont is a man of vast worldly experience, accustomed to handling these sorts of things. This is a very delicate matter, after all. Come," she summoned up a placating smile. "Admit that someone who has led the quiet, honorable existence of a country squire knows very little of such affairs. I am sure it will be a vastly uncomfortable journey, and I am also sure that your wife is greatly in need of your support at such a trying time."

The squire, who already begun to wonder just how exactly he was to begin tracking down the fugitives, paused to consider. He was not a man who willingly deserted his own fireside, even if it was to make a short journey to a nearby race meeting, and the certain unpleasantness to be encountered at the end of his proposed quest was rapidly losing the very small appeal it had held in the first place.

"If you think that the girl's uncle is likely to be more effective, then I suppose he could be sent for. But it is a tricky business, a very tricky business, indeed. Certainly this sort of escapade is nothing that my son would have indulged in on his own. Why—"

"Then I shall send word to London immediately." The marchioness rarely, if ever, resolved anything for herself, but when it was a question of ridding her drawing room of a large angry man, she was capable of more decisiveness than one might have supposed. "And the minute I hear anything or receive any news, I shall send word to Foxworth Hall immediately."

"If he does not find them soon, then . . . Oh, very well," the squire muttered as, favoring the marchioness with a curt nod, he stomped out of the room.

Fortunately for the marchioness's nerves, which were never in a very good state, Lucian was all that she had claimed him to be—as swift at formulating a plan and making arrangements as he was at responding to her initial summons. Two days after the marchioness had dispatched a footman to Mount Street with a frantic but garbled message concerning her daughter's whereabouts, he strode into the drawing room at Charlmont.

"What is all this, Louisa?" Lucian waved the hastily scrawled missive at his sister-in-law.

"Thank heavens you have come! They are gone, and Foxworthy is positively furious over it. He even has the temerity to tell me that it is all Arabella's fault, if you can credit such a thing."

"I can." He responded grimly. "From the looks of it, I would venture to say that she possesses twice the intelligence and three times the daring of young Foxworthy."

"Oh, surely not. Why, she can be the sweetest, most obliging—"

"—When she sees some advantage in it for herself. Now,

cut line, Louisa; this is not the time for dithering. When did you learn of her disappearance?"

"Never."

"What?"

"I mean, it was Squire Foxworthy's claim that his son was gone that occasioned my note to you."

"And no one ever thought to check if Arabella had disappeared as well?"

"No. I mean, it was the natural conclusion. That is, I believe the squire said his son had gone to Bath, which would of course lead one to think that . . . Lucian, you must understand, I had no choice but to summon you. If I had not, Squire Foxworthy was going to go after the pair himself!" The marchioness wrung her hands as she gazed piteously at her brother-in-law.

"Foxworthy go after them? Ha! No doubt Lady Catherine Granville as well, hoping to avert a scandal of ruinous proportions, has sent some representative of her own after them in the hope that her pupil can be safely retrieved before anyone is the wiser. I told you, Madam, that it was a most disastrous connection."

"But it was you yourself who said that we should send her away to school, away from his influence, so as to avoid this very situation," the marchioness wailed at his retreating back.

Lucian paused in the doorway. "Have no fear. I *will* find her, I *will* get her back, and there *will* be no scandal."

The door shut behind him, and a few minutes later, the marchioness heard the crunch of carriage wheels on the gravel drive. Sighing gustily, she took a restorative whiff of her vinaigrette and picked up the novel by Mrs. Inchbald that she had been perusing before her brother-in-law stormed into her drawing room.

With Lucian hot on the trail of the fugitives there was little else she could do beyond keeping her worries at bay with whatever distractions were at hand.

Chapter Seventeen

W hile the marchioness was doing her best to put all distressing thoughts and speculations from her mind, Lucian was entertaining one after another, each more infuriating than the last. Chief among them was the unsettling question of why it was the Marchioness of Charlmont rather than the proprietress of Lady Catherine's Select Academy who had been the one to write the letter informing him of his niece's disappearance.

What was wrong with him? Did Catherine not trust him to behave responsibly? Did she have so little confidence in him that she would prefer to solve a problem on her own rather than turn to him for assistance and advice, even though it was a question of his own niece?

Lucian ground his teeth as he flicked his whip over his team's heads. Undoubtedly she had been so intent on solving the problem as quickly and quietly as possible that it had never occurred to her to ask for help from anyone. Yes, that was it. It was not that she lacked faith in him, she had simply not thought of him. But why not? *You know why,* a cruelly honest voice inside his head told him. Yes, he did know why. Years ago she had trusted him, had had faith in him despite his reputation, and he had betrayed that faith.

Lucian smiled bitterly as he swept past a mail coach. The question was not why had she not come to him, but why should she? Because he wanted her to. Because he wanted to help her. He wanted her to rely on him, and he wanted to be all the things to her that he had failed to be before.

By the time he reached Bath, Lucian had had time to torture himself with thoughts of trust and betrayal. Despite the distraction of heavy traffic, he had agonized over her lack of trust in him, and then he had begun debating with himself endlessly as to whether her behavior showed lack of trust in him or duplicity on her part. In the end, as he stopped a moment at the top of Kingsdown to see all of Bath laid out before him, he decided that he would prefer to believe that it was her lack of trust in him rather than duplicity, anything to keep believing in her honesty and integrity. For if Lady Catherine could not be trusted to act honorably, who could?

This conclusion, however, did not keep him from fuming bitterly as he pulled up in front of number 16, the Royal Crescent and tossed the reins to an eager boy who hurried forward, or from snapping, "Lady Catherine, immediately!" at the butler who cautiously opened the door to him.

By the time Biddle had conducted him to Catherine's office, Lucian was seething with an angry frustration so overwhelming that it took every ounce of his self-control to hold it in check.

Catherine looked up in surprise as the door opened. The welcoming smile died at the sight of his compressed lips and the dark angry line of his lowered eyebrows. "My lord, whatever is amiss?"

"Where is she?" Lucian strode over to the desk and stood, arms crossed glaring down at her.

"I presume that you are referring to your niece?" Refusing to be intimidated, Catherine rose calmly and reached for the bell. "I shall send for her, though I suggest that you compose yourself. She is bound to be somewhat alarmed at your ferocious expression.

Catherine waved to one of the chairs in front of her and took her seat again behind her desk.

Grinding his teeth Lucian took the chair indicated, trying his best to match her air of cool deliberateness.

"The Marquess of Charlmont is here to see his niece.

Please inform Lady Arabella that he is here." Catherine nodded to the footman who had materialized in response to her summons and then turned back to her visitor. "I trust that all is well at Charlmont?"

"No. All is *not* well, and there is no use your pretending . . ."

"Uncle Lucian! I did not expect you. If I had known you were planning to visit, I would have been waiting for you."

If Catherine had not been so intent on retaining her air of calm hauteur at all costs, she would have laughed outright at the dumbfounded expression on the marquess's face. "Apparently your uncle was not expecting to see you here, my dear. You must give him a few minutes to recover from his astonishment."

Her acid tone was not lost on Lucian, who flushed uncomfortably as he fought to overcome feeling like some raw schoolboy called into the headmaster's office.

"Not expecting to see me? Why not?" Arabella's eyes widened as, the picture of innocence, she took the chair next to her uncle.

The silence that ensued while Lucian struggled to frame a reply was deafening. "Er . . . your mother sent for me. She was, ah . . . rather concerned for your welfare," he said at last.

"Mother? But why is she worried? I am quite well, and only last week I sent her a letter telling her so."

"That is just it. Nothing appeared to be amiss, but then young Foxworthy disappeared and . . ."

"Foxworthy?" Arabella echoed. The silence fell again. Clearly both women were well aware of the implications of Lucian's response, and just as clearly neither one of them was the least bit inclined to help him out with his explanation.

"Your mother assumed that his disappearance had something to do with you."

Again, his explanation met with blank stares.

"Ah, it was rumored that he had left for Bath, and his father, who was naturally surprised by this unexpected departure, called on your mother who then sent for me."

It was Arabella who broke the silence this time. "And, assuming the worst, you came chasing after me as though I were a naughty little girl. I am old enough to think for myself and to look after myself."

"You are nothing but a girl."

"And I believe that you were close to my age when you ran off with the upstairs maid," Arabella exclaimed triumphantly, if a little irrelevantly. "How can you sit in judgment on me when Charlotte Partington says you have had countless mistresses over the years?" she continued, warming to her theme.

"It is not the same thing, and you know it."

"Furthermore, everyone knows that you came to choose this place for me because Lady Granville is one of those mistresses and she asked you to see what could be done because she did not like having *her* name connected with *trade*."

"That is enough, Arabella." Lucian had at last gotten control over himself. His voice was as cold as ice and there was an air of deadly calm about him that made it clear to even the most casual observer that he was barely keeping his anger in check.

Abashed by her own boldness, Arabella cast a timid glance at her headmistress, who nodded at her pupil reassuringly. "You may go now, Arabella. The Marquess of Charlmont is just leaving."

Arabella rose quickly and, without a backward glance at either her uncle or Catherine, fled the room, leaving the two of them to confront one another.

The tension in the room was palpable as, white-lipped, they glared at one another across Catherine's desk.

"Catherine, I . . ."Lucian was the first to break the silence.

"I *said,* you were just leaving, my lord." If Lucian's tone had been icy, it was nothing compared to Catherine's.

"But please, I must explain . . ."

"There is nothing to explain. You proved yourself duplicitous ten years ago. There was no reason for me to believe that you would grow any less so over time. I am only surprised that you, who used to possess the values and opinions of a man of superior nature, should so easily accept the values and opinions of such a silly peagoose as Lady Granville. Now, if you refuse to do the gentlemanly thing and leave when you are asked to do so, then I shall."

He caught her by the wrist as she swept past him. "No! Wait! Catherine, you *must* hear me out! Yes, I came to the academy at the behest of Lady Granville. She is well aware that she is not looked upon with favor by the most fashionable members of the *ton,* and she was sick with worry at having her name . . . Well, never mind that. But I had no idea that it was *you* who were in charge of this establishment. If I had known that, I would never have agreed . . ."

"You fail to get my point, Charlmont. Whether or not you trust in my abilities to run an excellent educational establishment has nothing to do with the matter. That a man I *thought* was intelligent and principled should turn into such a gullible fool, *that* is the issue."

"It was not my mind that was involved in this case, but my heart."

Too late, Lucian realized his mistake.

Catherine's lips curled into a derisive smile. "Exactly. And here I thought that a man of your vast experience would be immune to the ploys of a pretty woman. But once a fool, always a fool." She wrenched her wrist from his grasp.

"I meant that I felt sorry for her, not that I cared for her." Lucian struggled helplessly to retrieve his position.

"Oh, I did not for a moment think you cared for her. You never did care for anyone but yourself. You were that way when I first met you, and as far as I can see, you have not changed in the least. Good day, my lord. You may show yourself out." Head held high, Catherine sailed to the door, opened it, and, without pausing for an instant, closed it firmly behind her.

Then, chin still set at a defiant angle, she crossed the hall to a deserted classroom, closed the door behind her, locked it, and burst into tears.

Chapter Eighteen

*L*eft alone to enjoy the full effect of his own blindness and stupidity, Lucian could do nothing for several minutes except stare blankly after her and nurse the sinking feeling that the door Catherine had shut behind her was a door closing on the rest of his life.

Not since he had received the news of his brother William's death at Waterloo had he felt so helpless, so alone, so despairing. In fact, that gray existence, filled with the corroding conviction of the meaninglessness of life, had continued to cling to him from the day he had heard William had died until the day he had walked into this very office and discovered that Catherine, his Catherine, was Lady Catherine Granville. Over time, to be sure, his despair over the loss of William had lessened in intensity, but it had not been until he had seen Catherine again that he had begun to hope that the sense of meaninglessness might disappear forever and he might still find hope for happiness in his life.

Now that hope was gone, and he himself had destroyed it. He had destroyed it with his own blindness, his own lack of faith, and his own distrust. What a fool he was! Only twice in his life had he found someone worth believing in, someone whose honesty he could admire, someone whose integrity was unassailable, and twice he had tossed that away through his own rash actions.

Slowly he made his way to the door and opened it. There was nothing to do now but return to London, which held even less appeal for him than it had the last time he had left Bath.

As he started to open the door, he caught a glimpse of skirt whishing by and, hoping against hope, he wrenched the door open, even as his consciousness was registering the color of the skirt as gray rather than the pale yellow sarsnet that Catherine had been wearing. He tried to catch himself, but it was too late, and he nearly collided with the mathematics instructress.

"I beg your pardon—Miss Denholme, is it?"

Margaret's initial expression of annoyance softened. She had little use for men in general, especially those whose jackets fit to such perfection and whose cravats were so exquisitely tied that it was clear they had little time to think of anything more serious than their outward appearance, but she was impressed in spite of herself. The Marquess of Charlmont had seen her only once, and at that time her name had only been mentioned in passing, yet he remembered it. "Yes."

"I . . . I wonder if you could be of some assistance to me."

She looked at him in some surprise, her eyes surveying him cautiously from behind her spectacles. "Perhaps."

If he had not been so overwhelmed with his own bitter self-recriminations, Lucian might have been amused by her less than forthcoming reply. Unlike their fashionable sisters, the females at Lady Catherine Granville's Select Academy clearly relied on their own intelligence to guide them through life and therefore reserved the right to make their own judgments. Quite obviously Miss Denholme's decision as to whether or not she would accede to his request had everything to do with the nature of the request and nothing to do with the person making it, regardless of his title, his wealth, or his exalted position in the world. It was as novel as it was refreshing.

"I wonder if you might tell me where I might find Lady Catherine."

Miss Denholme's finely arched brows rose at what she obviously considered an intrusion into Catherine's privacy.

Lucian smiled apologetically. "You are quite right in thinking that I have just been speaking with her. In fact, I at first thought when I caught a glimpse of you that you were she."

Margaret gave him a pitying look. "She is wearing yellow. I *never* wear yellow."

"Ah." He was silent, wondering what precisely he was to make of this highly irrelevant piece of information. "Naturally not, and you are quite right to avoid it. Gray is clearly far more becoming to a woman of your delicate complexion."

A faint blush crept into her cheeks and her gaze wavered ever so slightly.

Taking advantage of her momentary confusion, Lucian pressed his case. "Now, though it pains me to do so, I must admit that Lady Catherine is thoroughly and justifiably annoyed with me. I wish to offer her my utmost apology for having upset her, but knowing her to be a woman of singular determination—somewhat like yourself, I suspect—I am well aware that she will deny herself to me should I attempt to speak to her. Therefore, I must catch her unawares, and to do that, I need your help. Not, . . ."—he held up a placating hand—"that I would ask you to betray her trust. I would simply ask you to tell me where I might happen to encounter her. Believe me, I *must* see her. I *must* apologize for having misjudged her. I must make her understand that I . . . Well, never mind. But please, if you would be so kind, tell me how I may find her to say that I am sorry."

It was the words *please* and *sorry* that did it. So few men in general, and handsome ones with an air of authority in particular, ever used these words that Margaret found herself warming to him in spite of her natural distaste for fashionable gentlemen. Besides, he seemed to be so upset and so genuinely convinced that the fault was his. Such honest contrition should most definitely be given all possible encouragement. It was one of her father's cardinal rules and she was not about to break it now.

"Very well." She sighed. "But that is all I shall do. Lady

Catherine lives in the dower house, just past the gates of Granville Park. She usually leaves here an hour before twilight so that she can walk in her garden before sundown. However, she will not take kindly to any interruptions."

"I know." He shook his head ruefully. "But at the moment, she will not take kindly to me, no matter how I approach her. And now," he bowed low over her ink-stained hand," I am greatly in your debt. If I can be of any assistance in procuring you the latest mathematical treatises or secure you copies of the Royal Society's *Transactions,* I shall be happy to do so. You only need to let me know, and whatever you wish is yours."

Margaret's eyes gleamed appreciatively. Here was a gentleman who truly knew how to please a lady. She was beginning to understand why Catherine's face wore that special look whenever the Marquess of Charlmont's name was mentioned. "Thank you, I shall. But mind you," she added fiercely, "do not upset her further. She has had too many people upsetting her lately."

"I shall try." He knew Catherine's prickly independent nature well enough to know that he could not promise such a thing. "And I thank you. Lady Catherine is exceedingly fortunate in those she calls her friends."

Another quick bow and he was gone, taking the stairs two at a time in his eagerness to repair the damage he had done.

Buoyed up with renewed hope and filled with a restless energy that was in need of an outlet, Lucian hired the best hack the White Hart could provide and rode off in the direction of Granville Park even though it lacked at least an hour and a half until twilight. He rode past the gates to Granville Park and well beyond what he identified as the dower house, through the village of Granville itself, before turning around and heading back to the dower house.

Luckily enough, he was just coming over the rise of the last hill before the dower house when he caught sight of what had to be Catherine's carriage turning into the drive. Digging in his heels, Lucian urged his horse to a gallop so that he was just able to catch up with the carriage as it rolled to a stop in front of the wisteria-covered portico.

Hastily dismounting, he tied the reins to a convenient post, hurried to the door of the carriage before the coachman had time to descend from the box, and opened the door, holding out his hand to help Catherine down before she even knew what was happening.

In fact, her hand was in Lucian's before she realized that it was he and not John Coachman who was assisting her. "You!" She tried to snatch her hand away, but she was no match for a desperate and determined gentleman.

Since Catherine was not about to sacrifice what little dignity she had left or risk losing her balance by putting up a struggle while poised on the step of the carriage, she allowed him to help her down. But by the time her feet were both safely planted on the ground, he had drawn her hand firmly though his arm and was leading her toward the rose garden just visible at the side of the house.

Too stunned to speak at first, Catherine let him lead her down the gravel path; however, after they had gone a few paces she opened her mouth to tell him precisely what she thought of unwelcome gentlemen who accosted women on their very own doorsteps, but he laid a finger firmly on her lips.

"I agree with you that you have every right to be angry with me, and even more right to throw me out, but please, let me explain something to you. Many years ago, I, er, *knew* a young woman who made the unfortunate mistake of allowing herself to fall under the control of a most selfish and forceful man. He was older and far more experienced in the ways of the world than she and she was a spirited and intelligent girl so intent on escaping one confining and stifling situation that she fell into another that turned out to be a great deal worse than the one she had quit. Blinded by his superior experience and masterful ways, she failed to recognize his many defects and gave her trust to someone whom she would otherwise have avoided, someone who was inferior to her in almost every way."

His face grew grave as he paused for a moment, remembering. "She suffered a great deal of distress as a result of this rash mistake and, though I was ultimately able to be of some assistance in extricating her from her situation, it was not until after I myself had been the unhappy witness to all the misery that can be visited on one person by another, especially if that person is an older more experienced man who is taking advantage of a younger, innocent woman.

"Since that time, I have been bound and determined that no woman of my acquaintance would ever suffer such a fate, whether she was a duchess or a scullery maid, a close relative or the barest of acquaintances. Imagine what I felt, then, when I learned of young Foxworthy's interest in Arabella. It was abundantly clear to me from the outset that he cared nothing for her, and even more clear that he was a self-centered boor with no thought in his mind beyond his own pleasure and convenience. It was also equally obvious that Arabella was attracted to him by his undeniable good looks and by the possibility of escape he offered from her mother's nervous timidity and helpless ways and that she would not pay the slightest heed to any advice offered to her by interfering and well-meaning relatives. Therefore, the most practical solution to the problem seemed to be to remove her from the young man's sphere of influence.

"I admit"—he acknowledged Catherine's incredulous expression with a rueful shake of his head—"that the conclusion I arrived at was completely erroneous and the choice of action I selected was quite possibly the worst I could have picked. But you must realize that I found myself at the *point non plus.* And however misguided my actions, my intentions were good. At least I did something. I know my instincts were not wrong. That young man *is* after Arabella and he *will* ruin her life. He must not be allowed to. That is why I did what I did.

"Now"—he finally removed his finger from her lips—"you may say whatever you wish to say to me, but I hope that at least you will understand my reasons for doing what I did."

Catherine drew a long shuddering breath. She never wanted to see this man again, never wanted to give him the opportunity to hurt her ever again, but her innate honesty forced her to acknowledge the accuracy of his assumptions. "Your sentiments do you justice, my lord, but not your actions. I quite agree with you that young Foxworthy has designs on Arabella, that he is a brute, and that Arabella is dangerously foolish. Any idiot could see that. And any idiot would try to put a stop to such an improper and clandestine relationship. However, any idiot would have the wit to inform the headmistress of the establishment to which he was entrusting his niece of the impending threat offered by the situation instead of leaving the headmistress to sort it all out for herself and deal with the situation as best she could. And it *has* been dealt with, sir, no thanks to you. Arabella has seen young Foxworthy for the very selfish young man that he is, and it is most unlikely that she will entrust her happiness to someone who clearly does not give a farthing for it."

She looked Lucian squarely in the eye. "No, my lord, I may honor your reasons, but I do not honor your actions, nor do I appreciate your lack of faith or trust in me. Now, as I said before, if you do not leave, I shall. Nor do I ever wish to see you again. Arabella is no longer in danger, and I feel certain that all other matters pertaining to her education can be attended to by your agent or your secretary, so I bid you good evening."

And before Lucian could do anything to stop her, Catherine snatched her arm from under his and ran down the path and into the house, leaving him to make his way back to his horse and ride slowly, despondently, back to Bath.

He had never truly entertained the notion that he would be able to reestablish their friendship, for he knew her proud and independent nature. Still, he had hoped against hope that his explanation might at least have softened her a little toward him. He supposed that in a way it had. She had acknowledged the soundness of his thinking, but that, when he longed for so much more, was no consolation at all.

Chapter Nineteen

*O*nce she was inside, all Catherine's anger and the injured
pride that had supported her through the entire unnerving encounter vanished. She closed the door to the garden
behind her and collapsed against it as she fought to control
the sobs that threatened to overwhelm her.

Why had he not left her alone to think of him as a completely insensitive meddler? Why had he insisted on offering a sympathetic explanation for his behavior that made it
harder for her to dismiss him from her life forever?

Too exhausted and discouraged by the emotions of the
day and depressed by the prospect of a life that little more
than a month ago had seemed to hold a good deal of promise
but now stretched emptily before her, she waved away her
maid who had come to take her bonnet and pelisse and went
straight to bed without supper. Surely all she needed was the
forgetfulness of sleep. Surely things would look better in the
morning after she had had a chance to rest.

But the next day was, if anything, worse. Eager to return
to the distraction of work, Catherine would take nothing but
a cup of chocolate before hurrying back to the academy. But
when she arrived, it was to be greeted with the news that a
messenger from Lord Granville had just delivered a letter
for her.

Nerves already on edge after the events of the previous
day, Catherine found her hands shaking so badly that she
could barely open the letter. It was brutally brief and to the

point. In essence, Lord Granville, along with claiming ownership and control over everything she had once held dear,
now threatened to take over the academy. Having at last discovered that her great-aunt Belinda had died on the very
same day as her husband and having ascertained that no separate trusts had been set up especially for Catherine, Lord
Granville was claiming this inheritance as part of the
Granville estate. Therefore the academy belonged utterly
and completely to him.

"No," she whispered, dropping her head in her hands as
waves of despair washed over her. Too numb to think, too
helpless to do anything, she sat there as the world collapsed
around her. What was the point of doing anything, of fighting for anything, when Ugolino was determined to take it all
away from her?

"The Countess of Morehampton," Biddle announced
from the doorway.

"Oh." Catherine looked up to see Olivia's mother, exquisite as always, in a peach-colored carriage dress hovering
behind the butler. She had completely forgotten that it was
the day for the countess's weekly visit to the academy.

"My dear, I am interrupting you. Shall I go to Olivia and
return another time?" The countess spoke with the easy familiarity of one who was not only a regular visitor, but a
friend as well.

"No." Catherine sighed. "You are not interrupting anything at all. It is just life as usual."

Quick to hear the savagely sarcastic note in Catherine's
voice, the countess looked at her searchingly, her dark blue
eyes full of concern. "Not Ugolino! What, again? Will that
man never . . . Well, never mind. What is it this time?"

"He is claiming ownership of the academy."

"What? How can he? The presumption of that man strains
all credulity."

"He insists that because Great-aunt Belinda died the same
day as Granville died I was still married to Granville at the
time I inherited. Therefore, everything I inherited from her
became Granville's and thus became part of his estate,

which, unless it was specifically designated as being in trust separate from his property and set aside solely for me, which it was not, all goes to Ugolino." Catherine sighed again, more deeply, this time.

"But that is preposterous! You cannot let such a thing happen. You cannot allow that man to ruin your life any more than he already has. You must get yourself a lawyer."

"No lawyer will stand up for me against Lord Granville," Catherine protested wearily. "Any lawyer will just insist, as everyone does, that I should be thankful to be a widow whose income is sufficient to insure her comfort. He will tell me to enjoy my charming lodgings and be glad than I can afford a carriage."

The countess frowned thoughtfully for a moment, and then a sly smile crept over her face. "I know just the man. Though he read for the bar, he does not practice. Instead he offers counsel to those in need, counsel so clever that it has eventually saved many a life from ruin. Furthermore, he is a gentleman of rank who will not be the least intimidated or impressed by Lord Granville."

"But why should he care about me?"

"Because he is a man who abhors injustice as intensely as most men abhor a bad-tempered horse." She saw Catherine's skeptical expression. "It is true. I myself can vouch for his willingness to risk his reputation, even his life, for those unfortunate enough to find themselves at the mercy of someone who has power over them. I see that you are still unconvinced." The countess leaned forward, her face glowing with an intensity Catherine had never seen. "Then let me tell you a story.

"Years ago, before I was the Countess of Morehampton, I was an actress, a good actress, too," she added with a small, proud smile. "But even though I was a good actress, I would never have become a great one, I would have languished in the provinces without the tutoring and encouragement of Mr. Delahunt. He was the owner of a small traveling company that toured the Midlands. It was he who recognized my talent and tutored me in my craft. And it was he who eventually took me to London, hauling me from one theater to another, putting me before one manager after another, until at last one of them gave me a chance to prove myself. Prove myself I did. From then on, it was only a matter of time— and a good deal of work on my part, I might add—until I became known among the cognoscenti. I worked constantly and studied hard, and though Mr. Delahunt was instrumental in my eventual success, I earned it.

"And I was grateful to him for what he had done to encourage me and put me in the way of opportunity. Naturally enough, we became, ah, *intimate.* After all, what young girl, fresh from the provinces, could resist the allure of an older, more worldly man who was willing to devote himself to the management of her career? But as my success grew, instead of sharing in what he had created, instead of enjoying it, he became jealous of it and of me. He also grew mean and made spiteful, threatening remarks about the career that was now beginning to bring us wealth as well as acclaim.

"Though I was much admired, I stayed true to him and we lived together for several years. We even had a little girl, for I thought that a child would prove to him that he was everything to me. In time, however, he even grew jealous of her and the affection I lavished upon her. All my efforts to make things better were to no avail and things went from bad to worse. He began to drink and to beat me—not so that any marks would show, of course, for he was very careful to do nothing that would affect my career which was now supporting all of us."

"Finally I could take it no more. I told him that I and my little girl would leave him if he did not stop. He laughed in my face and declared that as my husband he was in charge of all my money. I could go nowhere without it, and he had it all. When I protested that I was not his wife, never having married him, he laughed again and told me that since we had been living together for years and shared a child, in the eyes of the law we were man and wife. I had no family to turn to, no friends outside the theater, and those I did have were afraid of a man who still retained some of his influence in that world. So, finding myself completely in his power, I remained.

"He grew worse and worse, and in my desperation, I offered to send our little girl away, thinking that perhaps if I were to focus all my attention on him, it would make him less jealous. He at last agreed to that and I sent her away with her nurse to live with the nurse's family in the countryside. It broke my heart, but I hoped that it would help keep me alive. I was right to do so, because when she left the beatings stopped—for awhile at least.

"But then I was given the part of Portia in *The Merchant of Venice*. The audience adored me, the world was at my feet. I had become everything he had said I could be, but it only infuriated him all the more.

"By this time, several wealthy men were beginning to take an interest in me, and strangely enough, that did not infuriate him so much as my artistic success did. Men admiring a beautiful woman was only the natural course of things and had nothing to do with my skill or talent; however, my popularity with the audience and the critics had everything to do with it, and that he could not bear.

"He even encouraged me to be friendly with these wealthy admirers, said it was another way for us to make more money and keep us in contact with wealthy patrons who could help him begin his own theater. I did not care for this, but I did his bidding and played the charming companion to these men.

"There was one among them, however, who stood out above all the rest. He was a man of wit and intelligence, someone who appeared to be more interested in my talent than my person, in talking to me rather than in making love to me. We became friends and soon, perceptive man that he was, he became aware of the fact that I was not only unhappy, but that I was afraid of my mentor.

"He asked me why I did not leave if I was so unhappy, and when I explained to him that I had no control over my money, he very kindly offered to purchase me a villa. I loathed the idea of being beholden to my friend for his kindness, but by then my life had become unbearable. I thought that if I were to give all my money to my mentor perhaps he would allow me to leave him.

"Somewhat cheered by this prospect, I broached it to my mentor one evening when I had made sure that I had ordered his favorite dinner, had the fire well laid, even wore my most becoming gown. In short, I did all that I could to put him in the best possible mood, but he would hear none of it. My earnings were now his livelihood, and as much as he resented my success, it was now his only claim to fame, as well as his sole support.

"He flew into a rage and beat me as he had never beaten me before. Then, leaving me nearly senseless on the floor, he stormed out to his favorite tavern. It took all the strength I had to pick myself up, gather what little jewelry I could lay my hands on, throw a cloak over my shoulders, and escape.

"I had nowhere to go, no one to turn to except my friend who lately had been so much less in evidence that I had begun to suspect he had fallen in love with another woman, a woman of his own rank and station in life. I was loath to ask his help, more loath still to call on him at his chambers in the most fashionable part of town, but I was desperate.

"He was kindness itself and would have sent for his own physician if I had let him, but I was too afraid of what it would do to his reputation and to my chances of escape should word get out where I was. I was badly bruised, but nothing more.

"He insisted that I must leave town and he also insisted on escorting me to whatever place of safety I chose. I, fool that I was, could think of no other place to go than to my daughter, who was still living with her nurse's family not far from here.

"There was no other choice. I had no money of my own, only my jewels to sell for coach fare, but I felt sure that my mentor would have every coaching office watched. In the end I was forced, most reluctantly, to accept my friend's offer of his escort.

"We left town that very night in his carriage, so worried

was I that I would be tracked down. By then my friend had
assured me that unless Mr. Delahunt and I had published our
banns and had exchanged marriage vows in a church, he
could in no way be called my husband; therefore he had no
legal claim to me or power over me or my money. Apparently my would-be husband had had no knowledge of Lord
Hardwicke's Marriage Bill that had been passed some fifty
years or more ago, or if he did, he was certain that I would
not have heard of it, since it had always been the custom
among country folk that a simple promise exchanged between a man and a woman in the presence of others consti-
tuted a marriage.

"I assured my friend that no banns had been published, no
vows exchanged—especially in a church—and no cere-
monies performed, but in spite of his reassurance that in the
eyes of the law I was nothing to Mr. Delahunt, I was still
very much afraid, for I knew his terrible temper and I also
knew his cleverness.

"I was right to be afraid, for the following day, while we
were changing horses at the Castle Inn at Marlborough, my
erstwhile husband appeared on a horse whose evident exhaustion attested to the intensity of his pursuit. He caught
sight of us just as my rescuer was handing me into the carriage for the last leg of our journey, and before either one of
us had a chance to think, he leapt off his horse, drew a pistol from his pocket, and rushed at us, shouting 'Unhand my
wife, you villain!'

"My rescuer, who was unarmed, faced our pursuer with
unimaginable coolness. 'She is not your wife, but a woman
wronged, a woman whom any gentleman would consider it
his duty to rescue from the clutches of a blackguard like
you,' he said. And then he grabbed the pistol which was now
pressed against his chest, wrenching it away with such force
that our pursuer lost his footing and fell, hitting his head on
the cobbles. He lay still as death, the blood from the wound
on his head quickly spreading a crimson stain all around it.

"I was too astounded to do anything, but my companion
never paused for a moment as, assuring himself that the man

was dead, he whipped out his handkerchief, bound his head, and threw him into the carriage.

"'I beg your forgiveness for forcing such an unpleasant traveling companion on you, but I think that this is the safest course of action for all concerned,' he apologized to me as he climbed into the carriage and banged on the roof for the coachman to whip up the horses. Before I could react, we were rattling out of the stableyard only a few minutes after our pursuer had entered it.

"We drove as though the devil were behind us, keeping an eye out for pursuers all the way, but no one followed us and we reached Morehampton without further incident. There I was reunited with my beloved daughter. My rescuer took the body to the local magistrate, who naturally was somewhat surprised to be confronted with a corpse on his very doorstep. Though he accepted my rescuer's story of self-defense, he nevertheless advised him to leave the country for some time, at least until all possibility of unpleasant inquiries had died down.

"So, my rescuer, having assured himself of my welfare and promising to have his agent recover what money of mine he could, bade me adieu and I settled into a quiet existence in the country with my darling daughter while he left for the continent.

"My rescuer was as good as his word, and many months later I did receive some money through his agent, enough to purchase a small manor house in the neighborhood.

"And you are familiar with the rest of my story. The manor house, which was at the edge of the Earl of Morehampton's estate, offered us the delight of frequent country rambles during which Olivia and I would often encounter the earl out with his dog and his gun. He was a lonely man whose wife had died many years ago. There were no children from that marriage, so he quite doted on Olivia. Soon he became a regular visitor to our simple home, and finding our company most congenial, determined to make it a permanent thing by asking me to marry him despite my background.

"Meanwhile, my rescuer traveled throughout the Mediterranean and the Levant, returning to London two years later. But his adventure with me, as well has his subsequent travels, had changed him. If he had been bored with the emptiness of fashionable life before he left, he was disgusted by it now and he determined to do something useful with his life, to put that clever mind of his to good use. Much to the dismay of his pleasure-loving peers, he took up the study of law, quitting the congenial company of Brooks's for the slightly more rigorous company at Lincoln's Inn. There he distinguished himself as much for his passion for justice as for his cleverness. It is this passion for justice that made him choose to remain an anonymous counselor to those who have no one else to turn to. To them he offers the advice to defend themselves in court. To the rest of the world he remains a shadowy figure known only as 'The Scourge of the King's Bench,' a title he infinitely prefers to his own, which is the Marquess of Charlmont."

"The Marquess of Charlmont!"

"Well, at the time this all occurred he was Lord Lucian Verney, but now he is the Marquess of Charlmont."

Chapter Twenty

$\mathcal{A}$ profound silence ensued, and the countess watched in fascination as a variety of expressions flitted across Catherine's face, expressions that made it perfectly clear to the former actress that the Marquess of Charlmont was something more to Catherine than the uncle of the academy's most recently enrolled pupil and Olivia's newest friend.

"He is the very person to advise you, Catherine. Besides his constitutional dislike for gross injustice and his abhorrence for those who abuse power and privilege, he would also feel that it was in his niece's best interest to have this academy continue to remain in your capable hands."

"A legal counselor," Catherine mused aloud, a ghost of a smile on her lips. But while she was absorbing this incredible piece of information, her heart was alight with happiness. The weight that had been pressing on it for the last ten years was suddenly lifted. He had not run off for love but to see justice done! She felt giddy with relief, and in spite of the dreadful threat looming on her horizon, carefree.

"And a very good one too, for he brings not only intellect, but passion to his chosen profession. They say that those he counsels never lose. I feel certain that he would not only dispose of Lord Granville's threat in short order, but he would probably be delighted to do so."

"No!"

The vehemence in her tone caused the countess to look at her in some surprise.

"I mean, there is no need to send to London for legal advice when I have my own legal counsel here in Bath. I shall just consult Mr. Barham, the solicitor who always handled Granville's affairs and now handles mine.

The countess lip curled. "Precisely. And he did not lift a finger to protect you against the highway robbery that Lord Granville has visited upon you since the moment you were widowed. Believe me, he will pat you on the head, metaphorically speaking, of course, tell you to be a good little widow, and advise you not to bother your pretty little head with things that do not concern you and that you cannot understand. Charlmont, on the other hand, will not.

"Believe me, Catherine, Charlmont saw with his own eyes what it was like to be a woman on her own with no property and no money. Since he rescued me, he has only seen more clearly the advantages that men of wealth and property have over those who possess neither, especially the women whose husbands own it all. He will understand, I assure you he will. But now I am afraid I must bid you good day as Olivia will be wondering what on earth has become of her mama who promised to visit her today."

The countess rose to leave, but paused when she reached the doorway. "Do let me know if there is anything I can do. I do have resources of my own, thanks to Charlmont, who secured them for me and then made certain that they remained within my control when I married Morehampton, and they are at your disposal."

"Thank you. You are very kind, but . . ."

"But you prefer to best Ugolino on your own. I quite understand, and I applaud your desire to do so, but do not let your pride deprive you of all that you have worked so hard to attain. The world needs Lady Catherine Granville's Academy because the world needs more women who are equipped to think on their own."

Closing the door gently behind her, the countess left Catherine to sort out the astounding information she had just been made privy to. Lucian had not betrayed their friendship after all, or at least, it had been higher concerns that had distracted him. He had been assisting a woman in peril, a woman who had been hesitant to ask for that assistance because she suspected that he had 'fallen in love with another woman, someone of his own rank and station in life.' Could that woman have been Lady Catherine Montague? Had he come to care for her after all, care for her the way she had cared for him?

For a moment, Catherine felt dizzy at the prospect, but cold reason quickly reasserted itself. This was a man who had first come to her academy at his mistress's request. He had come hoping to convince Lady Catherine Granville to give up her livelihood and her chosen task of educating young women, and he had come simply because a vain, silly woman was concerned for her reputation in the fashionable world.

Catherine gritted her teeth. And this was the man the Countess of Morehampton was suggesting she ask for help? Not only was it highly unlikely, it was a complete and utter impossibility. Lady Catherine Granville was never going to have anything to do with the Marquess of Charlmont ever again.

Snatching up a piece of paper from her desk, she dipped her pen in the ink and scribbled furiously, blotted the letter, sealed it, and rang her bell.

An enormously tall footman appeared. "Here, Thomas, take this to Mr. Barham in the Argyle Buildings and wait for a reply. I wish to impress upon him the urgency of the situation."

Mr. Barham's reply was prompt enough, and he agreed to wait upon his client in her office that very afternoon, but his response, when the problem had been fully laid before him, was nothing if not discouraging. "I do not know, my lady. Lord Granville's case seems very strong, and it certainly would never do to offend such a well-respected and powerful gentleman."

"It is the name and not the person that is respected, Mr.

Barham. How can you not see that, you who have served the Granvilles so faithfully all these years only to be summarily dismissed by him?"

The solicitor's sandy eyelashes blinked rapidly several times as he flicked nervously at a speck of dust on the sleeve of his coat. "It is not my role to question a client's preferences, and undoubtedly Lord Granville had his reasons for retaining another solicitor. After all, I was unknown to him."

"As was everything concerning the estate, which was all the more reason he should have kept you on. But that is neither here nor there. Great-aunt Belinda's will clearly states that her entire estate was to be left to me and me alone.

The solicitor shook his head. "That is as may be, but her intent counts for very little if Lord Granville is claiming it as part of your husband's estate."

"Then we must examine the situation thoroughly."

"You must be careful, Lady Catherine, very careful. For a widow in your position, any hint of scandal would be most injurious, most injurious indeed."

"Scandal, Mr. Barham? There are livelihoods at risk here. It is not only my livelihood, but the livelihoods of everyone in my employ from the instructresses down to the lowliest scullery maid, and you are concerned about my good name? Surely that has been unequivocally established over the last ten years."

"Ah, Lady Catherine, a woman's reputation is a fragile thing, a lovely thing, but fragile, very fragile indeed."

Catherine drew a deep, steadying breath as she rose majestically from her chair. "I thank you for coming to see me so promptly, Mr. Barham, but I can see that in this instance, I have no need of your services."

The solicitor rose also, most reluctantly. "But the academy . . . When Lord Granville—I mean, I can help with the disposal of . . ." He shifted uneasily from one foot to the other as his client's expression, which had been grim, now grew positively murderous.

"Get out."

"What? You can not mean . . ."

"I said, get out, Mr. Barham. If I need the advice of someone who possesses less courage and fewer resources than I do, I would have consulted my footman. Now, good day, Mr. Barham. You are free to return to the more respectable concerns of the rest of your clients."

The solicitor gasped, hemmed and hawed for the space of a second or two, then scuttled from the room with a great deal more speed than he had entered it.

It was at this inopportune moment that Margaret Denholme stuck her head around the door to inquire about the journey home.

"Men!" Catherine snatched up a satchel and began furiously stuffing account books and correspondence into it without the least regard for order or neatness.

"A useless set of creatures, to be sure," the mathematics teacher agreed readily, "but what have they done in particular to upset you this time?"

"Just being themselves—arrogant, spineless, meddling, unhelpful—you know, the usual."

Margaret was forced to be content with this sweeping generality in spite of her very clear conviction that some very specific grievances had prompted it. But it was equally clear that Catherine was in no mood to elaborate, so stifling her rampant curiosity as best she could, Margaret settled into what she hoped seemed like companionable silence during the carriage ride home.

It was not until they had halted in front of the vicarage that Catherine at last emerged from the fit of abstraction that had consumed her the entire time. "I may need to be out of town for a few days in the near future. I trust that you can see to the academy in my absence?"

Margaret turned, her hand still grasping the handle of the carriage door, and looked at her friend in some alarm. "Nothing serious, I trust?"

"No, just the usual—Ugolino and his greedy ways. I believe I must go to Oxfordshire to speak with Great-aunt Belinda's solicitor." Catherine did her best to sound nonchalant, knowing full well that a solicitor who had drawn up a will many years before his client's death was hardly likely to be able to help Catherine prove her case, but it sounded reassuring.

"Certainly. I shall be happy to take care of things while you are gone. Is there anything in particular you wish me to attend to?"

"No. Just make sure that Lady Arabella is fully occupied and well amused. I feel certain that she has seen through that selfish young man I told you about and now realizes that he was only after her for her fortune, but young women are very romantic creatures, and handsome, determined young men can be very persuasive. I do not think we have anything more to fear from that quarter, but it would be naive to dismiss it entirely."

"Very well, then. I shall keep my eye on her and I shall also instruct Olivia to take her shopping regularly. The shops on Milsom Street may fill a young woman's mind with frippery, but all in all, they can provide an excellent antidote to an unwholesome interest in an unsuitable young man."

"Thank you, Margaret. I know it pains you to suggest it, but the notion of shopping is a wise one and far more likely to distract Arabella's thoughts from dangerous channels than Euclid or Pythagoras. I promise to return as quickly as I can; my business is straightforward and should take little time or explanation."

Chapter Twenty-one

*B*ut the more Catherine considered it, the more she doubted that one solicitor would be more helpful than another. Certainly her own, who should to all intents and purposes have had her best interests at heart, had been worse than useless. Who was to say that Great-aunt Belinda's would be any better, if he were even alive? After all, the last and only time Catherine had seen him, he had barely looked more lively than the woman whose estate he represented. And besides, what did it matter if he was able to prove that it was his client's intent that her entire estate go to Catherine if she had neglected to set it up as a special trust for her great-niece and then had been so foolish as to predecease that great-niece's husband?

The journey from the vicarage to the dower house was no more than a mile, but it was long enough for Catherine, racking her brains for a solution to her problem, to recall how she had first learned of Great-aunt Belinda's death. It had not been the letter from the solicitor that had first brought her the news, but a hasty note written by her great-aunt's companion informing Catherine that her great-aunt had died in her sleep late the previous evening after having been ill for several days.

Late the previous evening! Catherine sat bolt upright as the carriage drew to a halt in front of the dower house. That was it! The academy was safe after all! Granville had died midmorning of that day and therefore *he* had predeceased Great-aunt Belinda by possibly as much as twelve hours.

Not waiting for John Coachman to open the door or put down the step, Catherine leapt from the carriage, brushing past Lucy who was anxiously awaiting her.

"Madam, I am so glad you are home, for . . ."

"Not now, Lucy, I am busy."

"But Mary . . . Yes, Madam. Very good, Madam." Lucy broke off with a crestfallen look. If Lady Catherine, who was always the soul of kindness and consideration, was uncharacteristically brusque, then undoubtedly there was a reason for it. Lucy's mistress never did anything without a reason.

The maid sighed and went to tell Cook to ready madam's supper. In good time Lady Catherine would explain it all, but in the meantime, Lucy's news would wait, for surely whatever was responsible for putting that determined expression on her mistress's face must be very important indeed to make her behave in such a way.

Meanwhile, Catherine raced into the library and tore open the top drawer of her husband's account desk. The battered old piece of furniture was one of the few things she had been able to convince Hugo to part with. It had stood in the estate office for as long as her husband could remember and every quarter day, she and he had dispensed the servants' wages from it.

Hugo, who employed the very expensive services of a supercilious agent, had had no need for such a desk, and his wife, shuddering delicately, had called it a hideously rustic bit of lumber that had no place in a gentleman's house. So Catherine had brought it with her to the dower house, taking strength and reassurance from its solid, utilitarian bulk and the memories of better days that it brought with it.

Hardly daring to breathe, she pulled out the packet of letters containing all of the correspondence that had to do with Great-aunt Belinda and sifted carefully through it, but the letter was not there.

Frowning in puzzlement, she carried the stack of letters

over to a chair by the window and searched through it more carefully this time, examining each piece of paper to make sure it had not stuck to the one below or above it somehow, but the letter still was not there.

Catherine's heart began to pound uncomfortably. She was a deliberate, careful person who took great pains never to misplace anything if she could help it, especially something as important as a letter announcing her great-aunt's death. Again, she searched through the stack. Again, she found nothing. She closed her eyes, desperately trying to recall every action she had taken with regard to the letter. Had she put it some other place for some particular purpose? But no, she remembered having received the letter and, after reading it, placing it in the bundle with the rest of Great-aunt Belinda's correspondence and retying the ribbon carefully around it. Then she had put it back in the desk drawer. When the letter from Great-aunt Belinda's solicitor had arrived, she had added it to the bundle. The letter from the solicitor was still there; the companion's letter was not. Catherine was certain that she had never had cause to remove the companion's letter from the bundle.

Was it possible? Could someone else have removed the letter? No! Such disappearances were the stuff of gothic tales, not a widow's simple, quiet existence.

"Madam?"

Catherine looked up to see Lucy hovering in the doorway.

"Your supper, Madam. It is ready. Would you like me to bring it to you here?"

"No, thank you, Lucy, I am just coming." She saw the maid's anxious expression. "I am sorry, Lucy. You had something to tell me when I first arrived, but I had something else on my mind. What was it you wished to say?"

"Oh, I suppose it is nothing much, really, Madam." Lucy looked gratified that her mistress had remembered. "But it is Mary. She seems to have just up and left us without so much as a by-your-leave. Her few belongings are gone. She said nothing to anybody, and after you were so kind to take her in when Lord Granville let her go. The ingratitude of some people—but then she always was a sly little thing."

"'A sly little thing.' Hmmm."

"What is it, Madam?" Attuned to her mistress's every mood, Lucy felt rather than saw the arrested expression on Catherine's face.

"I wonder." Catherine stared thoughtfully out the window for a minute or two. "Can you discover, without anyone's being the wiser of course, if she happened to stop by Granville Park after she left us?"

"But why would she stop at the Park if they were so unfeeling as to let her go without a reference in the first place?"

"Because I am not so sure that they *did* let her go. She may very well have been in their employ when she came to us."

"What? How?"

Catherine smiled grimly at Lucy's astonishment. "I will say this once, and only to you, Lucy, for I have no proof, but a certain document is missing. It is a document I placed carefully in my desk some time ago and I have not taken it out again. Now that document is missing, and so is the maid who showed up suddenly on our doorstep not long ago, which leads me to the possible conclusion that she stole the document, a document whose contents would put an end to Lord Granville's latest and nastiest scheme. Now, do you think you can find out if she returned, even for a moment, to Granville Park after leaving us?"

Lucy's eyes sparkled mischievously. "But of course I can. John Coachman's nephew is a stableboy at the Park. He is a likely-looking lad who never misses a thing. He will be able to tell us. Shall I send for him?"

"No. Do not do anything that might cause comment. But if John were to happen to hear in the course of things that his nephew happened to see Mary at Granville Park after she left here, it would go a long way toward clearing something up for me."

"Very well, Madam." Lucy brightened as a sudden thought struck her. "Now, Sukey in the kitchen was quite friendly with Mary when she was here. She was always begging Mary to tell her how they did things at the Park, as though Mary would know." Lucy sniffed disparagingly. "Perhaps Sukey knows where Mary is."

"I think it is best if you say nothing at all to Sukey about this. All we need to ascertain at the moment is if Mary returned to the Park. John Coachman's nephew is as reliable a source as any and less likely to be noticed than others might be."

"I understand, Madam."

Catherine barely touched her supper that evening, picking at it here and there as she leafed through "Minutes of the Evidence taken before the Committee Appointed by the House of Commons to inquire into the State of Mendicity and Vagrancy in the Metropolis" in *The Edinburgh Review.* But her mind was not on the words before her. In fact, she hardly saw the pages at all as she flipped through them one after another. What was she to do now that the letter was gone—either destroyed or in Hugo Granville's possession, but most certainly not in hers?

How was she to prove that she did have sole right to Great-aunt Belinda's fortune? Clearly it was a waste of time to worry herself over the loss of the companion's letter now that it was gone, but at least thinking about it had not been entirely wasted, for she was able to recall its contents in minutest detail. Great-aunt Belinda *had* died before Granville. Of that Catherine was now absolutely certain. She just had to find another way to prove it.

Unfortunately, Catherine was also able to recall that the companion, a Miss Harriet Smith, had mentioned accepting another position somewhere in Lancashire. While it was possible that someone in the neighborhood near Great-aunt Belinda's handsome manor house might remember where that position was, it was also highly unlikely. Great-aunt Belinda had been a woman of scholarly and reclusive habits who had shown little patience with the mundane interests and trivial concerns of her neighbors. She had employed only the smallest of staffs, all of whom were undoubtedly dispersed far and wide to other households.

The most Catherine could hope for was to discover that the exact time of her Great-aunt Belinda's death had been recorded somewhere, in the parish register, perhaps. She knew that Margaret Denholme's father, who was most punctilious about such things, insisted on absolute accuracy and detail in recording the time and cause of death in the registers. For others, though—in her own native parish in Yorkshire, for example—the simple notation of the date of burial sufficed. If luck were with her, the vicar in charge of Great-aunt Belinda's parish would be a man who subscribed to the Reverend William Denholme's view of such matters.

Whatever the case, it was clear to Catherine that it was incumbent upon her to travel to Oxfordshire, for there was no one else she could trust to carry out such a delicate and time-consuming investigation. She had warned Margaret Denholme that such might be the case; now all she had to do was prepare the staff at the dower house.

"But, Madam," Lucy protested, "what if John Coachman's nephew brings him news of Mary? John Coachman will be gone."

"His news will just have to keep until I return. With any luck, the journey I am about to take will provide me with the same information that was in the document Mary took, if indeed she took it. Remember, I have no proof as yet, only my suspicions, so we must proceed with caution. In the end it will be sufficient to know that Mary returned to her employer after she left us at the dower house."

"Very good, Madam. I shall ask Cook to prepare a hamper for the journey and I shall see to it that your clothes are packed. Will we be staying long?"

"Not if I can help it, Lucy. It is less than a day's journey, and once there, I expect to spend no more than a night, two at the very most."

Hoping to save herself time in her investigation, Catherine returned to the library to reread all the letters in the bundle she had labeled "Great-aunt Belinda." Sifting through them carefully, she searched for the names of anyone, a vicar, a local merchant, an acquaintance of any sort, who might be able to tell her more about Great-aunt Belinda's last day, but there was no one. Even the solicitor who had informed Catherine of the contents of her great-aunt's will appeared to have been in Oxford on business at the time of his client's death.

Worn out by anxiety, her eyes tired from reading and rereading the letters, Catherine went to bed that night exhausted and discouraged. The next day, however, as the carriage rolled down the drive, her spirits lifted somewhat. At last she was doing something to foil Ugolino and his nefarious plots. Even if she was ultimately unsuccessful, at least she was actively resisting him, and it felt good to do so. Surely now that she was putting her own mind and energy to work against him she would win in the end. After all, Ugolino was only as good as the people he employed, and none of them, not even he, was as good as Catherine was when she put her mind to a thing.

Catherine would have felt a good deal less optimistic if she had seen the face at the dower house kitchen window watching closely as the carriage rolled down the drive and turned left onto the Bath road. As the carriage drove out of sight, the face disappeared from the window and Sukey raced to the stables, a piece of plum tart carefully concealed under her apron.

To most people, a piece of plum tart, no matter how large, did not constitute a large enough bribe to risk losing employment, but to the scrawny lad who had been cleaning out the stables at the dower house for less than a week, plum tart was a generous reward indeed for a two mile dash to Granville Park and back just to pass along the simple message "The mistress has gone to Oxfordshire."

Chapter Twenty-two

*T*he journey to Oxfordshire passed without incident, and once she had resigned herself to the fact that there was nothing she could do until they reached Bampton, Catherine actually began to enjoy watching the passing scenery.

It had been more than two years since she had done anything more out of the ordinary than trace the road between Bath and the dower house back and forth and back and forth until she knew every tree, every fence, and every cottage in every season and in all kinds of weather. Now it was a delight to feast her eyes on different church spires, unfamiliar village greens, and houses she had never laid eyes upon. For a time she was able to forget altogether the very reason for her journey until, as the western sky was beginning to change from blue to pink, they drew up in front of the George and Dragon.

The George and Dragon was a respectable enough looking inn, clean but modest, and the landlord welcomed them with the unfeigned interest of someone unaccustomed to travelers who stayed longer than the time required for a change of horses or a quick meal.

His wife showed Lucy and Catherine to two large comfortable rooms at the front of the house, chatting with all the pleasure of a sociable woman constrained by the limited custom of an inn in a small rural village located some distance from the major thoroughfares to London, Oxford, Bath, or Gloucester.

"Of course I knew of Lady Belinda Montague, a fine

enough looking woman in her day, but headstrong, very headstrong." The landlady pulled back the curtains and flung open the windows to let in the fresh air. "With her looks and her fortune, she could have had her pick of any number of eligible gentlemen in the area, but none of them ever did appear to 'come up to scratch,' as they say. It was the general opinion in these parts that she was too clever for most of them, but it is my way of thinking that she preferred to conduct her own life just as she wished without the possibility of interference from any man. A husband would have been an awkward interruption to her way of life. She was forever studying, she and that companion of hers."

"A Miss Smith, I believe." Seeing her chance, Catherine stepped in to direct the tide of reminiscence into more useful channels.

"Yes, Smith. Miss Harriet Smith, that was it," the landlady agreed.

"Do you know what became of her?"

"No. She left not long after Lady Belinda died. I do not know where she went, not to family, for she had none. I believe she took another position, up north somewhere."

"Then she must have realized that Lady Belinda's illness was a grave one if she left for another position so soon after."

"Well, Lady Belinda was rather frail for some time so I suppose it is possible that Miss Smith was looking for a position, but Mr. Jenkins, the apothecary, said that it is often so with strong-willed people; they linger on through an illness that would have killed less determined people.

"Then her death came as no surprise to anyone?"

"Dear me, no. In fact, I cannot say exactly when it happened for sure. She was so rarely seen in the village, keeping to herself as she did. Even the burial was the quietest of affairs. She and the vicar were not on the best of terms, you see. In addition to being exceedingly strong-minded, she was something of a freethinker as well, I believe. Dr. Stevenson did not approve. Being rather high church and all, he would have found opinions like hers rather difficult to take even in a gentleman, but in a woman—well, you can imagine. But he did his Christian duty."

"Dr. Stevenson," Catherine remarked thoughtfully. "Perhaps he can tell us more tomorrow."

"I am sure he would if he could, but the good man was buried himself not two months ago and we have as yet to see his replacement. It is hard, this being such a small parish and all; it would take a most dedicated young man indeed to take it on."

This was discouraging news, indeed, but Catherine refused to be daunted by it. Surely a vicar who was "rather high church" and conservative enough to disapprove of her great-aunt's freethinking ways would have been a stickler for detail as far as recording dates and times of death in the parish register.

With this optimistic thought in mind, she consumed the simple but hearty supper of pigeon pie and gooseberry fool the landlady served them and retired early, determined to start her inquiries as early as possible the next morning. If all went well, they could even be on the road before noon and at home in their own beds by the very next evening.

The morning dawned most promisingly and after providing the travelers with the simple breakfast they had requested, the landlady sent a lad from the stable off with a note for the sexton, then directed Catherine toward the lane that led to the church.

"It is not far, my lady. You can see the steeple just over there, and it makes a very pleasant walk on such a fine day as this."

Lucy, who much to her horror had noticed a tear in the lace on her mistress's nightcap, remained at the inn to repair the damage while Catherine, happy to indulge herself in the fresh air and exercise after a day confined in a carriage, took her time as she strolled along what amounted to little more than a country lane that led to the rose-covered walls of the churchyard and the dark green mass of yews by the lych-gate.

Before entering the gate, she paused to watch a pair of but-

terflies flitting by and listen to the song of a distant lark, mar-
veling at the simple pleasure to be had from such exquisite
but common things. When had she stopped taking pleasure in
such simple experiences? And when had she stopped even
taking the time to seek them out? When had she become so
busy that she no longer appreciated the beauty in the ordinary
objects surrounding her, the loveliness of all that nature had
to offer?

Was it when Granville had died? No, she had mourned the
loss of his friendship and his support, his appreciation for her
capabilities, the inspiration of his integrity, but he had never
shared her delight in the music of birdsong, the riot of color
to be found in a garden, the perfumes of the flowers and the
fields. Was it when she had become so involved with running
the academy that she had little or no thought to spare for anything else? No, in a way the responsibilities that came with
running Lady Catherine Granville's Select Academy for
Genteel Young Ladies had actually invigorated her and given
her back some of the energy that seemed to have drained
from her after Granville's death.

When, then, had she lost her exuberance, the sheer joy of
existence, of being alive in a world filled with beauty, poetry,
and music wherever she looked, whenever she took the time
to stop and observe, to savor and appreciate? It was well before Granville's death—before Granville, even.

It was . . . Catherine stifled her train of thought as firmly as
though she were shutting her own front door behind her
when she left for the day. No, she was not going back to that.
No matter how much the Countess of Morehampton might
speak in his defense, explain his sudden disappearance from
Catherine's life, exclaim over the good he was doing now.
No, no matter how responsible or honorable he had become,
Lucian Verney was not going to have the power to affect her
as strongly as he had before, the power to fill her life with
laughter, and excitement, and . . .

Desperate to wipe such treacherous and unnerving
thoughts from her mind, Catherine ran the last few yards to
the door of the church where the sexton was waiting for her.

"Mrs. Barnes sent word as you was coming, my lady. I have the register right inside and all, but if you will excuse me I have a grave to be digging out back. Ned Thatcher's third wife, poor man. Wasn't married more than a year when off she went in an apoplectic fit. The vicar from over at All Saints agreed to do the service, seeing as the curate's off at the other parish and we have no one to replace Dr. Stevenson. I will just be out back if you want me." And pointing to an enormous leather-bound volume lying on the pew closest to the door, he picked up the spade he had left leaning against the doorway and whistling loudly, went back to his work.

Catherine nearly staggered under the weight of the thick brass-cornered volume that must have held the records of all Bampton's inhabitants since shortly after the Conquest, if the thickness of it was anything to go by. Puffing slightly, and trying not to smear dust on her pelisse, Catherine carried it over to an equally ancient lectern placed conveniently under the light streaming in through high arched windows. Carefully opening it she found the page with the last entries and smoothed it out in front of her.

Bampton was a small village, and though its inhabitants celebrated their normal share of life's important events—births, marriages, and deaths—they hardly filled one page in a year, so Catherine did not have far to look to find the entries from two years ago.

Finding the page with the year of Great-aunt Belinda's death clearly marked, she slowly ran her finger down the entries, carefully reading each one so as to be sure to make no mistake. In no time at all she found it, "March 20, Lady Belinda Montague, well advanced in years, and for a considerable time unwell, languished until ten o'clock in the evening."

"Ten o'clock in the evening," Catherine whispered jubilantly. "At least twelve hours after Granville died!" But as she was reveling in the happy thought that the academy was still legally hers, she felt a stunning blow on the back of her head. Her hand slipped from the register, she felt herself falling, and then the whole world went black.

Chapter Twenty-three

*C*lutching the stout cudgel in his hands, Fogle stared at the inert form crumpled on the floor at his feet. He hoped he hadn't killed her. She was quite a pretty thing, really, if you liked your women slender and clever-looking. He hadn't intended to hurt her, but he had had no choice. The master had said to find the page in the register and take it, but she had gotten there before he had, and there was no telling what she would have done with the information once she had found it. He was sure she had found the information she was looking for because he had heard her whispering "At least twelve hours before Granville died" as he had crept silently up on her from the back of the church.

Yes, Lord Granville would be most displeased if Fogle had managed to kill her into the bargain. Not that there was any love lost between the two of them, Lord Granville and the lady, no love lost at all, but a murder in the family was not at all respectable, even if you detested the person, and to Lord Granville, respectability was of ultimate importance. It was to him what religion was to most people.

When the boy from the dower house had come to tell them that the lady had left for Oxfordshire to investigate further into her great-aunt's death, Lord Granville had ordered Fogle to follow her and find out what she was up to. He had even furnished him with one of the horses from his own stable and Fogle had ridden like the wind. But the horse had cast a shoe at Chippenham and Fogle had been forced to stop and have it attended to. By the time he had reached Bampton, the ladies had retired to the inn and, not wanting to attract any unwanted attention to himself, Fogle had been forced to spend an uncomfortable night under a hayrick.

Lord Granville had been entirely correct in guessing that the lady's first move would be to consult the parish register. During his interview with Fogle, he had muttered something under his breath about headstrong young women who lacked the proper respect for the heads of their families, refusing to take the word of the man of the family and haring off on their own line of inquiry without consulting their betters. He had therefore instructed Fogle to arrive at the church before the lady and snatch the appropriate page before anyone was the wiser.

"Now, Fogle, I have chosen you for this task because you are a resourceful man and, furthermore, you are a man who can read. This is the name you are looking for." Lord Granville had thrust a paper under Fogle's nose with the name "Lady Belinda Montague" clearly written on it. "And this is the year you are looking for. Once you find it, I want you to remove that page and bring it to me, but mind you, do it carefully. I do not want anyone catching sight of you. No one is to know that you have been there at all."

They would know that he had been there now, Fogle thought ruefully. Even if he were fortunate enough that the lady remembered nothing of the incident, she would be very much aware for some time to come that she had been dealt a solid blow on the head. If only he had not slept so late this morning, but tired out by his long ride and kept awake a good deal of the night by the unfamiliarity and the discomfort of his surroundings, Fogle had at last fallen asleep well after midnight and well after his usual bedtime.

Sighing heavily, he straightened and stepped gingerly around the body. There was nothing for it but to continue with the task he had set out to do. He scanned the page of the register that the lady had been reading and found the name he had been told to look for. Pulling out a pocket knife, he slowly, delicately, began to cut the page out of the register when he suddenly became aware of the sound of approaching hoofbeats.

He paused for a moment, waiting for them to continue on past, when much to his dismay, they stopped in front of the door. Hastily, he tore the knife down the edge of the book's spine, snatched up the page, thrust it into his pocket, and darted out the door to the side, congratulating himself on having had the forethought to tie his horse in a concealing clump of trees well beyond the churchyard.

Carefully pulling the door securely shut behind him, Fogle could just make out the sound of footsteps echoing down the aisle and a muffled exclamation before he scurried off toward his waiting horse, threw himself on its back, and galloped off across the fields in the general direction from which he had come.

"Catherine!" Lucian sank to his knees next to her. Gently lifting her hand, he slid off her glove and searched desperately for a pulse. It was there, faint but steady. Overwhelmed by a relief so strong it took him completely by surprise, he continued to kneel there for a moment, staring down at her, the delicate arch of her brows over fragile translucent lids, the dark sweep of her lashes against the pale cheeks, the beautifully sculpted lips that parted slightly as the faintest of breaths whispered between them. He had had no idea how worried he was about her until he saw her lying crumpled and helpless on the floor in front of the lectern.

"Catherine, my poor girl, my dearest girl, wake up." Gently, carefully, he slid one arm under her shoulders and drew her to his chest, cradling her there, warming her, hoping desperately that somehow she would be aware that someone had come to look after her.

The ghost of a smile twisted his lips. Looking after was the last thing Lady Catherine Granville wanted. The Countess of Morehampton had been abundantly clear on that point when he, in response to her note, had been admitted to her drawing room the previous day, travel stained, but eager to do whatever he could to help.

"She won't thank you for your interference, you know—

or mine, for that matter." The countess had greeted him with the easy familiarity of an old and trusted friend. "She is determined to handle this situation all on her own. And she needs to handle it all on her own in order to prove to herself and to Lord Granville that she can stand up to him, that she is a force to be reckoned with in her own right, but, oh, Lucian, I am afraid for her. He is not a nice man, and she has been tempting fate for some time now by refusing to recognize any authority he might have as head of the family." She glanced anxiously up at her visitor. "Does he have any authority? Legally, I mean."

"I do not know, Miranda. I would have to look at her husband's will and her marriage settlements. But legally he does not have the right to resort to fraud and subterfuge as your letter seems to suggest he is doing. Now, what is it you would have me do?"

"I hardly know. I would like, for her sake, to have her extricate herself from her predicament all on her own, but I know the world, Lucian, and I know that no matter how clever or how resourceful Catherine is, as a woman on her own, she is at a severe disadvantage. She needs someone with your knowledge to help her, someone who commands the universal respect that will give her claims validity in the face of Granville's bullying.

The countess's blue eyes twinkled. "I do believe that she understands that, but where you are concerned, she is particularly loath to accept any assistance whatsoever, which is precisely why I wrote to you. Furthermore, if my instincts are correct, which they usually are, I do believe she is not indifferent to you."

"Ah."

The twinkle deepened. "Nor do I believe that you are indifferent to her. In fact, when I mentioned the name Lucian Verney, her reaction led me to suspect that she had once been quite familiar with that name. She only betrayed herself by the faintest of blushes, a barely perceptible shortness of breath, but a woman notices these things, especially a woman who has spent much of her life upon the stage.

"What would I have you do?" The countess tilted her head consideringly. "Follow her, of course, but discreetly, rendering her assistance only if necessary. If she needs none, why, then I shall just have to think of some other way to bring the two of you together. Now, be off with you. You have a journey to Oxfordshire to make and I know that you are longing for rest before you leave."

He had taken her suggestion and made an early night of it, leaving the White Hart on horseback early the next morning well before daylight with instructions to his valet to follow at a more leisurely pace in his carriage. He arrived at the George and Dragon only to discover from the landlady that Catherine had gone to the church, and he quickly followed her there and arrived . . . too late.

A faint moan brought Lucian abruptly back to the present.

Catherine's lids fluttered, and for a moment she gazed up at him blankly. Then recognition dawned. "You! What are you doing here!"

"Hardly the welcome that one who finds you alone, knocked senseless, and helpless might reasonably expect." Lucian replied sardonically. But his words were belied by the warmth in his eyes. In the brief moment when she had first recognized him he had seen, or hoped he had seen, the gladness in her eyes. For one brief second he had felt, or thought he had felt, her hand grasping his for strength and reassurance.

She struggled to sit up. "No . . . I mean . . . how did you know that I was here?"

"Gently, my girl, gently." Still holding her close, he eased her into an upright position. "You have had quite a knock on the head, and redoubtable though you may be, I feel sure that, along with whatever preceded it, it must have had some ill effect on you. Here." Carefully, he undid the ribbons of her bonnet, lifted it from her head, and ran gentle fingers through her hair.

"Ouch!" She winced uncomfortably.

"Quite a bump. It is a lucky thing you did not do yourself

further injury when you fell, for I feel certain that it must have been quite a blow to render you unconscious."

"I. . . ." She frowned in an effort to recall the events before the world had gone black around her. "I don't know what happened. One moment I was standing there reading the register and the next . . . The register!" Catherine struggled in his arms. "I must get the register."

"Easy, easy. You are not as completely recovered as you might think." Slowly, still holding her close, Lucian raised her to her feet.

The accuracy of his words was quickly borne in on her as the world revolved dizzily around her for several seconds before righting itself.

"Now, what was it about the register?" One arm around her waist, the other clasping her hand, he led her over to the lectern where the register still lay open.

Catherine glanced eagerly at it. "I was right, after all. See, here. . . ." Her eyes fell on the few remaining bits of torn page still left in the spine of the book and she burst into tears. "Oh, no! I have lost the proof. I have nothing to show for it now."

Lucian gathered her in his arms. "Hush, my poor girl. Hush now." Ever so carefully, he pulled her head against his shoulder and gently stroked the back of her neck until the sobs that shook her had subsided.

At last she looked up at him and, fiercely dashing away the tears from her cheeks with one hand, she fished for her handkerchief with another.

"Here." He pulled in immaculate square of linen from his own pocket.

"No. It is bad enough that you found me helpless on the floor. At least allow me the dignity of using my own handkerchief."

"Very well, then." He grinned. "I am relieved to see that you seem to have suffered no permanent ill effects from your unnerving experience and remain the damnably independent woman you always were."

Catherine sniffed disdainfully, but her eyes filled with

tears. "Whatever am I to do? I cannot let that man win! He is a . . . He is . . ."

"I know. I know." Lucian led her to a convenient pew and sat down with her. "He is a villain of the worst sort, for he hides a thief's heart under the trappings of respectability, and now he has the title to make it even more respectable. Believe me, Catherine, I know about these things. I have been fighting against such things with all my might these past six years or more. And that is why the Countess of Morehampton sent for me. She knows what the world is; she has seen what it takes to win against men like Lord Granville, and she knows I can help you. Together, you and I can find the evidence that will prove the falseness of his claims. Together, we can establish your irrefutable right to what was always yours, and he will never be able to threaten you again."

Chapter Twenty-four

Together. The word warmed her heart. He had not said "I," but "together." And he had not said he had come to "rescue" her, but to "help." The distinctions were small, but to Catherine they made a world of difference.

In fact, he *had* rescued her. How long had she lain unconscious on that cold stone floor, and how much longer might she have lain there if he had not appeared? She had no notion. But he had arrived, strong, comforting, and infinitely reassuring in a world where the ground seemed to be constantly slipping out from under her feet, a world where she always seemed to be taking one step forward and two steps back. Yet he had not asked her, as so many would have, why she had not asked for help, why she had not consulted with someone older or more experienced. He had simply accepted the fact that she had taken the investigation on all by herself as though it were the most natural thing for a single woman to do. And now that she had failed, he was offering her his assistance.

Catherine smiled tremulously at him. "I expect you are wondering why I did not ask for help, or . . . at least bring someone with me."

"On the contrary, I know precisely why you did not. In general you are used to relying on your own resources, and in general you are absolutely right to do so. There are few people so well equipped to handle whatever life may throw in their paths as you are."

The words brought a hot flush of gratitude to her cheeks. "I had no idea Ugolino would ever threaten me in any way. I thought he was nothing but a greedy, pompous fool who worshipped respectability and the honor of the family name."

"True. But even pompous fools can turn dangerous when threatened with loss of respectability or when they see the opportunity to indulge their greed."

"And yet you were prepared to try to talk Lady Catherine Granville into changing the name of her academy in order to preserve that respectability, or at least Lady Granville's." Catherine wondered what devil had prompted her to mention that unfortunate episode, but she could not say. Surely she neither knew nor cared what Lady Granville was to the Marquess of Charlmont or he to her? But an insistent little voice in her head told her that she cared very much.

"Touché." Lucian grinned as he led her back down the aisle of the church and out into the sunlight. "You never were one to let a fellow get away with inconsistencies of any sort." His face grew serious. "Truthfully, though, I felt sorry for her."

"Sorry for her! Sorry because she was so beautiful and enchanting, no doubt." What had come over her, Catherine wondered. Why, she sounded almost acerbic!

"In a way." He remained thoughtful. "She was so worldly in her ambitions, yet so ingenuous at the same time, for she truly believed that her beauty and her charming manners alone would give her the entrée to the *ton* that she so desperately craved. Yet there was a certain gallantry as well in her determination that I quite admired. It was rather touching, really. And then, you know me, I never had the least use for it all anyway, so it was rather amusing to beat them at their own game. When I left town to visit the academy the first time she was on her way to becoming fashionable and I was free again to do as I pleased, and, in the course of it,"— he paused to look deep into Catherine's eyes—"I found you again, and for that alone I am forever indebted to her."

It was not at all the answer she had expected. Catherine

had been waiting for some cynical denial of the relationship, some reference to Lady Granville's being indistinguishable among the scores of other beautiful women he numbered among his flirts, but the sheer honesty of his answer caught her off guard and made her believe him when he told her he was glad to find her again.

She stood there mesmerized by the look in his eyes, which was both heartwarming and frightening, heartwarming because the light in them told her how much she meant to him, frightening in the intensity of feeling behind that look. Suddenly shy and unsure of herself, Catherine tried to pull her hands away, hands she had not even realized he was clasping in his until that moment.

But instead of letting her go, he pulled her to him so that she could feel the beating of his heart against her cheek. "I did not know how much I had lost until I found you again," he whispered against her hair.

He held her a moment longer and then, sensing her uneasiness, sighed and let her go. "But now, my girl, there is work to be done, and I am a boor for distracting you from it. Come, let us speak to the landlady at the George and Dragon."

"The landlady?" She hated her voice for squeaking the way it did, as though she found being held in a gentleman's arms most unnerving, which indeed she did. It was a relief to have him return to the normal half-teasing, half-businesslike tone of voice he normally used with her.

"Yes. Aside from ladies' maids, the landladies of this world are the single greatest source of information about the goings-on in any community. I feel sure that if there is any servant or any distant relative of a servant who once worked for your Great-aunt Belinda who remains in the vicinity, Mrs. Barnes is bound to know. I am sure that with the proper questioning, she will eventually be able to furnish us with some useful scraps of information she did not even know she possessed."

"Mrs. Barnes? How do you know her name is Mrs. Barnes?"

Lucian raised a quizzical eyebrow. "Oh ye of little faith! Surely you know me well enough to know that the landlady already considers me a most delightful gentleman, so affable, and not at all high in the instep. I made her acquaintance before I came upon you crumpled on the floor in front of the lectern. It was she who directed me to the church."

"I was *not* crumpled. I am not such a helpless . . ." but she thought better of it. When Lucian had found her, she truly had been helpless, and she had been so reassured by the strength and comfort of his presence and the warmth of his arms around her.

"Well, prone, then. But here we are. Let us see what she has to say."

"I would dearly love to help you, my lord, but try as I can, I can think of no one who can tell you anything about that day. Miss Smith, of course, went to the position up north I spoke of, and her maid, Prue, went to a brother somewhere in Shropshire, I believe as well as the coachman who left to look for work. I am that sorry, my lord." The landlady shook her head sadly. "No, stay a minute. Yes, perhaps there *is* someone. The cook, Mrs. Elkins, now shares a cottage over in Lane End with her sister. She might just possibly know something."

"Thank you, Mrs. Barnes." Lucian executed a truly exquisite bow. "You are a local treasure, it is plain to see."

"Why, thank *you*, my lord." She chuckled, dropped a flirtatious curtsey, and then proceeded to give them directions to Lane End.

"Honestly," Catherine muttered in disgust. "She might at least have acknowledged my presence, but with you in the room, I simply ceased to exist. 'I would dearly love to help you, my lord. Thank you, my lord.' You should be ashamed of yourself, carrying on with her like that."

"People are more forthcoming with information if they are encouraged, you know. Sometimes, given the proper inspiration, they can come up with information they did not even realize they had."

"Encouragement!" Catherine gave a most unladylike snort. "Dalliance, more like."

"Come along. Let us find Lane End. I know from former days that you are a positive glutton for fresh air and exercise, and as it is not far, I propose we walk there."

They set off at a brisk enough pace, but the fineness of the day, the beauty of the countryside, and the pleasure of intelligent conversation were infinitely seductive, and as they made their way toward the cottage, arguing over the findings of the committee looking into mendicity and vagrancy in the metropolis, the walk turned into a saunter and the saunter into a stroll.

Pausing at the rose-covered gate that opened on the path leading to the cottage, Lucian regarded his companion with a critical eye. "You should take holidays more often, you know. Distraction from your work and your responsibilities puts the glow back in your cheeks and the sparkle in your eyes. You look as though you are once again enjoying life the way the Catherine Montague I once knew did."

"Holiday! You call this a holiday?"

"There, you see. Of late you have been forced to take life so seriously that you even turn a walk in the country into a task to be completed."

"But it *is* a task to be completed, and a very critical one too, I might add. Besides, I did stop to enjoy the countryside."

"When?"

"Not long ago, before I was so rudely brought back to the present reality by a blow to the head."

"Ah." He regarded her with a curiously arrested gaze. "And what did you enjoy?"

"The butterflies, the birds, the flowers, oh . . . a hundred things."

He smiled as he ran a caressing finger down her cheek. "I am glad. You are too full of beauty yourself not to be able to enjoy it elsewhere."

There was no telling how long they might have stood

there gazing at one another, but the creak of the cottage door brought them back to the task at hand.

A tiny white-haired, rosy-cheeked old woman stood in the doorway. "Good day to you, sir, madam. What may I do for you?"

"And a good day to you, mistress," Lucian replied. "We hope that you may be of some assistance to us."

"I?" The white-haired lady looked doubtful in the extreme.

"Yes. Does a Mrs. Elkins live here?" Lucian flashed her a reassuring smile.

"That would be my sister."

"I believe that she was a cook for some time to my Great-aunt Belinda Montague." Not to be outdone this time, Catherine stepped forward and favored the woman with what she hoped was her own reassuring smile. "We were just wondering if we might have a word with her."

"Just a minute. Oh, where are my manners?—I mean, do come in please, sir, madam." She led the way into a tiny but immaculate room where a fire glowed brightly on the hearth despite the warmness of the day. "May I offer you any refreshment? My sister makes a most excellent blackcurrant cordial."

"Thank you, no. We will not trespass long on your time, but we were hoping she might be able to answer a question or two." Catherine tried to sound politely regretful rather than eager for information.

"If you will excuse me, I shall fetch her." The little lady ducked behind a flowered curtain to the left of the fireplace only to reappear a moment later followed by an exact duplicate of herself.

"Betty, this gentleman and this lady have come to ask you some questions about Lady Belinda."

Lucian stepped forward. "Do not be alarmed, Mrs. Elkins. It is a simple matter, really. We promise not to keep you, but Lady Catherine here is most anxious to know about the day her great-aunt died. It is rather important, you see, and though you may not have seen your mistress a great deal after she became ill, we know that a cook who works at the very heart of the household, especially a small one, is often more aware of its comings and goings than most people might think."

"You have that right, sir. Though, by that time, I was getting along in years myself and not what I once was. But what is it that you wish to know?"

"Well, we know that she was ill for some time before she died." Catherine ventured encouragingly.

"Yes, madam, an inflammation of the lungs. She fought against it, she did, and I made every delicacy I could think of to build up her strength, but it did no good. Why, the last night I do not think she even touched the tray I sent up."

"But she was alive when the tray was taken up to her?" The studied casualness of Lucian's tone might have fooled the two women, but to Catherine, the tense angle of his head, the tightness of his jaw, and the brightness of his eyes reminded her of a cat about to pounce.

"Oh, my, yes. The girl that took it up to her told me that Miss Smith tried to persuade the mistress to take a bite of custard, but even that was no use. And then much later when Prue went back to collect the tray, she met Miss Smith on the stairs coming to tell the coachman to fetch the doctor because she thought the old lady was getting worse."

"And what time would that have been?"

"Let me see now, sir. Except for the tray, Prue had done all the washing up and swept the floor. I would say that it was somewhere between nine and ten o'clock in the evening."

"And one more question, if you would be so kind, Mrs. Elkins." Lucian nodded encouragingly. "What was the doctor's name. Does he still live in the vicinity?"

"Dr. Taylor. But he was not able to come until after midnight on account of Mrs. Trimble's having her baby—a most difficult delivery indeed, though to see the lad now you would never know it—so he did not arrive until well after midnight and by then my lady was already gone."

"And the doctor?" Lucian prompted gently.

"—lives at the other side of the village just on the Gloucester road, about three miles from here."

"Thank you, Mrs. Elkins. You have been extremely helpful, most helpful indeed." Lucian shot Catherine a triumphant look. "And you have vindicated my faith in cooks as the source of all knowledge in a household. Now we shall trespass on your time no longer. I bid you both good day." A quick bow and a smile to the pair by the fireside and Lucian ushered Catherine back out of the cottage.

The door had barely closed behind them, however, when she turned to him. "What was that look for?"

"What look?"

"That triumphant smirk when Mrs. Elkins told you where the doctor lived."

"Stop being so prickly, my dear. There is not the least need for it. I was merely letting you know how delighted I was to hear that the good doctor has not moved on as so many others in the case appear to have done. If you will think about it, you will realize that a determined lawyer might cast doubt on the reliability of Mrs. Elkins as a witness. She is, after all, quite old, and all her knowledge comes from hearsay. Dr. Taylor, on the other hand, is presumably a respected man of science. If he is ready to swear that your Great-aunt Belinda was but recently deceased when he arrived, then I believe we can prove your precious Lord Granville's claim to be quite without merit, parish register or no parish register."

"But do you think the doctor will be able to swear to such a thing?"

"If he is worth his salt he will be. But let us first fortify ourselves with a little refreshment before we go consult the good doctor. No?" He could not help laughing at her eager look. "You always were a little terrier, weren't you, once you had got your teeth into something. Very well, then, we shall go this moment; however, for this journey, I suggest we take the carriage."

The doctor was not only at home but very clear about the time of his patient's death. "Yes, it was a busy night, that night, what with the difficulties of Mrs. Trimble. She was in a bad way or she would not have called for me—a staunch believer in the efficacies of the midwife, that one. It cost her a good deal of pride to call for a doctor, believe me. Young Trimble was born half an hour or so before midnight so I must have stopped by the manor house at some time after half past twelve. The old lady was dead, of course; no surprise, given her age and the illness, but Miss Smith, who was ever punctilious, wanted a doctor's opinion."

"And in your opinion, sir, how long had the lady been dead?"

The doctor looked sharply at Lucian. "A matter of some importance, I gather?"

"Important enough to ask you to swear to it, if need be."

"Well, let me see. The body was cold, so she had been dead some time, but it was not stiff, so I should say it had not been more than a couple of hours—somewhere between ten and eleven o'clock in the evening, I should say."

"And would you swear to it?"

"Certainly, I would swear to it." The doctor was indignant.

"Then that is all we need, and I thank you very much for your time, sir."

"There." Lucian smiled down at Catherine as the housekeeper showed them out. "And *now* may we have some refreshment?"

Chapter Twenty-five

*I*t was far too late in the day to set out for Bath, and Lucian, after noticing how Catherine winced as she removed her bonnet, insisted on calling for the doctor.

"It is just a bump on the head," she protested, "nothing more."

"That is as may be, but you are looking quite done up, my girl, and I would feel a good deal better if you allowed Dr. Taylor to take a look at your head."

Catherine looked mutinous, but by this point, she was too tired to argue and she meekly allowed the doctor to be sent for, undergoing his examination without a murmur of protest.

After gently probing the bump, peering into her eyes, and having her look at his finger as he waved it back and forth in front of her face, the doctor pronounced her fit as a fiddle. "There is no sign of concussion," he reassured Lucian, "and other than the headache that is to be expected after one receives a significant blow to the head, the lady should suffer no ill effects from her mishap other than to wonder why someone should wish to do her such a mischief in the first place."

"Which is precisely why I wanted you to swear to the time of Lady Belinda Montague's death. In fact, if you would be so good, Doctor, as to sign this statement I have drawn up for you . . ."

The doctor shot Lucian another penetrating look, took

the paper, read it carefully, and scrawled his name at the bottom.

"Thank you, Doctor. That piece of paper should do more toward making this patient heal than any medical assistance you could possibly have rendered her." Lucian smiled as he folded the paper and handed it to Catherine. "And now, my girl, you must rest."

On principle, Catherine voiced her protest, but it was a very weak one. The events of the day, coupled with her injury, as well as the wild range of emotions that had buffeted her from hope to despair, along with other deeper feelings which she did not even wish to contemplate, had thoroughly worn her out and she soon retired to her chamber and Lucy's expert care.

In fact, she only intended to take a short nap and was utterly appalled to discover that it was morning when she next awoke. "What? I have not slept through the entire night!"

"Indeed you have, Madam, and a very good thing it is too. You were that exhausted." Lucy smiled comfortingly at her mistress as she handed her a pot of chocolate.

"Breakfast in bed? I am not an invalid." Catherine sat up, preparing to swing her feet out of bed, only to be pushed firmly back against the pillows.

"Begging your pardon, Madam, but his lordship gave strict instructions as to how I was to coddle you."

"Lord Charlmont? He is still here?"

"Yes, Madam, and most attentive he has been too, checking in now and again to see that you were sleeping soundly."

"He watched me sleep? What business is it of his?"

Lucy turned quickly away to hide a knowing smile. "His lordship explained to me what happened yesterday and naturally, being the fine gentleman that he is, he was most concerned about your health."

"That is outside of enough!" Catherine jumped from the bed. "Help me on with my clothes, Lucy."

And not ten minutes later she was confronting Lucian

over rashers of bacon and eggs in the taproom. "There was no need for you to look after me, my lord. I thank you for doing so, of course, but I am perfectly capable of looking after myself, and . . ."

"—Journeying back to Bath on your own. I know. But I mean to accompany you. There, see? I knew you would not be pleased to hear that."

He rose and walked around the table to look anxiously down at her. "Yes, you are looking fit as a fiddle again, in spite of the knock on the head. But did it never occur to you that I might be doing this not for you, but for me?"

"For you?"

"Catherine,"—he took her hand in his—"you are one of the people I admire most in this world, and, as you know, there are precious few people I admire. I care what happens to you. I enjoy your company, and I want you healthy and happy so I can continue to do so. Now, as you undoubtedly spurned the chocolate that was sent up to you, let me order you some breakfast."

And so it was that an hour later, after seeing that Lucy and the few belongings they had brought with them were settled in Catherine's carriage, he handed her into his own and climbed in after her.

"I know that you think I have been odiously high-handed during this entire affair," he began, settling himself comfortably in the seat opposite her."

"Not odiously, perhaps, but certainly high-handed."

"But I have a constitutional dislike of bullies and an even greater dislike of injustice, so I felt bound and determined to join you in the fight against both the bullying and the injustice that have been visited on you. However, I am not the only one who has been high-handed in this affair. The Countess of Morehampton has been equally determined to interfere on your behalf against the despicable 'Ugolino,' as I believe you call him."

He leaned forward to take her right hand in both of his. "Let me explain to you about the Countess of Morehampton. I think that you can see, from her eagerness to throw us together, that I mean nothing to her and she means nothing to me. She never did mean anything to me beyond the fact that she was a gallant hard-working woman who was being brutally used by a selfish and despicable man."

"Oh, I was attracted to her at first. She was clever and witty, a woman who for the most part thought for herself. Until then, I had never met anyone like her. My previous experiences with women, numerous though they might have been, all revolved around my physical attraction to them, and in turn the social and pecuniary advantages they thought they could reap from me by becoming either my wife or my mistress. Miranda Delahunt was different. She wanted to profit from my intelligence, to learn from my experience. She sought me out for advice, and I sought her out for intelligent conversation, until that is, I met you."

Lucian grasped Catherine's hand more tightly and looked deep into her eyes, willing her to believe his every word. "With you I discovered the true joy of friendship, of being challenged by someone who could think and analyze and appreciate as well as I could. I came to admire your spirit, a spirit that refused to take advantage of birth and fortune but insisted on defining itself on its own terms. You were so like me in so many ways, hemmed in by your class and your wealth, longing to prove yourself by accomplishing something truly worthwhile, by giving something meaningful to the world. How could I not be immediately attracted to you; how could I not care about you?

"I am ashamed to say that when you appeared on my horizon, I rather forgot about Miranda until she came to me one day in desperation, frantic to escape from the oppressive cruelty of her husband. I knew her story, of course, that he had recognized her talents, brought her to London, and helped her to realize her potential. I knew she was not in love with him, but until then I had not been aware of the extent to which he had made her suffer simply because she was more successful than he was.

"It was the meanness of it all that tore at my heart. She freely acknowledged her debt to him, was more than willing to repay it, to give him all that she felt she owed him in return for her freedom, but that was not enough. He wanted her soul. He wanted complete and total control of her. He was so deeply jealous of her success that even though he himself had contributed to it, he was willing to destroy her, just to keep her from enjoying it, just to keep her from taking pride and pleasure in all that she had accomplished.

"In addition to making her suffer, mentally and physically, he had the advantage over her of being a man of the world, which he exploited to the fullest degree. I was sickened and enraged by what I saw, and naturally I offered her whatever assistance lay in my power to help her escape from the hell that her life had become. I had no way of knowing, of course, that I would become embroiled in her life to such a degree that I would be forced to flee the country. And because my disappearance was so closely connected to her and to her good name, I felt I was not at liberty to explain myself to anyone, whatever it might cost me. And believe me, Catherine, it cost me a great deal."

Looking up into the gray eyes that bored into hers, Catherine could feel his resolve, feel his conviction that there had been no other course of action for him to take other than the one he had taken.

"Catherine, I am not excusing myself. I am only telling you this story to explain to you why I have acted as I have now, even though it may seem to you to be somewhat highhanded. I have seen what unscrupulous men can do to women's lives, and how men who do not even have much power in the world can ruin the life of an intelligent and resourceful woman. That is why I am determined to help you defend yourself against the schemes of Lord Granville. And that is why I now offer you all the skills I have at my disposal to help you see to it that from now on you have the right to conduct your life as you see fit, without interference from anyone."

He ran one hand distractedly through his thick, dark hair. "I can see that you are still not convinced. Do you know what I did when I at last returned from the continent?"

She shook her head slowly.

"I decided to be useful; I decided to do something serious with my life. I went to Lincoln's Inn and for three years I dedicated myself to learning the law with the best of them. For three years I gave up every other pastime. My face disappeared from the gaming room at Brooks's, the races at Newmarket, my box at the opera. As far as the *ton* was concerned, I might have remained on the continent, so little was I to be seen in its usual haunts. But when I was called before the bar, there was no one else called who had a more thorough knowledge of the law than I did. And since that time I have done my level best to put it to the best use I could.

He paused and stared out the window at the passing countryside for some time— for so long, in fact, that Catherine thought he had finished. But then he turned back to her with the oddest expression on his face, half-hesitant, half-defiant. "And do you know the one thought I have carried with me all these years? The measuring stick that I have used to judge myself?" His voice, usually deep, authoritative, and assured, wavered oddly as though he was unsure of himself.

"Nnnooo." Again, Catherine shook her head slowly.

"It was the thought of all our discussions of the Speenhamland System, the Poor Laws, and the reforms we dreamt of, the schemes we came up with to improve society. I asked myself at every juncture, *What would she say? Would she approve of what I am doing?*

A faint smile tugged at the corner of his mouth. "And now I think you just might approve. The world does not know me, but it knows my work. I am known only as 'The Scourge of the King's Bench,' not so much because of my clever advice, but because of my willingness to give counsel to those who have none, or those who are forced to mount their own defense without the wit or experience to do so. Perhaps my greatest triumph was to help a woman save herself from the jail sentence her husband thought he had so cleverly arranged by having her jewels stolen. They were jewels left to her by her mother, so they possessed considerable sentimental as well as monetary value. Now, the husband, knowing how eager she would be to bring about their return, arranged to have them stolen. Once they were gone, he, in the guise of sympathy, suggested that she advertise a reward for their return in the newspaper. But when the supposed thief came to collect the reward, the husband had not only the thief arrested but his wife as well, who having paid the reward was arrested as an accessory because she was offering money in return for what she knew to be stolen goods. In desperation, the poor woman turned to me and I suggested to her that since she had in fact paid a just value for these goods instead of one below or above, she could claim she was not an accessory. It is a very fine point of law indeed, but she won. I tell it to you now to prove to you that even something as seemingly simple as buying back one's own jewels can lay one open to trouble in the eyes of the law. So I beg you, Catherine, please call on me immediately should Lord Granville make any further difficulties for you."

She was too overwhelmed by it all—his story of the Countess of Morehampton, the tale of the woman and her jewels, her own recent upsetting experience—to do anything more than nod dumbly. And inconclusive as it was, Lucian was forced to be content with that.

For the rest of the journey, he did his best to distract her with questions about the academy, the curriculum she had selected, how she and the instructresses decided upon their materials, how she had arrived at the salaries she paid them, which educational theories she subscribed to. "For though I see much of Rousseau and Madame de Genlis behind your obvious desire to offer an education that will bring out the innate abilities of each individual pupil, you appear to differ from them in your equally obvious belief that women are just as capable of learning as men, and of learning more than the few skills that will make them delightful companions for their husbands. On the other hand, though you seem to believe, along with Hannah More, that a well-educated woman can have a profound influence on those around her, you seem to carry it a good deal further than she."

It was Catherine's turn to smile. "Far enough so that some day, I hope, there will no longer be women who will require rescuing from men. You had better hope, for your sake, my lord, that I do not succeed too well too soon."

He laughed. "On the contrary, I would be delighted if your success were to deprive me of much of my work. You already seem to have succeeded to a considerable degree with my headstrong young niece, though how you accomplished it, I have yet to understand. Not only did she recently send me a letter describing several books she is reading, but my sister-in-law reports that young Foxworthy has returned to the vicinity and is comporting himself with what can only be described as sullenness and ill humor— clear indications that his suit did not prosper. I do not know what magic you and your academy worked, but I can only say I am exceedingly grateful."

"No magic, my lord. Just showing her that exchanging one despot for another is not acquiring one's liberty."

"So you think me a despot, do you? Let me tell you, my girl, watching over Arabella's welfare was not of my choosing. I would as soon as . . ." Then, catching sight of the twinkle in her eye, he chuckled. "Well, even *you* must admit that the girl is a handful."

"That I do. But she is fortunate to have someone as clever as you to assume the burden of looking after her. Even she admits to that."

"Arabella admitted that?"

Catherine nodded.

"To you?" He was absurdly pleased and touched that she should mention it to him. "Thank you for that. And thank you for all you have done for her, and for me."

He reached out a hand and tilted her chin so she was forced to look him squarely in the eye. "I am sorry I ever doubted you about Arabella and Foxworthy. I was a fool to do so. It has been so long since I had faith in anyone—but that is no excuse. Will you forgive me?"

She nodded, and for just a moment she had the oddest feeling that he was about to kiss her, but then he appeared to think better of it.

Chapter Twenty-six

$\mathcal{T}$hey had both become so engrossed in their conversation that it hardly seemed as though any time at all had passed before they were turning into the gravel drive of the dower house.

"Thank you. It was extremely kind of you to rush to my aid as you did." Catherine took Lucian's hand as he helped her down from the carriage, but when she tried to retrieve it, he grasped it even more firmly in his and led her toward the rose garden.

"It was not kind. I was concerned about you." He turned to face her, taking her other hand in his. "Catherine, I *want* you to succeed. I believe in what you are trying to accomplish. Do not dismiss me as though I were just some gallant who offered you the normal gentlemanly assistance. I care what happens to you and your dreams."

"But why?"

"Because you want to make the world a better place, and so do I. We are alike in that, you and I, as we are alike in so many ways, ways that make us different from the rest of the world. Being different can be very lonely. I came to Oxfordshire because I did not want you to have to fight your battles alone. I wanted to share them with you. Even more important than hoping I might be able to help you triumph against Lord Granville's despicable attempt to deter you from carrying out your purpose and continuing to run the academy, I wanted you to know you had my entire support. And I wanted to share the struggle with you."

She stared at him mystified.

"Confound it all, Catherine, I *care* about your happiness, I *care* about your success, and I *care* about you!"

But still she appeared to remain unconvinced.

Completely and utterly frustrated, Lucian pulled her to him and pressed his lips to hers.

The kiss was meant to prove his commitment to her in a way that words could not, but the instant his lips touched hers, something happened. An overwhelming longing swept through him as he felt the smoothness of her skin under his hands as they slid from her waist up the slender column of her neck to cup her face. The scent of rosewater, the softness of her hair against his cheek, made him ache with a tenderness and a desire he had never known before.

Slowly his mouth moved against hers, tasting her, savoring her. As her lips opened gently under his, he grew dizzy with the urge to make her part of him, part of his life, never to let her go again.

Her eyes closed and her head tilted back inviting his caress. Lucian buried his hands in the rich brown curls and trailed kisses along her jaw to her ear. Then, with a sigh that was more of a groan, he pressed his lips against her forehead and pulled her to him so that her body was molded to his, the long, slim line of her thigh pressed along his, so that he could feel her heart beating against his chest.

"Catherine, I beg of you," he whispered in her ear, "let me care about you. Do not dismiss me as you dismiss others who seek to offer you inexpert help. I *can* help you and I want to help you."

She felt rather than heard his words, felt them in the breath on her cheek, the rumble of his voice in his throat, passionate and pleading. But she was too far gone to respond. She had never felt this way in her life, not even in her most intimate moments with her husband.

Granville had been tender and respectful. He had made her feel safe and comfortable, but he had never made her feel the way she did now, as though she were a bird, poised at the edge of a cliff, ready to sweep off the precipice to be caught and borne up higher and higher by the wind rushing up beneath her wings. She had never felt so alive. All her senses tingled with an energy and a vitality she had not thought existed. Suddenly everything she wished to do, everything she wished to become, seemed possible. She felt excitement flowing through her, and a desperate longing to cling to Lucian, to meld his strength with hers, to be carried away by his belief in her, and his belief in them.

A cool breeze ruffled her hair. Daylight was quickly fading. She felt the slight chill of the mist rising from the meadow over where the shadow of the trees had blocked the sun. It brought a chill to her flushed cheek and reason back into control.

No, she had never felt this way before, except perhaps once before, during her one and only Season when she had been in Lucian's arms. It was just a waltz at one of the countless balls she had been forced to attend, except this one had been magic because he was there and he had asked her to save the last waltz for him. The opening strains of music had swept them into a world of their own. Nothing else had existed but his arms around her, the gray eyes smiling down at her, telling her how much she meant to him. And then he was gone the next day.

There was a reason she had only felt this way once before in her life and that was because it was not real. It was only the desperate joy of the moment, the passionate hope that such closeness could last forever, but she knew that was not true, that it was impossible. Such intensity could not possibly sustain itself. Life was not like that. The feelings she was experiencing now were not real for the very simple reason that they did not last. She knew that from her own experience.

Gathering what little strength she had left, Catherine drew a deep, shuddering breath and pulled away, away from the warm lips that demanded a response, away from the hands whose touch was magic itself, away from the dangerously welcoming shelter of Lucian's arms.

"No."

"No?" He tilted his head, a wicked little smile quirking the corners of his mouth.

"No. I mean, thank you. Thank you for your offer to help, but no."

His dark brows rose quizzically and a dangerous gleam stole into his eyes, a gleam that unaccountably made her heart beat faster.

"Thank you for caring about me—I mean, the academy, and, er, what becomes of it, its success. Your support means a great deal to me." She drew herself up with what she hoped was regal calm as she struggled to sound gracious but dismissive. "But now I must bid you adieu so that I can read over the reports Miss Denholme will have left me to prepare for work tomorrow."

And then she fled, like the rank coward that she was, hurrying up the stairs to the small terrace that overlooked the rose garden, wrenching open the French windows that opened from the library out onto the terrace. Once inside, she scrambled up the stairs to her bedchamber and shut the door behind her, leaning against it while she tried to catch her breath and fighting to keep her shaking knees from buckling underneath her.

Lucian remained staring thoughtfully off into the gathering gloom, the smile slowly fading from his lips. It was a rare moment in his life that he found himself at such a standstill, rarer still that he found himself put there by a will as strong, if not stronger, than his own.

What was he to do now? How was he to convince Catherine to trust, not only in him, but in the feelings she had for him? Clasping his hands behind his back, he strolled slowly, reluctantly, back down the path toward his waiting carriage.

There was no use remaining. He knew she would not see him. He had glimpsed that look of panic in her eyes as she had pulled away from him. Brief though it had been, he had seen it, and he knew what it meant. All too well he knew what it meant, for he had experienced that same sort of panic when Lady Granville had smiled possessively at him the last time he had run into her in Bond Street. It was the panic of an independent spirit that feared, above all else, losing that independence.

Catherine was a woman who could be justly proud of her accomplishments, none of which would have been realized without that independence and determination, and she was not going to allow anything to threaten that independence, even if it was her heart's desire.

At the moment, she just did not happen to understand what was her heart's desire, just as Lucian had not fully appreciated what was his heart's desire until perhaps an hour ago. Then he had kissed her and so much that had been nothing more than vague thoughts, feelings, longings, and desires had coalesced into one vision startling in its clarity and simplicity.

What he needed, what he wanted, what he had longed for all his life, was Catherine. Rationally, he had begun to suspect this quite some time ago, when his rediscovery of her had brought back all the painful, provocative memories of their first relationship and reaffirmed his original undeniable attraction to her wit and her spirit. But he had not been fully emotionally aware of this until the Countess of Morehampton had forced him to recognize how completely his happiness was tied up with Catherine's happiness and well-being. The kiss had pushed him over the edge to the further revelation that it was not only the desire for Catherine's happiness that drove him, but his own sense of incompleteness without her. Or to be more precise, he was in love with her, had always been in love with her since the moment he had first met her.

As he settled back against the maroon leather squabs of his traveling carriage, Lucian could not help reflecting how cynically he had doubted the existence of love. Yes, he would admit that there was love of money, love of power, love of social position, he had seen them a hundred times among his peers, and countless women in the grip of one or all of these had declared themselves to be in love with him. But being in love, truly in love, had seemed an impossible dream. No one had ever proven its existence to him in a way that he had found to be the least bit convincing. Now he knew why. There *was* no way of proving its existence to another person. One was either in love, or one was not. And he was in love with Catherine.

Now all that remained was to convince her that she was in love with him, that she wanted to spend the rest of her life with him as he wanted to spend the rest of his with her. For the moment, however, there was nothing to do but respect her wishes and leave her alone to return to her work while he returned to his own work in London.

He tried to ignore how depressing a thought it was as he ordered the coachman to head for Marlborough and the relative comfort of the Castle Inn, where he could at least be assured of an excellent meal and a decent bed for the night.

Chapter Twenty-seven

$\mathcal{A}$s she rose the next morning, Catherine tried to tell herself that she was in a most cheerful frame of mind. After all, she could now draft a letter to Lord Granville informing him that she had been able to procure proof from a reliable witness that her great-aunt had died after her husband, leaving no question as to the disposition of Lady Belinda Montague's fortune.

But somehow the prospect of foiling yet another of Ugolino's schemes to force her into quietly respectable widowhood did not bring Catherine the pleasure she had thought it would, and no matter how she threw herself into her work in an effort to recapture her energy and enthusiasm, it was simply not the same. She felt both listless and restless at the same time, and no task that she selected brought her any sense of satisfaction.

Her dissatisfaction was so palpable that even Margaret, usually absorbed in her own work, remarked upon this unusual state of affairs. "Perhaps you should have allowed yourself to rest a day to recover from your journey to Oxfordshire. You are looking sadly pulled, you know," the mathematics teacher observed, casting a critical eye over her friend as she paused in the door of Catherine's office some two days after Catherine's return from Bampton.

"Pooh. I am not such a poor creature as to be worn out by a simple carriage ride." Catherine jumped up and hurried over to take the list of supplies Margaret had been checking over.

But despite this sudden display of energy, Margaret remained unconvinced. "You *were* able to accomplish all that you hoped to during your journey, were you not?" she asked anxiously.

"Oh, yes. Everything is quite settled now, thank you." Catherine sat down and stared at the list in front of her, effectively discouraging all further discussion.

Margaret left, but still Catherine's eyes refused to focus on the list. Instead, she kept seeing Lucian's face as he had swept her into his arms, feeling his lips on hers demanding an answer she was afraid to give.

She shivered at the memory. Even thinking about it two days later she felt weak with longing and with a desperate yearning to believe that the incredible way her body had reacted to his touch was not just the illusion of senses disordered by exhaustion, tension, and desire, a yearning to ignore the past, forget that he had disappeared completely from her life ten years ago and never once attempted to contact her until he had appeared in her office three months ago, a yearning to live only in the moments they had shared since she had returned to consciousness in his arms to find him looking down at her as though she were the most precious thing in the world to him.

Catherine longed to believe that those moments that had culminated in the kiss in the rose garden were the beginning of the way life could be—rich, joyful, a world of shared pleasures as well as shared interests and shared values, but she could not risk it, would not risk it. It had taken her too long to forget Lucian the first time, too long to replace her daydreams of ecstatic happiness with the more solid, sober reality of mutual respect and shared responsibilities that Granville offered. And there had been nothing wrong with that way of life. She had been content, had felt useful, productive, and respected.

But were you happy? a treacherous little voice inside her whispered, a voice that echoed the doubts Lucian had expressed about her marriage to Granville. She knew that contentment and happiness were not the same thing, but she also knew that she had actually experienced one and had only dreamed about the other. And now, she was a fair way toward reestablishing that contentment on her own terms, as soon as she had convinced Lord Granville for once and for all that she was free to conduct her life as she saw fit and nothing could stop her. Better to pursue that certain goal of contentment than to risk everything on the chance of happiness, a happiness that depended so critically on someone else who had proven unreliable in the past.

Sighing, Catherine rose and shoved the list aside. It was no use trying to force herself to deal with it now. She could no more concentrate on it than she could fly. Perhaps tomorrow, once she had settled all this in her mind, she would be able to tackle it with renewed vigor and revived intelligence, but for now, it was time to return to the dower house, eat a light supper, and go to bed and pray that she would not dream of a dark, angular face whose penetrating gray eyes looked into her very soul.

But the next day brought no relief. In spite of her good intentions, Catherine found her mind wandering off into daydreams at the most inconvenient times—as she was giving Cook instructions for the week, while she was showing Lady Nettleton around the academy and answering questions about the desirability of education for young women, even during a discussion with Margaret about the possibility of adding Greek and Italian to the curriculum.

"I do feel that any female academy bold enough to include Latin in its course of study ought to include Greek as well. It will instill just the intellectual discipline and rigor in our pupils that we are hoping for," the mathematics instructress insisted.

"But will they enjoy it?"

"Enjoy it?" Margaret looked at her friend with as much astonishment as if Catherine had suddenly grown another head.

"Will it make them happy? Will it enable them to appreciate the beauties and pleasures in life to a higher degree?"

Margaret snorted. "Of course not. But we are not here to help them enjoy life."

"Would you not agree that the aim of education is to help one live life to its fullest?"

"Er, yes . . . I suppose so, but that is not the same thing as enjoying it or being happy."

"Is it not? How sad. For if we cannot enjoy our lives, what is the purpose of living them?"

"To be useful, naturally, to be upright and Christian in our thoughts and actions, to set an example for our fellow creatures, and to take care of those too poor to take care of themselves."

"In short, to conduct ourselves with the rigid respectability that Ugolino expects from the widowed Lady Granville herself."

"Now you are being absurd. Of course one should not follow such a narrowly righteous path as that man expects—a more falsely pious—well, never mind. What odd humor has gotten into you, Catherine? You are not yourself lately."

"No, I am not." Catherine smiled reflectively. "But I think you will agree that what differentiates Ugolino's false piety from your father's true Christian charity is his utter lack of sympathy and compassion for his fellow man. He lacks the softening sense of humor that makes us accept and even love one another's weaknesses. He is a man who derives no joy from even the simplest of life's pleasures, and therefore he cannot bear to have anyone else enjoy them either. We do a great disservice to our girls if we educate all that capacity for joy right out of them."

Margaret stared at her companion. "And do you know of anyone—anyone who is not a useless sybarite or a deluded fool, that is—who *does* enjoy life? I think it highly unlikely."

"Highly unlikely, but not impossible. But then, he is a highly unlikely individual—passionate, but principled; idealistic, but alive to all the ugly realities of the world and determined to change them."

"And I suppose that this paragon exists somewhere outside of your vivid imagination?" Margaret sniffed.

"Oh, he is not a paragon, not by any means. But he does exist outside of my imagination, and I have no doubt that he is managing to enjoy himself thoroughly at this very moment."

But accurate as Catherine's observations usually were, this one was definitely not. Lucian was sitting in his chambers at Lincoln's Inn frowning heavily at the document in front of him. It was a case brought to him by a Mr. Salt, a solicitor who could usually be counted on to bring him only the most interesting and complex of cases. But despite the complexities of the case and the vexed issue of whether it was murder or suicide that was responsible for the death of a young wife whose husband had run through the fortune she had brought to the marriage, he could not focus his attention on it, for his thoughts kept drifting back to another young woman who had brought a fortune to her marriage and lost it as well.

But the thought of Catherine, while it brought a smile to his face, also brought sadness to his heart. The smile was for her indomitable spirit and the courage with which she insisted on standing up for herself and making her way in the world. And sadness was also for the way she insisted on standing up for herself and making her own way in the world, for it meant that she would not share her world with him for fear that somehow he would take all that independence away from her.

The worst of it was that he understood her position completely and sympathized with it wholeheartedly. He could understand her fear that he would interfere in her affairs. And he might very well interfere, as he had done in Oxfordshire, in order to help her, especially in matters where he knew himself to be an expert. What she did not know was that he was perfectly willing to consult her in her areas of expertise and defer to her judgment when it was a matter of her knowledge and experience being superior to his.

He wanted her to continue doing her part to nurture and educate women to become as strong and independent as she was, but he also wanted her to enjoy it more. Why could she not understand, as he was coming to understand, that life, even with its problems and worries, could be so much richer, fuller, and more rewarding if there was someone to share it with, someone to discuss it with and hold close at the end of the day?

When his brother William had been killed, Lucian had felt much of the purpose and meaning slip from his life. William, an even crazier idealist than Lucian, had been the one person whose opinion he had valued. William had given him a standard to measure himself by, something to live up to. Catherine did the same thing for him. And William had laughed. He had seen the irony in life, the humor of it all. Since boyhood, even in the most dire situations—as they accidentally set fire to a potting shed or sank their rowboat— Lucian had been able to glance over at William, see the answering gleam of humor in his eyes, and burst out laughing. No one else had ever shared that with him, except Catherine. Having lost both William—and Catherine, once already—Lucian knew how very precious and rare such camaraderie was, and he did not want to lose it again or be forced to live without it.

But how was he to win Catherine's trust? Shaking his head wearily, Lucian again tried to focus on the document in front of him. Then, suddenly, he knew what he must do. He had to ask her for *her* help in solving one of *his* problems. He had to share the problems of the case he was studying with her and ask her advice. How simple, and yet how miraculous that the thought of asking for her help could brighten his world to such a degree.

Suddenly his life, which had seemed so gray and monotonous after his return from Bath, was filled with possibility. He had something to look forward to, something to anticipate.

What was he waiting for? Filled with a heady exuberance, Lucian gathered up the papers in front of him and headed back to Mount Street to tell his staff to prepare for another journey to Bath. But when he arrived at his own doorstep, his butler handed him a letter. Lucian glanced at the address. Bath had come to him!

He tore open the letter, scanning it quickly. A slow ironic grin spread across his face. After all the years that the matchmaking mamas of the *ton* had done their level best to see Lucian Verney leg-shackled, who would have guessed that it would be Hugo Granville who would reunite him with the love of his life. "Gilmore, see to it that my things are packed. I am going to Bath."

"Yes, sir. Very good, sir." Not by so much as the flicker of an eyelid did the butler betray his satisfaction at this news. Nor did he betray his conviction that it was not his lordship's niece that was the reason for this sudden journey or the lifting of his master's somber mood, but the niece's headmistress.

Gilmore was the soul of discretion, but he was a shrewd observer and a keen student of human nature. Naturally a man in his exalted position did not indulge in idle gossip or listen to vulgar hearsay, but he had seen enough over the last three months to know that his master had at last discovered a woman worthy of him. The brittle cynicism had slowly softened into ironic humor, and the bleakness that had lurked in the back of the gray eyes had finally disappeared as the man who had thoroughly enjoyed life reappeared, a man Gilmore had not seen since his master had left for the continent ten years ago.

Chapter Twenty-eight

*H*ugo Granville's name might have been silently blessed in London, but it was most definitely being cursed in Bath. "That pompous, punctilious, interfering . . . ogre!"

"Whatever is amiss now?" Margaret asked as she came in with the account books that Catherine had sent a maid scurrying to request from her.

"Ugolino!" Catherine stormed, taking the account books from Margaret's hand, slamming them down on the desk, and then proceeding to clear a space for them by sweeping papers into ever increasing piles on the floor around her desk.

"Well, it is really Farmer Griggs,"—Catherine paused to catch her breath—"but it is Ugolino at the bottom of it. Farmer Griggs called at the dower house this morning and, finding I had already left, came here. It seems that Lord Granville has discovered that Farmer Griggs has offered shelter and support to Betty and her illegitimate baby, and he"—Catherine ground her teeth in frustration—"considers it his moral duty to order them out of the community so as not to be a bad influence on other young women who might see that Betty has been accepted without punishment for her licentious behavior and therefore, seeing no penalty connected with this behavior, might embark on a similarly dissolute path."

"Naturally, Farmer Griggs protested that it was his right

to shelter whomever he pleased in his own house, in addition to its being a simple act of Christian charity to offer aid and comfort to a homeless woman and her child. And then Ugolino had the audacity to point out that some of Farmer Griggs's fields are actually land leased from the Granville estate and therefore Farmer Griggs does not have quite so much right as he thought he did to behave as he pleases. Ugolino actually threatened to take the land back immediately if Farmer Griggs did not instantly comply with his wishes. Can you credit the monstrous ill nature of that man? Will he never leave me alone?"

"Actually, he *is* leaving you alone," Margaret pointed out logically, as she watched her friend furiously clearing a working space around the account books on her desk. "And you cannot really call a man 'punctilious' and an 'ogre' at the same time."

But she received no thanks for this reasonable observation. "I know." Catherine snapped. "Literally speaking, he is *not* interfering in my life; he is interfering in Betty's and the Griggses', but you know he would not if they had no connection to me."

"True," Margaret was forced to concede. "But there is really very little you can do about a contract drawn up between Farmer Griggs and Lord Granville."

"How can you say that? I am responsible for introducing Betty and her baby into the Griggses' household, and if Ugolino wants to improve the moral tone of the neighborhood by threatening Farmer Griggs with taking back the Granville land he rents if he does not get rid of Betty and the baby, then I am responsible for any loss of income he might suffer. I had hoped that by going over the academy's books I might discover some way to make up for Farmer Griggs's loss of income, but I cannot. We do not make enough ourselves to compensate him to that extent. I gave them to you in the hopes that perhaps you might see something I had overlooked since you are so much cleverer with figures, but . . ."—she looked pleadingly at the mathematics instructress—"you could find nothing?"

"Nothing." Margaret responded firmly. "At least not the sort of sum you asked me to look for. To find a sum that large you would be forced to resort to highway robbery."

"Maybe I shall."

"Catherine! You cannot do anything more to help Farmer Griggs, believe me."

"Oh, no?" Catherine took up her pelisse which had been casually tossed over a chair, pulled it on, and stuffed her bonnet on her head, securing it with a hopelessly lopsided bow. "Watch me! I am not giving in to that man even if it means resorting to the law."

"You do not seriously think that Mr. Barham would be so rash as to stand up to Lord Granville?"

"Barham?" Catherine snorted derisively. "I am not so naive. Not Barham. The Marquess of Charlmont."

"The Marquess of Charlmont! What would you want with . . ."

"He read for the bar. I need legal counsel from someone who will not be intimidated by Ugolino. It makes a good deal of sense to me. Now, if you will excuse me, I am off to reassure the Griggses." And she stormed out, leaving her friend staring after her openmouthed.

But by the time her carriage had turned into Farmer Griggs's immaculately kept farmyard, Catherine's self-assurance, fueled mostly by righteous anger, had slowly seeped away. How could she ask a man to risk so much of his livelihood? But what would become of Betty and the baby if she did not? Perhaps, if she looked carefully at the academy's books one more time, she could find a way to support Betty and the baby, but deep down inside Catherine knew that Betty would never accept such obvious charity.

More than once, Betty had told her "I like working, my lady," both at the dower house when she was looking after Catherine's chickens, and later after she had become a valued member of Farmer Griggs's household. "It makes me feel like I am someone to know that I can do something."

How well Catherine had understood that feeling, and how much she sympathized with the young woman's wish to look after herself and her baby. *I will not let that young woman down,* Catherine resolved as the carriage slowed to a halt. *But how am I to keep this from her? If she discovers the trouble she has brought to these good people, she will feel it is her duty to leave them.*

Fortunately, however, Farmer Griggs was in the yard examining the shoe of one of his draft horses when Catherine arrived. "Good day, my lady." His honest, weather-beaten face, usually the picture of good health, looked gray and careworn. "You know I would do everything I could to keep them here if it were in my power." He came straight to the point. "The Missus is powerful fond of that baby, and Betty is as good and honest a worker as I could hope to find in many a day, but the fact is, I can not afford to lose the income from that field. As you well know, the Griggses have had this agreement with the Granvilles long as I can remember, before my grandfather's time. Maybe we should not have counted on it as much as we have, but we have done well by the Granvilles, and what with buying my new team this year and those sheep the year before last, I have nothing left to spare. I need every bit that field produces."

"I know. I know, and I will not ask it of you, if it comes to that." Catherine summoned up an encouraging smile that was totally at odds with the anxiety gnawing at her stomach. "But I hope it will not come to that. If you can but stand firm for a few more days, I think I know someone who can help us."

"Who? There is no one in these parts strong enough to stand up to his lordship."

"A friend." Catherine could not help but smile at the thought. She nodded. "A good friend who understands such things."

"Ah." There seemed nothing else to say. Farmer Griggs could only hope that Lady Catherine's trust in her friend was well placed.

But later on that evening, as he recounted the story to his wife and Betty over supper he began to consider the conversation more thoroughly. "A "friend," she said it was who might help us, 'a good friend who understands such things,' and she smiled kind of funny-like. I wonder. It must be a gentleman, for who else could possibly make Lord Granville listen to reason?"

The anxious little group at the farm was not kept in suspense very long, for not a week after her conversation with Farmer Griggs, Lady Catherine appeared in his farmyard again.

This time, however, she was not in her carriage, but in a beautifully sprung black curricle with bright yellow wheels pulled by "as sweet a pair of goers as it has ever been my pleasure to see," the farmer later told his cronies in the taproom of the Green Man.

And her companion had been just as impressive as his equipage and his cattle. Tall and dark-haired with eyes that missed nothing, he handled his team with the ease and assurance of a born whip.

"Top of the trees, he was, but not the least high in the instep," Farmer Griggs had continued with his story. "Spoke to me like a real gentleman, he did, all about the fields I rent from his lordship and the longstanding agreement. You would not think that a nob like that would know so much about country matters—more than Lord Granville, I am willing to bet, the new one that is—but he did."

"Who was he, Tom?" one of the eager listeners, unable to bear the suspense any longer, had wanted to know.

"He was the Marquess of Charlmont, which is a most powerful family in its own right. But what is more to the point, as her ladyship says, this man knows the law, and people's rights, and he is not afraid to stand up for people like you and me. Her ladyship says that that is what he does in London."

"And why would a nob like that want to help you, Tom?" another onlooker wondered.

Farmer Griggs stared meditatively at his tankard of ale. "Well, lads, her ladyship says it is because he doesn't like bullies, and he is all for fairness. But it is my opinion," he paused for effect, "that he is sweet on her ladyship."

"Ah." There was a general chorus of approval.

"But what does she think of him?" A waggish man in the corner spoke.

"Now *that* is a question," another chimed in. "She is a lady as has a great deal of spirit—too much of it for his new lordship's taste at any rate."

A ripple of laughter greeted this sage observation.

But Farmer Griggs held up his hand. "Let me just say— and then we won't speak of it again as it isn't respectful— let me just say that I think her ladyship finds that there is a lot to admire in this gentleman. After all, it is not often that she asks for help or advice from anyone."

The listeners in the room acceded to his dictum and the talk turned back to the usual topics of the weather and the price of corn, but the curiosity of the neighborhood had been aroused and they did their utmost to keep an eye out for the out-and-outer who was not only going to stand up to his lordship but seemed to have won the approval of Lady Catherine in the process, a feat that completely overshadowed any other claims to fame that the gentleman might have.

Happily oblivious to what others might be saying about her relationship with the Marquess of Charlmont, Catherine, too, was arriving at the conclusion that she approved of him very much indeed.

It had been a most lowering experience to discover how much she was counting on his help as she waited anxiously for a reply to her letter. It was even more lowering to feel her heart pound and her breath come in short, ragged gasps at the sound of a carriage pulling into the dower house drive late in the evening, a few days after she had sent her letter to London.

She rose shakily to her feet. Could he have come so quickly? Surely it could be no one else at this time of night, but he must have set out for Bath the instant he received her letter.

Fighting to gain control over her body, which seemed to have dissolved into a weak, quivering mass, Catherine made

her way to the door as best she could. There he was, curly
brimmed beaver tilted at a rakish angle, springing down
from his carriage as though he had not spent the entire day
on the road.

"You came!" It was all she could say. She cursed herself
for sounding so grateful, but it was true, she was inordi-
nately glad to see him.

"Of course I came." He took both her hands in his, smiling in a way that reduced the few remaining bones in her
body to jelly. "Now tell me all about it."

"What? Oh yes, Ugolino. Well, come in and sit by the
fire." She nodded to Lucy, hovering in the background, and
while the maid ran off to procure refreshment, she led him
into the library.

He had listened carefully to the entire sordid tale without
comment until she had finished. "Hmmm." His eyes nar-
rowed as he sipped thoughtfully on his port. "I may or may
not find a legal way to keep him from forcing his will on
Farmer Griggs, but failing that, I have other ways of, er *in-
fluencing* him."

"Oh?" Catherine looked at him anxiously. His grim expression made him look truly formidable.

"Let us just say that my constitutional dislike of people
who abuse their power and their privilege will not let me
allow Lord Granville to get his way in this case, a way,
which from all that you have related to me, is neither responsible nor charitable. At any rate," he smiled reassuringly at her, "we will not let Farmer Griggs suffer for his
kindness."

"I shall call on you tomorrow at whatever time you think
best and we will go see what we can learn from Farmer
Griggs. Now, I must go and get some rest if my mind is to
be sharp tomorrow."

It was not until he rose and headed toward the door that
she saw how tired he was. The deep-set eyes were shadowed
with fatigue and the lines of his face were more clearly
etched than she had ever seen them. A sudden rush of gratitude warmed her, and unexpected tears stung her eyes. She

leaned against the heavy oak door as he stepped out into the gloom. "Thank you for coming," she whispered. "Thank you so very much."

"Anything for you, my love," he murmured in reply. His lips brushed her forehead softly. He turned and walked swiftly toward his carriage, feet crunching on the gravel. She remained in the doorway as he climbed into his carriage and watched as he rolled off down the drive until the twinkle of the carriage lamps was no longer visible.

Chapter Twenty-nine

Somehow, just his being there made everything better, and the feeling of hopelessness and gloom that had settled over Catherine since her visit to Farmer Griggs suddenly lifted. She was not alone any more. Someone else was by her side in her struggle with Lord Granville. Just the knowledge that Lucian was there and that he believed in her made her feel oddly invincible, whether or not his legal knowledge proved to be effective.

Anything for you, my love. Had she heard him correctly, or had it merely been the whisper of a passing breeze and her own desperate fancy? Giving herself a mental shake for indulging in such romantic foolishness, Catherine lit a candle and made her way slowly to her bedchamber. She, too, needed rest if her mind was to be sharp the next day.

But once in bed, she found that sleep was impossible. She lay there haunted by visions of an angular face etched with lines of exhaustion but filled with a grim determination to help her win her battle against Ugolino. *Anything for you, my love.* Could it be true? And if it were true, how could she ever repay him?

But as quickly as Catherine asked herself that question, she had another vision of Lucian looking down at her, face softened by tenderness, eyes alight with a longing she did not dare name, a longing that she too had felt, a longing so elemental that it brought both fear and joy to her heart.

Was it true, then, what she had felt so long ago the first

time she saw him, that they were meant for one another? The misery she had suffered after being left without a word had made her scoff at such a romantic fallacy, the fantasy of an inexperienced girl who knew nothing of life's realities. But now, as she lay there remembering the look, the touch, the taste of him, she wondered if perhaps she had not been so very wrong that first time after all. Tomorrow, she reminded herself, tomorrow would bring the clear light of day, and reason would once again reassert itself. Then she would not be so affected by her own exhaustion and worry. She would see him again as he was, a man, not her savior, not her soul mate, just a man and nothing more.

But the next day did not bring the counsel Catherine had expected. A messenger brought a note from Lucian suggesting they call on Farmer Griggs that afternoon when she and he had finished their daily tasks.

"Now, we will enjoy this drive and think of nothing more serious than the beauty of the countryside," Lucian admonished as he helped Catherine into his curricle that afternoon.

And indeed she did, as they bowled smoothly along the road, past rich green fields dotted with sheep, up the slope to the top of the hills ringing the Avon's lush valley and overlooking the city laid out below.

They arrived at Farmer Griggs's, and Lucian, whose easy manners and genuine concern soon made the farmer comfortable, questioned him closely about the fields in question. "Now, if I am not much mistaken, the fields you are speaking of lie in that direction." Lucian pointed off toward the dower house.

"That they do, my lord. They are between my land and her ladyship's, along the road here."

"Ah. And was there a verbal agreement with the late Lord Granville about this, or do you have a lease?"

"Oh, I have a lease, my lord. His late lordship insisted on it. He was a true gentleman, that one."

"And may I see the lease?"

"Yes, of course, my lord. I shall just fetch it from my

desk." The farmer hurried off and was back within a few minutes, bearing a yellowed piece of paper with a seal on it.

"May I take this with me to examine it?"

"Certainly, my lord. Do you think it will help?"

"I very much hope so. I shall certainly do my utmost to see that you keep your rights as well as Betty and the baby here at the farm."

"Oh, thank you, sir. We will all bless you for it." Much reassured by Lucian's quiet confidence, the farmer waved them on their way.

Catherine, however, was not so sanguine. "Do you really think you can do anything? Surely if there is a lease, Hugo must have his own copy and knows that he is within his rights as a landlord. He is a dreadful bully, but he is far too concerned with his good name and reputation to break the law."

"You might be right, but he certainly sailed very close to the wind when he tried to claim your inheritance from your great-aunt Belinda as part of your husband's estate. We shall see. I am not in Chancery, but I know enough about wills and estates to have an idea that may help us in this instance. Now, I also need a copy of your husband's will. Do you have one?"

"Certainly, in the strong box, in the library."

"Then let us go there, if we may."

They were soon ensconced in the library, Lucian with the two documents spread out before him, and Catherine leaning over his shoulder. Not a sound broke the silence as he read, frowning in concentration. "I gather that the large Palladian villa just visible from the road is Granville Park?"

"Yes. Granville's great grandfather began building it and his grandfather finished it."

"Then this house, judging by its style and its proximity to the road was here before the park was built."

"Yes. This was the original manor house and dates back to the beginning of the family's fortune, when the first Lord Granville was rewarded by Henry the Seventh for his support."

A slow smile spread across Lucian's face. "Then, if I am correct, and I think I am, this is the Granville Manor referred to in both the lease and your husband's will, which gives you life interest in the house and its lands."

"Yes." Catherine nodded thoughtfully. "Do you mean to say, then, that—"

"—That the land Farmer Griggs is leasing is actually part of Granville Manor? Yes. And," the smile grew broader, "if I am correct, the present Lord Granville not only has no jurisdiction over these fields, but he has been collecting rents that belong to you, if he has been collecting the rent, that is."

Catherine snorted in a most unladylike manner. "Not collect rents? It is highly unlikely. Ugolino is the most clutch-fisted . . . Of course he has been collecting rents."

"Then I think that it is fair to say that not only does he owe Farmer Griggs an apology, he also owes you some money."

"Truly? How delightful!" Catherine could not help executing a gleeful jig.

Lucian laughed. "I do not believe I have ever seen you look so happy. I shall have to see what I can do to make sure that it continues. Seeing justice done appears to bring you more satisfaction than jewelry and carriages bring to other women. You are a rare woman, Catherine, and you have very expensive tastes, which I long to gratify."

His tone and his words were teasing, but the look in his eyes made her cheeks grow hot. What would it be like to be gratified by him? She could not help thinking of his lips on hers, of the slow, sensuous way they had trailed kisses down her neck, making her ache with longing, of how her body came alive at his touch, which was infinitely comforting and infinitely disturbing at the same time. What would it be like to cast her fate to the winds, to give in to longing and desire, to be swept away by pleasure without a thought for anything else?

In all her life, Catherine could never remember having ever let herself go or given herself up to the joy of the moment without a thought for the morrow. She had never indulged in a whim or an urge without thoroughly examining the consequences. And what had it brought her in the end? Happiness? No. She was content enough with her life, especially now that Ugolino seemed to be at bay. She was proud of what she had accomplished. But was she happy? Did she wake up every morning filled with delightful expectation as she once had briefly, ten years ago? No.

For a moment she saw her life stretching endlessly before her. Once it would have been enough to contemplate the shaping of young women's lives, continuing with the sort of good works she and Granville had done, but now it filled her with a sense of the emptiness, the sameness of it all.

Almost she wanted to throw herself into Lucian's arms and think of nothing more except this one moment in time. It would be heaven to know he was there whenever she was worried or tired or overwhelmed by life, to know that there was someone to hold her, to help her, to stand by her and share it with her as he had today. But was it real? And would it last beyond today? Could she bear it if it did not?

"Catherine?"

"What?" She had been so embroiled in her own thoughts that she had almost forgotten he was there looking down at her with that disturbing light in his eyes.

"I want to gratify them—all your wishes, that is."

"No. I mean, I do not need someone to do that."

"But I *want* to. I know you can look after yourself, and many others at the same time, but I want to look after you, share your problems and your successes because I care about them. I care about you. I love you." He cupped her chin with one hand and tilted her face so that she had to look up at him. And then he saw that her eyes were swimming in tears.

"I don't know . . . That is, please, I need to be alone. I need to think."

Desperate as he was to convince her that the two of them belonged together, he could not help smiling tenderly. "Of course, my love, but I can tell you from my own experience, that in this case, all the thinking in the world will not give you the answer."

He yearned to pull her into his arms, to kiss her breathless, to prove to her what he knew all the reason in the world could not explain, but with a supreme effort, he restrained himself and leaned forward to kiss the top of her head.

Then, drawing a deep, steadying breath, he straightened and mustered up his most businesslike voice. "With your permission, I shall take these documents back to the White Hart with me, look them over thoroughly, and draft a letter to Lord Granville."

"That would indeed be most helpful." Catherine smiled at him, grateful for his understanding.

But when he had left, she sat down at her desk and let the tears roll slowly down her face. Better than anyone, Lucian appreciated the conflict that was raging within her. The mere fact that without a murmur of protest, he had accepted her need to be alone showed beyond all doubt that he understood and sympathized with the war between her independence and her longing to share, her fear of losing herself and her longing to be with him. How could she not love a man like that? And she did love him. She had always loved him.

Finally, wiping away her tears, she stood up and walked over to the French windows, stepped out onto the terrace, and, taking a deep breath, inhaled the scent of the roses in the garden beyond. Why was she agonizing over it all? She had lost him once and survived. She could do so again, but in the meantime, it was time to enjoy the world around her. It was time to live.

Chapter Thirty

$\mathcal{A}$nd Catherine's very first act after arriving at this resolution was to take a brisk walk across the fields to Farmer Griggs's to play with the baby and share Lucian's discovery with the anxious little group that gathered around the kitchen table as soon as she appeared.

"That is wonderful news, my lady! We have been that worried." Mrs. Griggs beamed as she brought Catherine a glass of her blackberry cordial. "Tom has been going over and over the account books to see if we could manage without that field, and Betty has been saying that she must look for employment in Bristol or somewhere where no one knows her. It has been a dreadful time."

"It does my heart good to be your tenant once again, my lady, indeed it does." Farmer Griggs was less effusive than his wife, but his relief was palpable. "And the marquess, is he sure he is right?"

"The marquess is the sort of man who would not have said such a thing unless he were quite sure, but apart from the legal issues involved, he assured me that even without that he would make Lord Granville see that it was not in his best interests to threaten you."

"Well, to be sure, the marquess does look like a man who knows what he is about and not likely to take no for an answer, I expect."

"Very true." Catherine smiled. "The marquess does not

take no for an answer, and he most definitely does know what he is about."

Farmer Griggs shot a meaningful look at his wife. "A good man and a true gentleman, the marquess."

"Yes . . . a good man." Catherine, who had been holding the baby, returned him to his mother. "And now, I must get back to my own duties. I am afraid I have neglected the academy shamefully through all of this.

The Griggses thanked her again, and feeling more light-hearted than she had for quite some time, Catherine headed back to the dower house. In fact, she was feeling so optimistic that she could even bear to glance off in the distance without a qualm at the classical lines of Granville Park just visible beyond the trees that lined its long curving drive. "And that is the last I shall be forced to deal with you, Ugolino," she muttered triumphantly as she strode along the path through the fields.

But there she was wrong, very wrong. For not twenty-four hours later as she was sitting at her desk in her office at Lady Catherine Granville's Select Academy, Biddle appeared in the doorway. "Lord Granville to see you, my lady," he announced with his usual impressive gravity.

The butler barely had time to deliver his message before he was shoved aside by the portly, puffing figure of Hugo, Lord Granville. "This is an outrage! Have you lost all sense of decency? Have you no better respect for this family and its tradition than to go rallying tenants against landlords? I knew that you had very little, if any, consideration for the proprieties, but I had no idea that you were an outright Jacobin!" He gasped, still catching his breath after the climb up the stairs.

It was only by picturing the granite-faced image of the Marquess of Charlmont that Catherine was able to calm herself enough to reply. "Quite the contrary, my lord. I have every respect for tradition. And tradition holds that the rights and holdings of the original manor house are to remain together intact. I would suggest that in this instance it is you, my lord, who lacks the proper respect for this family and its history."

Hugo's pale protuberant eyes were bulging, and his fleshy face was mottled with rage. If Catherine had not been so desperate to maintain her own dignity, she would have laughed outright, for he looked like nothing so much as an angry carp.

"You will not get away with this. I will see to it that you cease this scandalously disrespectful behav—"

"You will do nothing of the sort." An icy voice behind him broke into Lord Granville's tirade. "And it is you who will cease the disrespectful behavior. You will start giving the respect she deserves to Lady Catherine, now, or you and your precious reputation will be very much the worse for it." Immaculately attired in an exquisitely cut coat of blue Bath superfine, biscuit-colored pantaloons, and a cravat of dazzling whiteness, the Marquess of Charlmont strode into the room.

"Who, may I ask, are you? And how dare you interfere in a private conversation?" Hugo's efforts to sound imperious merely wound up sounding petulant in the face of Lucian's cool authority.

"I am serving as counsel to Lady Catherine and as such I have come to advise her that she need have nothing further to do with you. I am also the Marquess of Charlmont, and I make it a point never to have anything to do with people who conduct themselves as uncivilly as you seem to consider it necessary to do. Now, if you feel that you must bully someone, I suggest you go elsewhere but leave defenseless farmers, unfortunate females, and perfectly respectable widows alone."

For a moment, there was utter and complete silence. Lord Granville's jaw flapped frantically, but not a sound issued forth. "Perfectly respectable, you say?" He at last managed to spit out. "What sort of person runs a school, I ask you? Some poor down-at-heels governess who is no better than she should be. But a Granville? Never!"

"The Marchioness of Charlmont may, and she will, if she

will have me." Lucian raised a quizzical brow at Catherine who was too bemused by the entire exchange to do anything but stare at both of them.

"The Marchioness of Charlmont? What does the Marchioness of Charlmont have to do with this?"

"Nothing, perhaps, if Lady Catherine can not find it in her heart to make me the happiest of men. Or perhaps everything if she can. But in either case, she will continue to remain the much respected proprietress of Lady Catherine Granville's Select Academy for Genteel Young Ladies because, from what I have seen, the academy is doing an excellent job of educating young women. And England has a desperate need for well-educated young women."

Lord Granville caught sight of Catherine's dumbstruck expression. "Marchioness of Charlmont, bah! You are just saying that in the hopes of making her your next mistress, and as head of the Granville family, I refuse to allow you to sully the name with such cheap propositions."

"If your concern is for the Granville name, sir, I would first look to my own wife's conduct, if I were you, and leave off harassing Lady Catherine."

"My wife? How dare you, sir!"

"Let me explain something to you, Granville." Lucian took a step closer to the infuriated gentleman, and his voice grew deadly soft. "Lady Granville, in pursuit of life as a fashionable member of the *ton*, is bringing more dubious renown to the name than Lady Catherine is in her pursuit of female education. There are rumors linking Lady Granville's name with several gentlemen of the *ton*, and believe me, I know whereof I speak, for I am one of those gentlemen."

"Now, if you do not leave Lady Catherine and your neighbors in peace, I shall see to it that the vague rumors about your wife's activities become common knowledge, and then the reputation of the Granville name will truly not bear looking into. I trust you understand me."

Lord Granville blanched, but he stood his ground. "Fine words, sir," he spat with a venomous glance in Catherine's direction, "with which you no doubt expect to win the approval of your next mistress; however . . ."

"The next Marchioness of Charlmont, you mean. If you *ever* whisper a word against Lady Catherine again, I assure you that I will gladly defend her honor, whether she consents to become the Marchioness of Charlmont or not."

However verbally aggressive he might be, Lord Granville was utterly and completely lacking in physical courage, and there was no mistaking the very real menace in the Marquess of Charlmont's expression. "You—you have no right . . ." he stammered, edging toward the door.

"Then I suggest that, in the interests of keeping yourself in one piece, you quit this room immediately."

But before Lucian had finished his sentence, the man was gone.

Lucian turned to Catherine. "There. I do not know why I did not think of that before. If I had challenged that villain to a duel at the outset, I would have saved us all a good deal of trouble."

"You—you did not have to do that." Catherine found her voice at last.

"Well, it was a trifle rough and ready, I admit, and far less elegant a solution than those that I usually favor, but effective, nevertheless."

"No, I mean what you said about the Marchioness of Charlmont. There was no need for it. You do not know the extent of Ugolino's vanity. Despite his low opinion of me he will now be claiming that he is related to the Marchioness of Charlmont, and all the world will think that you and I . . ."

"And he would be absolutely correct; that is, if you will have me."

"If I will have you? But I do not need to be married to be respectable. It is no longer an issue since you put the fear of a duel into Ugolino."

"Precisely, my love. I would hope that you would be married because you wish to be, because I love you, and,"—he pulled her close and looked deep into her eyes—"because I hope you love me too."

"I do not know. I do not know." She twisted her hands in an agony of indecision.

"Do not know if you love me or do not know if you wish to be married to me?"

"I . . ."

"Do you know what I think?" He kissed her gently, slowly, on the lips, and then tracing her jaw line with his lips to her ear, he whispered. "I think, perhaps, you have loved me as I have loved you, since the moment I saw you, since the moment I recognized a kindred spirit among all the fashionable aspirants for the *ton's* attention. But"—he pulled her closer to him—"loving someone and sharing one's life with that person, giving up one's independence, are different things altogether."

His eyes smiled down into hers. "I have had my independence, as have you. I have accomplished many of the things I set out to accomplish, as have you. Yet, when I saw you again, I realized how empty my life has been without you. I want to share it with you, enjoy it with you. I want you to help me, advise me, share your knowledge with me, as I hope I can do with you."

"But the academy. I cannot just abandon it."

"I should hope not. I hope that you make it the premier female educational establishment in all of England. I hope that it is so successful in fact that every marchioness in the land will feel compelled to establish one of her own, so successful that Lady Granville will be continually pointing out that she is closely related to the proprietress of Lady Catherine Granville's Select Academy for Genteel Young Ladies.

Catherine chuckled. "Now *that,* sirrah, is doing it much too brown."

"But it is not doing it much too brown to say I love you." He tilted her head up and pressed his lips against hers, not gently this time, but passionately demanding, persuading, pleading.

And she was powerless to resist. His very touch made her feel as though they belonged together. It always had. She had tried to deny it after he had disappeared from her life, had continued to deny it through eight years of marriage, but when she had first seen him standing in the doorway of her office three months ago, she knew that she had been lying to herself for all those years.

His hands slid down her shoulders to her waist, pulling her to him as though to make up for all those years away from her. "Catherine, please, say you will marry me. I never want to be without you again. Say you will take the risk to be with me for the rest of our lives."

It was, as always, his complete understanding of her fears and hesitations that finally won her over. And after all, as she had already asked herself over and over, what did she stand to lose? Nothing, except what she had lost before. But what she stood to gain was the happiness that she had never found anywhere else but in his company. "I will marry you."

"And I promise never to let you out of my sight again." He smiled down at her. "And I know an excellent man of law who can draw up the marriage settlements to your great advantage."

"But what does the 'Scourge of the King's Bench' know about Chancery, my lord?"

"Enough to know that marriage to you is the most ambitious and rewarding case he has yet taken on."

Catherine laughed and gave herself up to the joy of loving him at last.

Signet Regency Romance
by
Evelyn Richardson

A Foreign Affair
0-451-20826-9

Fortune's Lady
0-451-20552-9

REGENCY ROMANCE
Now Available from Signet

The Rules of Love
by Amanda McCabe

As the author of a book on etiquette, Rosalind Chase
can count every rule that handsome Lord Morley
breaks. But when she can't get him out of her mind,
Rosie begins to wonder if she's ready to
break all the rules of love.

0-451-21176-6

The Rejected Suitor
by Teresa McCarthy

When the Earl of Stonebridge returns from war, he
vows to win over the girl he left behind. All he has to
do is remind her of the love she once felt for him. And
with his kisses, she might just remember.

0-451-21180-4

Allison Lane

Emily's Beau

0-451-20992-3

Emily Hughes has her sights set on one man: Jacob Winters, Earl of Hawthorne. But her hopes are dashed when she discovers that Jacob is already betrothed. She will have to forget Jacob and marry another, which is just what she plans to do—until one moonlit kiss changes everything.

Also Available:

Birds of a Feather	0-451-19825-5
The Purloined Papers	0-451-20604-5
Kindred Spirits	0 451-20743-2

Available wherever books are sold, or
to order call: 1-800-788-6262

S908